Peggy-
Trust in the Lord with

All Your Heart !

Proverbs 3:5

by

LeighAnne Clifton

LeighAnne Clifton

Published by Pen It! Publications, LLC in the U.S.A.
812-371-4128 www.penitpublications.com

ISBN: 978-1-954868-07-6
Cover Design by Donna Cook
Edited by Dina Husseini

Acknowledgments

I make it through each day by my faith and trust in Proverbs 3:5. I'll admit it's sometimes easier said than done, but God is so good. He's walked beside me, sometimes carrying me, through highs and lows, and the journey to publishing this book is no different. Looking back at the long process, I so clearly see His hand guiding me, holding me back when I wanted to run ahead and closing the doors that weren't right. He gets all praise and honor for whatever good this book brings into others' lives.

A special thanks goes out to the beautiful ladies who read this book long ago and provided invaluable feedback. My sister Laura, dear friend Jane, and niece Mary gave me perspective, wisdom, and, most importantly, their time. I can never thank you ladies enough.

To my kids, Bryce, Allee, and Hamilton – Thanks for bearing with me as I learned to be a mom (and a mother-in-law!). You are my blessings, my inspiration, and my joy.

You wouldn't be reading this book if it hadn't been for Debi Stanton and the amazing folks at Pen It! Publications. Donna's beautiful cover art, Dina's thoughtful editing, and all the behind-the-scenes unsung heroes of the publishing company made my dream become a beautiful reality. For that, I'm forever grateful!

Dedication

Never in a million years would I have considered pursuing this dream of writing without the constant encouragement of my husband Bill. He believed, even when I lost hope, that God would see this through. I love you, Billy, and I thank you for your unwavering support.

Table of Contents

Chapter 1

Shattered World

Arms crossed and nostrils flaring. Alexandra Powell fumed watching her mother pack. The sweetness of the birdsong and the fragrance of daffodils floating in the open window were no match for Alex's foul mood. Karen packed for another out-of-town job, leaving the town of Woodvale, North Carolina, behind, again. Alex couldn't remember her mother refusing a client to attend a PTA meeting or a dance recital.

Karen lugged more clothes from her well-stocked closet to her bulging suitcases, preparing for an extended absence. Alex recalled the other times this scene had played out when Karen left before an important milestone in Alex's life.

"Mom! Prom is next weekend." The whine crept into her voice despite her best efforts to control it. "Will you be back in time?"

Karen looked upward, heaving a huge sigh. "Yes, Alex. I'll be back. I won't miss it."

Alex plopped onto her mother's bed while Karen zipped three pieces of luggage. Two weeks ago, Karen had promised Alex to squeeze prom dress shopping into her schedule, but she'd called from out of town and told Alex to go without her. A client needed Karen for several more days. Although devastated, Alex had pretended to laugh it off, as she had done with Karen's countless absences throughout her life.

Alex's many years working with her step-father J.T.'s construction crew had developed her carpentry skills and nourished her confidence. She'd soon be waving goodbye to life in a small Southern town as it disappeared in her rearview mirror. She couldn't wait. The biggest drawback to her new independent life in California would be leaving the construction business. Alex doubted Karen would know she'd left.

And, if Alex had to guess, she was willing to bet Karen wouldn't be around on prom night.

∅ ∅ ∅

Prom day. Cloudless and sunny. A perfect April day. As Alex predicted, Karen called before breakfast to announce she wouldn't be able to break away from her job in Nebraska. She gushed her apologies, asking Alex about her dress and dinner plans, but she cut her daughter off mid-sentence to hurry to an important meeting. Alex tried to remain strong and stoic, having anticipated this very occurrence, but the crushing blow cut her to the core. Her mother would miss her prom—of all nights.

A single silent tear rolled down Alex's cheek as she disconnected the call. She brushed the tear away with one quick swipe of her hand and drew in a deep breath.

"No more expectations," Alex said to the pitiful-looking girl staring back at her in the mirror. "Starting now, you get out there! You live your life! *And* you dang well enjoy it! Who cares if she doesn't want to be a part of it?"

She punctuated each command with a jab of her pointed finger. Though her voice cracked a little on the last part of her pep talk, it almost worked. She made it through the day with barely a thought of Karen.

Decorating for the prom at the school gym that morning had gone off without a hitch. The *Evening in Paris* theme came to life under Alex's imaginative and organized guidance as the decorating committee chair. The students had worked like a well-oiled machine to create the illusion of Paris right in the gym, setting the stage for a magical evening.

When Karen bailed on the dress shopping trip, Alex's best friend Brittany had accompanied Alex. She'd helped Alex choose a simple dress. It was a pale shade of aqua with a beaded satin bodice and a full pouf skirt of matching shimmery tulle. It fit her to perfection, and highlighted her gorgeous chocolate-colored eyes. Slipping into the dress, Alex twirled and kicked, happy she'd chosen a dress with a short skirt, which freed her from the limitations and hindrances of yards and yards of fabric. Her thick brown curls cascaded from a ponytail secured high on top of her head. Brittany, more adept than Alex at makeup application, performed a mini-makeover with stunning results.

Slipping the backs onto her large rhinestone earrings, Alex checked her appearance one last time before heading downstairs to await the limo that would take her friends, both guys and girls, to their evening's destination. As she neared the bottom, she saw J.T. smiling up at her, hands clasped behind his back. J.T. had always been the carpool parent, chef, and homework helper, the parental figure Alex trusted to listen to her problems and celebrate her successes.

"Hi, J.T.," she said, puzzled but returning his smile. Sometimes grownups acted so weird.

"Hi, sweetheart. You look beautiful," he said. Alex could see his eyes starting to get misty. "I wish your mother could see how pretty you look."

"Please, don't," was all she could muster. If she tried to say more, she'd lose it, and she didn't have time to rehash Karen's most recently broken promise. Neither J.T. nor Alex could do anything about it now.

"I know y'all aren't doing the date thing tonight, but I didn't want you going to your prom without this." As he spoke, Alex watched him bring from behind his back a clear floral box that he'd been hiding. In it nestled a corsage of fragrant white roses and delicate gypsophila. Aqua ribbon the exact color of her dress looped in and around the blooms.

J.T. carefully lifted the delicate creation from the box and slipped the corsage onto Alex's wrist. She inhaled the sweet scent of the roses, tears stinging her eyes at the kindness of the gesture. She blinked them back in an attempt to prevent her mascara from running.

"J.T., you didn't have to do this."

"I know," he said, staring at his feet, "but I never went to my own prom. My girlfriend got sick. It's been fun watching you get ready for yours. And, besides, you are practically my daughter."

With this last statement, he looked up, shrugging one shoulder while he tilted his head. Relief flooded Alex when the doorbell rang and released her from the awkward moment. She thanked J.T., gave him a quick hug goodbye, and hurried to the limo with the other two girls who'd already been picked up. Off they went, leaving J.T. to wave alone as they drove away.

"Karen," J.T. spoke into the cool early evening, "you've really messed up this time."

3

✂ ✂ ✂

After a midnight breakfast hosted by a group of parents, the limo driver delivered all the kids back to their respective homes. Alex's feet ached and exhaustion seeped into her bones, but these temporary maladies paled in comparison to the glow of contentment and happiness. She basked in the memories of the evening as she walked to the front door.

She smiled remembering her friends' reactions when they first stepped into the transformed space. The beauty and elegance of the Paris theme had exceeded Alex's expectations, and the night couldn't have gone better. Alex danced almost every dance; thankful she'd chosen a short dress. She flitted about with little effort, unlike her friends who scooted around uncomfortably in skin-tight sheaths or mermaid gowns.

When she opened the door, Alex was surprised to hear the television still blaring in J.T.'s den. She thought he'd have long ago headed upstairs to bed, even if he were still waiting up for her. She assumed he had a full day of appointments tomorrow.

Alex slipped off her shoes, tucked one finger through both heel straps and tip-toed across the wood floors toward the staircase, peeking into the den as she passed by. J.T. sat on the sofa, his elbows resting on his knees and his head in his hands. He was still awake but disheveled - shirt untucked, no shoes, hair tousled as if he'd run his hands through it many times. His body shook, leading Alex to believe he might be crying. An empty bottle of wine sat on the coffee table in front of him. Alex didn't see a wine glass.

"J.T.," Alex whispered, "are you all right?"

He jumped at the sound of her voice and stared at Alex with a mixture of confusion and guilt, as if caught doing something he shouldn't. He stood, waved his arms wildly, and sputtered that everything was going to be okay. She thought he said her mom's name, but his speech was so slurred, she couldn't be sure. Alex set her shoes and bag down at the door and approached him, careful not to make a sudden move or noise.

"You've got a busy day tomorrow. Why don't you go upstairs and turn in, J.T.?" This behavior was completely out of character, and Alex

4

began to worry. She wanted him to sleep off whatever had gotten into his head.

As she got closer, she noticed another empty bottle underneath the table. *What had he been doing?* This was so unlike anything she'd ever seen him do. He never had more than one glass of wine. Maybe two on a special occasion.

She reached past him to start cleaning up the mess. As soon as she did, his demeanor changed as though someone had flipped a switch. He whipped his hand out and grabbed her by the wrist, so lightning-fast she had no chance to dodge the snare. Alex had trusted J.T. all her life, but in an instant, fear and panic overtook her. A longing look burned in his eyes, and he yanked her down onto the sofa with him. Alex bit her lip, stifling a scream. She knew it would do no good. Their neighbors lived so far away nobody would hear her. Besides, at two o'clock in the morning everyone had been asleep for hours.

"That's right. There's no need to scream," J.T. said, an eerie calm descending over him as he caressed her hair with one hand while maintaining his iron grip on her wrists with the other. "You know I'd never hurt you."

"J.T., I think you need to just go upstairs and go to sleep," Alex said, crying now from the crushing pain in her wrists and the suffocating fear welling up from deep within.

The next few minutes seemed to happen in sickening slow motion, later to be played over and over again in Alex's mind. His huge form loomed over her. His weight pressed her down. The stench of his alcohol-tainted breath choked her. The leather upholstery gripped the bare skin on her back. Helpless, Alex wished for her spiky-heeled shoes she'd left at the door, desperate for anything she could use as a weapon. In the back of her mind she knew what horror this man-turned-stranger was bent on, but she refused to make it easy for him.

Despite her determined struggle, though, Alex couldn't match J.T.'s power and patience. He simply waited for her fighting spirit and adrenaline-fueled strength to play out. As she lay crying, the man she'd loved as a father for as long as she could remember, the man she'd trusted to protect her, that man, in his drunken haze, shattered her world and took from her what no one could ever give back.

Chapter 2
Self-Preservation

Alex escaped up the stairs, summoning the last of her energy, and locked herself in her room. One goal possessed her: to cleanse herself of the atrocity she'd just endured. Her body wracked with sobs, she scrubbed herself underneath the steaming hot shower in the bathroom adjoining her bedroom until her skin was raw and the water ran cold.

This can't be real. This has to be a nightmare. I'm going to wake up soon.

If only she understood why. But would understanding make the pain of J.T.'s assault easier to bear? He had raised her as his own daughter since she was six years old. She had been his protégé in the business since she turned twelve. As companions and friends, they spent time together when Karen traveled. Never had tonight's horrific deed been foreshadowed in any way.

Alex stepped out of the shower to dry off, trying to avoid her reflection in the mirror. Horrified, she caught a glimpse of the ugly purple splotches already forming on her wrists where his steely grip had bound her. Alex donned fresh panties and pajamas as fast as she could.

Despite the weight of complete exhaustion, sleep eluded Alex. Huddled beneath the covers of her warm, comfortable, familiar bed, Alex should have been reliving the beautiful memories of her prom. Instead, her mind played over and over again the most devastating event of her entire life. It occurred to her a horrible crime had been committed, she was the victim, and the perpetrator lived under the same roof. But never once did she consider contacting the authorities.

Besides, who would believe me?

Highly respected in the community, J.T. came from one of the founding families of Woodvale. No one would believe her if she recounted tonight's events to them. The chief of police and J.T. had a standing golf game each month. And, he'd built a mansion on the lake for the city attorney. No, she needed to figure this one out on her own.

☙ ☙ ☙

A flash of lightning quickly followed by a booming clap of thunder awakened J.T., who still lay passed out on the den sofa. Startled by the rumbling noise, he stirred and attempted to determine his whereabouts. He tried to blink, but it felt as if sandpaper lined his lids. A hundred drums pounded in his head, and he moved his tongue around in an effort to relieve the feeling of cotton having been shoved in his mouth. Rising to a sit, he saw crushed white rose petals, bruised and browning, scattered on the floor beside the sofa. Questions swirled in his mind.

Two empty wine bottles served as an accusing reminder of why he felt so utterly rotten. He hadn't indulged so excessively since college when he'd learned he couldn't drink away the memories. He adhered to a strict two-drink limit. So, what went wrong last night? He wracked his brain, but it was impossible to think when it felt as if his head could explode any second.

Rising shakily in search of the aspirin bottle, he saw Alex's shoes and purse in the doorway to the room. That's when glimpses of last night returned in sickening, nightmarish flashbacks. That's when he realized where the rose petals had come from.

"Oh, God! What have I done?" he moaned, trying to piece together the few images his alcohol-impaired memory would allow. "Please, don't let me have hurt her," he silently begged, appalled even further by the thought.

J. T. jumped at the ringing phone interrupting his thoughts. Through a crackling connection, Karen informed him the weather had delayed her flight. She wouldn't be home until the evening. He promised to have dinner waiting, trying frantically to somehow sound calm, normal. Inside, terror at the thought of harming Alex in his drunken state gripped his gut. And yet, he needed to know the truth. He checked his watch. Almost noon already. J.T. had no idea what time Alex had gotten home, but she should be awake by now. He sighed and placed a foot on the first stair, but turned and went to find the aspirin first.

Alex awoke to the sound of her cell phone ringing. Opening one eye to peek at the lit screen, she saw the caller ID indicated Brittany was awake and ready to talk. Alex groaned and rolled over, pulling the pillow over her head. A fitful sleep had finally overtaken her a scant two hours earlier, and she was in no mood to talk.

The ringing stopped, only to begin again after a three-second pause.

"Aahh!" Alex cried, rolling over and tapping the screen. "Hello," she said more brusquely than she intended.

"Well, aren't you just about as sunny as the weather today?" Brittany asked, sarcasm gushing through the phone.

A pang of remorse jabbed at Alex. Her best friend had no clue about last night, and Alex knew she shouldn't make Brittany pay for her own emotional pain.

"Sorry, Britt," Alex said. "I'm a little grumpy from all the work and lack of sleep." The lie rolled off her tongue as if it were true. "What's up?"

"You wanna hang out and study, maybe go catch a movie later? My folks were going to grill steaks tonight, but I think this weather might change those plans to a pizza night. You in?"

Brittany's usual cheerful personality, obviously not deterred in the least by a little thing like a thunderstorm, poured through the receiver. Alex, on the other hand, struggled to form a coherent sentence. She concocted a lame excuse about wanting to be home when her mom returned from her trip, hung up the phone, rolled back over, and pulled the covers over her head.

A few minutes later, Alex heard him moving around downstairs. Though hunger gnawed at her belly, going to the kitchen terrified her. How would she ever face him again? Shame and humiliation crashed over her like a tidal wave, causing her stomach to churn and all previous thoughts of food to vanish.

Alex couldn't make her mind grasp why had he done this awful thing. She had loved and trusted J.T. like a father since he and Karen had met. He had always protected and cared for her, giving her the attention she needed, even when her mother didn't. He'd taught her how to frame a house, refinish a piece of furniture, and keep the company's books. When Alex had a problem, she confided in or sought advice from J.T. rather than her mother.

Not only was he more available than Karen, but he also genuinely listened and offered thoughtful opinions. Now all those years building trust were scattered to the wind with one searing, hurtful act. It stunned her to discover her world could turn upside down in an instant.

✄ ✄ ✄

As J.T. trudged up the stairs, he thought back to his dreams from the night before. Maybe they could be more accurately described as nightmares. His high school days still haunted him sometimes, but many years had passed since he'd allowed himself to remember. On most days, he pushed the memories away by immersing himself in his work.

The bigger and more ambitious a project, the more concentration it required, therefore, the less time and energy he had available to dredge up ghosts from the past. Those ghosts did nothing but cause him trouble, like last night. Precisely how much trouble, he had yet to determine. A disturbing premonition that he had crossed the line rattled his confidence half-way up the stairs. He couldn't remember where the alcohol-fueled dreams had ended and the terrible reality had begun, but he needed answers, no matter how difficult.

He reached the second-floor landing and braced himself for the worst. He knew his life might be about to change forever. He tapped on Alex's door. No answer. He tried again, louder this time.

"Who is it?" she called through the door. Fear echoed in her voice.

He closed his eyes and tilted his head back, taking a deep breath, hoping to gain a measure of strength from it.

"It's me. Can we talk?"

"Go away."

✄ ✄ ✄

When she heard him mount the stairs, Alex got out of bed to reassure herself the door remained locked. She stood mere feet from

10

it; arms wrapped across her midsection in a protective grip. Her body quaked and the tears flowed unchecked.

"Honey, I just want to say I'm sorry if I did anything stupid last night," he began.

She snapped. The hurt and grief morphed into a white-hot rage. *Stupid? He thought what he'd done to her was stupid?* Alex flung open the door with all of her might and glared at him, her tear-streaked face and bed-tousled hair giving her an almost deranged aura. Her screeching voice completed the picture of one who has taken total leave of her senses. Livid and fueled by the adrenaline pumping through her food- and sleep-deprived system, she could be silent no longer.

"Stupid?!"

One hand gripped the doorknob in the event she needed to shut it quickly. She might appear to have lost her mind, but in truth, she was well aware of the situation in which she'd placed herself. She felt vulnerable and exposed facing her attacker. Alex drew a deep, calming breath to regain control of her emotions. It almost worked.

"You believe what you did to me was 'stupid'?" she whispered.

"Now listen," he said, attempting to explain as he advanced toward her.

Alex slammed the door, striking him in the forehead and banging the lock into place before he could recover his wits.

"Alex, that was uncalled for. Open the door this minute. We need to talk," J.T. demanded.

"No, J.T. There's nothing to talk about," she said, now in complete control of her thoughts and feelings, at least for the moment.

"Alex, I need to know. What happened?" He sounded as if his head were leaning on the door. His voice was so quiet, however, Alex strained to hear him. What was he talking about? After the heinous thing he'd done, he wanted her to say it out loud for him? What a sick man he was. She didn't know him at all.

"You raped me, J.T."

☙ ☙ ☙

He had no recollection of how he got down the stairs, found his keys, got in his truck, or started driving. All he knew was he had to get out of the house. He had to think. Instinctively, his mind had whipped into damage control mode.

11

What had he done? What would happen to him? To their family?

He'd cleaned up the wine bottles and rose petals before confronting Alex. Karen knew he didn't handle alcohol well, so if she discovered he'd been drinking, she would launch into a tirade. He'd dispose of the evidence while he was out.

Alex said she just wanted to be left alone, and he gladly accommodated her. She'd be living at home only a few more months, and J.T. felt pretty sure she wouldn't tell her mother about last night. It wasn't like they were close. But what about her friends?

If she told her friends, they would tell their parents, jeopardizing J.T. Wickham's position as a respected citizen of Woodvale. He didn't need any whispered rumors or nasty gossip tarnishing his name...again. He needed to be proactive about this and take control of the situation. If he were completely honest with himself, he was terrified.

By the time he returned home, he'd formulated a foolproof plan. Karen would go for it, he was certain. He walked in the back door to find Alex in the kitchen spreading peanut butter on a slice of bread. Her head jerked toward him, such terror shining in her eyes he thought his heart would break. He'd never had any children of his own, so Alex came as close as he could imagine. He had messed this up beyond explanation. How did he allow things to go this far?

J.T. never quite recovered from the heartbreak he'd suffered in high school. Afterwards, he'd left Woodvale for college, earning his business degree. He'd embraced his confirmed bachelor status until he met Karen. Something about her beauty and confidence combined with her determination to make a name for herself drew him in. His mind drifted to the early days of their relationship.

Karen had moved to Woodvale when Alex was five, the raw, painful memory of divorcing Alex's deadbeat dad still stinging. And though Woodvale provided the slower pace Karen had sought for herself and her daughter, the real estate market paled in comparison to what she'd left behind in Charlotte. Still, she possessed that rare gift of salesmanship. She made a decent living in their new hometown.

Woodvale brought Karen and J.T. Wickham together. J.T. hailed from a long line of Woodvale Wickhams who had built the town from the ground up. Fresh out of college, he'd assumed control of the family's lucrative and booming land development business. When his go-to realtor retired, J.T. began shopping around for another firm to help sell the luxury homes, office buildings, and shopping complexes he built.

He'd been immediately attracted to the lovely brown-eyed, brunette Karen when they met at a posh groundbreaking celebration for one of his new shopping centers. His fit, athletic build disguised the fact he had ten years on Karen. His tanned skin and salt & pepper hair complemented his clear blue eyes to perfection. Karen later admitted to him she felt an immediate attraction as he approached her with two glasses of champagne. Within weeks, they were dating each other exclusively. Six months after their initial meeting, they were married.

Karen kept her realtor's license at first, but soon her talent for interior design blossomed. J.T.'s knack for selecting the right location for the next investment combined with Karen's superb taste in outfitting each place to highlight its best features soon made the Wickham name synonymous with high quality and outstanding design. It wasn't long before people from all over the country clamored for Karen to decorate their homes and offices.

Growing to love Alex as his own daughter had been an added bonus J.T. had never expected when he married. And now, no amount of apology or explanation could change or fix what he'd done. He had destroyed a relationship of trust he'd spent most of Alex's life building, and second chances didn't come easy.

Or did they? He was going to have to try.

"I'll be done in just a sec," Alex said, snapping J.T. out of his reverie as she rushed through her task. "I needed some food. I haven't eaten since midnight."

She sprinkled cinnamon and sugar on the peanut butter, a snack J.T. had made for her since she was a little girl.

"I'm making spaghetti for dinner. Your mom should be home soon," J.T. said in a quiet voice, not daring to move any closer for fear of spooking her.

"This is fine. I'm going back to my room to study. Tell Mom I said hi." Alex turned and beat a hasty retreat.

"I suppose that could have been worse," J.T. said to the empty kitchen.

Five seconds later, J.T. welcomed Karen home. She launched into a detailed description of her trip and the job she had completed. She complained about the weather that delayed her return, raved about the scenery in Nebraska, and described in detail her luxury hotel accommodations. After talking for a full thirty minutes, she asked about Alex.

"She's in her room studying. The prom was last night," J.T. replied, his back to his wife as he prepared dinner, hoping his voice didn't reveal his guilty conscience.

"Oh, that's right," she said, tapping her head with a manicured hand. "I forgot. How did it go? Did she look cute? What color was her dress again? Red or something like that?" Karen asked as she opened the pantry door.

"She looked gorgeous," J.T. said, trying not to choke on the words. "Her dress was blue. I think she called it aqua, or something like that. What are you looking for?"

"The bottle of wine left from the dinner party we had a couple of weeks ago. I was thinking a glass might be nice with the spaghetti. Oh, well. I don't see it. We must have polished it off. I'll just head upstairs and take a quick shower while you finish dinner, if you don't mind." Her voice trailed behind her as she disappeared from the kitchen, luggage in tow.

J.T. released the breath he'd held through the entire exchange. He had to pull it together. If a few simple questions about how Alex had looked and where a bottle of wine had gone made him this edgy, he was sunk for sure. This called for drastic action.

He shook some pepper into the sauce, turned it on low to simmer, and put a loaf of garlic bread on a baking sheet. As the pot filled with water for the pasta, he considered when to set his plans into motion. If his calculations were accurate, he should have nothing to worry about.

Both his marriage and his reputation around town would be safe and well-protected. Everything he had worked for all of his life wouldn't go up in smoke over one horrible action committed in a drunken stupor. He heard Karen's footsteps coming down the stairs and prepared for the sales job of his life.

Karen sauntered into the kitchen in baby blue sweats, an oversized t-shirt and flip-flops. When working, she looked like a model for an upscale boutique, but not at home. With still-damp hair and no traces of her make-up, she looked much younger than her late forties.

"Can I do anything?" she asked, taking a seat at the kitchen table.

J.T. brought the salad bowl and veggies over to the table, and they began to chop and drop them into the bowl. "So, I've been thinking," he said, attempting a nonchalant tone as he tore lettuce piece by piece.

"Yeah? About what? Do you have a new project coming up?"

"Not exactly, although part of my idea may involve some work for you," he said, glancing at her to gauge her reaction.

She stopped chopping the cucumber, set the knife down and turned her undivided attention on him.

"What have you gotten me into? I am not doing another one of those charity auction things. Or hosting a tea party with all of the stuffy old ladies in town. Oh, my gosh. I swear, J.T., if you signed me up for any such nonsense…"

Karen seemed to be considering the dreadful possibilities of what he might have wrangled her into. As he scooped the pasta into bowls and ladled out hefty portions of sauce, he chuckled, which he knew would only heighten her misgivings about the whole situation. He returned to the table, set down their dishes, and dug in with gusto, ignoring her insistent demand not to be wrangled into an unappealing activity.

"J.T. Wickham, you tell me this instant what you have up your sleeve. I'm too tired for any more of your shenanigans!"

"Well, now. There's a word I haven't heard since my grandmother was around," J.T. said, knowing her curiosity outweighed her irritation. "But if you must know, I thought we could throw Alex a party. Since she turns eighteen the day after graduation, it could be kind of a graduation and birthday party combined. She won't get to come home much, being all the way out there in California, so it'll be a nice way for her to have a last hurrah with her friends before they all go their separate ways."

Karen pondered the idea for a moment while J.T. worried she would squelch the whole plan. But ever the gracious Southern hostess eager to display her wealth under the guise of hospitality, Karen erupted into a thousand ideas for themes, decorations, food, music.

His cryptic smile put the brakes on her endless stream of chatter. "You can start making your lists after dinner, because I've only told you half the surprise."

She set down her fork and leveled a questioning look at him, one well-plucked eyebrow arched high.

"Spill it, mister," interest shining in her eyes as she rested her elbows on the table and folded her hands beneath her chin. She seemed willing to hear him out. A good sign for J.T.

"Well, you'll be hitting the big five-oh next year. I thought we could celebrate your birthday a little early and kick off our empty nest years at the same time."

He reached into his back pocket and produced an envelope with their travel agent's logo embossed on it.

"What is this?" Karen asked, her curiosity obviously piqued.

"It's two tickets for a cruise. And not just any cruise. We're going to Alaska and then taking a train through the Canadian Rockies. Doesn't that sound fantastic?"

He leaned over to kiss her, and from her smile, he knew he had hit the jackpot.

"When do we leave?"

"The day after Alex's birthday. She's going to the beach with her friends for their graduation trip, so this is the perfect opportunity for us to get away."

He'd planned every detail with care. Weeks ago, Alex had asked him about going on the beach trip and, while Karen was gone, he gave his permission.

"The main thing left for you to do is to pick a date for her party," he said, as he reached for her bowl, clearing the table.

"I think I'll go talk to her about it now." Karen rose. J.T. hadn't seen her this excited about anything involving Alex in a very long time.

"You know what," J.T. said, "she got home pretty late last night and has hardly been out of her room all day. Why don't you wait until in the morning?"

"Maybe you're right," she agreed. "I think I'll head on up to bed myself. I'm beat."

She stood on her tiptoes and planted a kiss on his lips before slipping out of the kitchen. J.T.'s heart pounded until he thought it would beat out of his chest. Could he ever pull this off? Could he hide what he had done from the people of this town? Would he be able to live with the guilt? He decided right then and there he could and he would.

✄ ✄ ✄

"How about a surprise party?" he asked as he snuggled beside Karen in their king-sized bed. He could tell from her breathing she wasn't asleep, so he guessed she was lying there thinking about the party. He guessed right. Bolting upright, she switched on her bedside lamp, eyes wide.

"Do you think so?" she asked. "How would we know who to invite?"

"I think it'd be great. And Brittany could help us pull together a list of their friends. We could invite some of our colleagues who've known her all her life for the graduation part of the party. Why don't you sleep on it?"

J.T. leaned over to kiss Karen good night. He could tell he'd started even more wheels spinning in her brain. She would go for the surprise party idea, which was great because he needed her to.

J.T. knew Alex better than Karen did, and Alex couldn't stand for people to make a fuss over her. She didn't mind being the one working hard for other folks, whether it was building them a home, fixing them a meal or working on prom decorations.

But if he and Karen approached her about a birthday or graduation party in her honor, the idea would die a certain death right there. Alex's dislike for the spotlight didn't fit into J.T.'s plans at all. He lay there with his own thoughts brewing.

This party was exactly what he needed to demonstrate to the people of Woodvale his generosity and love toward Alex. That way, if by chance any word of the horrible thing he had done to her somehow circulated around town, he'd have concrete ammunition to refute it. Not to mention the years of caring for her and raising her as his own daughter.

Those facts, of course, made what had happened last night all the more difficult to understand and explain, both to himself and to Alex. Neither Karen nor Alex had any notion of the ghosts that still haunted him from the past, which in no way excused his conduct. Somehow, though, he had to keep himself in the clear. Self-preservation fueled him now, plain and simple.

J.T. drifted to sleep praying the past didn't visit him again tonight in his dreams. He knew he couldn't explain his screams to Karen.

Ø Ø Ø

Karen and J.T. set the party date for the weekend before graduation. Karen convinced Brittany to take Alex out for a girls' afternoon of manicures and movies before heading back to the Wickhams's home for the big bash. Each guest received a phone call from Karen imploring them to keep the event a secret. J.T. witnessed the stress of relying on others not to spill the beans agitate her nerves almost to the point of illness. A week before the big day, she announced she'd resigned herself to the cat getting out of the bag as a risk one took when planning a surprise party.

J.T. gave Karen free rein regarding the party budget. The more she spent, the more it soothed his conscience. She obsessed over every small detail, from decorations to food to music. Karen enjoyed a famous reputation in Woodvale as the consummate hostess, and she had no intention of this event being anything less than her very best.

ⵖ ⵖ ⵖ

Alex remained oblivious to the party preparations. For her, the month of May meant the end of school and all of the associated tests, senior activities, yearbook signing, awards day, and, of course, her job. The breakneck pace and packed schedule left her little time to consider what J.T. and her mother spent their time doing. In fact, she did everything she could to avoid them.

As salutatorian, she had the honor of speaking at graduation, which required much time preparing, revising, practicing, and stressing over her speech. Although graduation loomed several weeks away, Alex believed in tackling a task without hesitation. She threw herself into the crafting of her speech with a level of passion unusual even for her.

She wanted her words to inspire her classmates to *do* something with their lives, not simply give them two minutes of meaningless fluff. Who was she kidding, though? Most of the kids in her class would stay in Woodvale, get dead-end jobs, have 2.3 kids, barbecue on the weekends, and sit in carpool lines every afternoon. They could live that sad, predictable story if they wanted to.

Not Alex.

She dreamed big: engineering degree by age twenty-two, company president by thirty. What she couldn't foresee was the lesson regarding the volatility of plans and the utter lack of control she had over any of them.

Chapter 3
Girl Time

Brittany patted herself on the back at the masterful and sneaky way she'd arrange their half-hour drive to the neighboring town of Clairdon, home to the closest mall and movie theater. When Brittany suggested to Alex that they treat themselves to a girls' day the weekend before graduation—Alex resisted at first. Her excuse of still needing to study for one more final exam and wanting to put some finishing touches on her speech caused Brittany's big brown eyes to fill with tears and full lip to slip into a pout. Brittany knew Alex couldn't resist this ploy.

"How does your mom ever win any arguments with you, Britt?" Alex asked her, laughing as she slammed her locker and shoved her books in her book bag.

"Oh, she's totally immune. I wish it worked as well on her as it does on you," she replied with a wink, turning to go to her next class.

Brittany felt confident that Alex didn't suspect a thing.

☙ ☙ ☙

Party day finally arrived.

The late May sky held puffy clouds, a gentle breeze blew in from the east, and the sunshine hadn't yet begun to toast the town, as it would in a few short weeks. Karen and J.T. sat on the front porch enjoying their coffee, both marveling at the weather, while being careful not to mention the party in case the guest of honor slipped outside unannounced. They needn't have worried.

Karen panicked when Alex, who had burned the candle at both ends for weeks, slept until almost nine. The caterers were scheduled to arrive around eleven to begin setting up tables and decorating, and a thousand things had to be finished before the guests arrived. She headed upstairs to Alex's room to hurry her out of the house. She and

Brittany had to be leaving by ten. Karen's insistent knock on Alex's bedroom door was acknowledged immediately.

"Come in," Alex called.

She sat at her computer, tapping away at the keyboard, intent on completing her speech. When she didn't look up, Karen suppressed a rush of irritation.

"Alex, you do realize Britt will be here to pick you up in about half an hour?"

Karen attempted to remain calm, but she wanted to toss Alex's clothes at her, carry her into the bathroom, and turn on the shower, *but* she didn't dare.

In an uncharacteristic burst of maternal insight, Karen considered how withdrawn Alex had been over the last few weeks. She attributed it to Alex's growing apprehension over moving across the country. If anyone had told Karen the real reason for Alex's subdued behavior, she wouldn't have believed it.

"Yes, ma'am. Britt called. She's running a little late, but she'll be here right at ten. I'm using these extra few minutes to work on my speech. Let me save this file, and I'll get going."

Karen watched Alex's fingers make several quick keystrokes before she shut the computer. Then her daughter hurried toward the bathroom. Within a few seconds, Karen heard water running. Satisfied things were going according to plan, she returned to her preparations downstairs.

When Brittany arrived, Karen watched Alex, freshly showered and long brown locks pulled into a high ponytail, bounce down the front porch steps. Brittany had convinced Alex to bring something a little nicer to wear for dinner than the T-shirt and jeans she'd thrown on. Alex of course had no idea they would be returning to her own house for that dinner.

"You girls have a good time today. Do you have spending money for the mall and lunch?" J.T. asked.

Karen noticed an almost imperceptible flinch from Alex when J.T. spoke. She assumed that whatever disagreement they'd had while she'd been gone must have been a doozy. Besides, Alex's moods flipped so fast these days, who could keep up. Karen knew she couldn't.

"Yes, sir," she said, making no eye contact as she moved toward Brittany's car.

Crossing her arms, Karen tried to recall when this ice war of Alex's began. Maybe she'd ask J.T. about it while they put the last-minute touches on the party. Better yet, she wouldn't spoil this day with such depressing talk. There'd be plenty of time to discuss it later.

As soon as the girls drove away, the party prep kicked into high gear. Over the course of the day, Karen's watchful eye and professional touch transformed the Wickhams' backyard and pool area into a springtime fantasy garden. Tonight, hundreds of paper lanterns would shimmer in the old oak trees, dozens of tables would groan under the weight of mountains of delectable gourmet food, soft drinks would overflow ice-filled tubs, and endless pitchers of tea and lemonade would flow freely.

But the cake. Karen had made sure this birthday cake rivaled any upscale wedding cake her guests may have enjoyed. A DJ would keep the dance floor hopping. Karen stepped back, surveying the final effect with a critical eye. Only then could she sigh with deep satisfaction at how beautiful everything had turned out. Alex had better appreciate the time, effort, and money invested in making this evening perfect.

Karen had always substituted her money for her time where Alex was concerned. To her thinking, everyone won using her approach. Alex received the thanks for Karen's generous donations, and Karen pursued her career unfettered by whiny kids and mouthy teens. She wondered if Alex appreciated the investment she'd made in Alex's schools, teams, or charity projects. Just thinking that Alex could be ungrateful after all Karen had done irritated her.

Karen remained blind to the fact that the camaraderie between Alex and J.T. had developed over the years as a result of sharing time together in her absence. Karen shared very few interests with her daughter and had surprisingly little knowledge of Alex's day-to-day life. Refusing to fret over things she couldn't change, Karen shrugged and checked her watch, wondering how much longer until the guests began arriving. Smiling, she prepared to receive the well-deserved praise for this fabulous party. She had just enough time to change clothes and freshen her perfect makeup, stepping into the often-repeated and flawlessly executed role of hostess.

ⵁ ⵁ ⵁ

In Clairdon, the girls went non-stop all day long. Alex, amused at Brittany's packed itinerary, played along. They started with some hole-in-the-wall antiques shops on Clairdon's Main Street, followed by coffee at a nearby café before zipping out to the mall. Hours ticked by while they window shopped, tried on clothes, and made up funny stories about passers-by as they caught their second wind on the benches in the center of the huge walkways. Although it was a little late for lunch, they decided on a quick salad at the food court.

"I'm starving, but I don't want to spoil my dinner," Brittany said.

"I would agree with you if I knew a few more details about dinner," Alex said, trying to sound annoyed at her friend.

They found a table and set down their trays.

"Hey, I'll be right back. I've got to scoot into the ladies' room," Brittany whispered. "My little monthly friend showed up a few days early. That's why I was late picking you up this morning. I had to scramble around and take care of things."

Throughout her explanation, she grabbed her purse off the back of the chair and rose to make her way to the food court restroom.

Brittany's comments set off a lightbulb in Alex's brain, followed by a wave of nausea that left her weak. School, graduation, and, if she were honest with herself, her own pity party had consumed her every waking thought of late. She'd thrown herself into busy-ness, but she hadn't considered something that should have raised red flags following J.T.'s attack.

Wracking her brain to remember, she recalled thinking what a lucky break not to have any blemishes on her face for prom night. This meant she must've had her last period about two weeks before that fateful night. Alex didn't know if she'd be able to finish her salad.

Two weeks late. She was never late.

Oh, please no, she thought, sitting alone and contemplating her next move.

When she saw Brittany bouncing back to their table, Alex decided to formulate a plan without her friend's knowledge and put on the bravest face she could muster.

"Who licked the red off your lollipop?" Brittany's concerned scowl solidified in Alex's mind the need to keep her friend clueless to Alex's suspicions.

"What? Oh, nobody. I was just thinking."

Alex pushed her food around to make it look as if she had eaten. Brittany's animated chatter, alternated with shoving huge forkfuls of salad in her mouth, indicated she remained oblivious to Alex's dark mood until she halted mid-sentence and pointed her fork at Alex accusingly. Alex thought Britt didn't notice, but Britt noticed everything. She always had.

"What got you so down in the dumps while I was gone? We were having a great time and then, all of a sudden, you're a Debbie Downer? I thought I'd broken you out of the funk you've been in." She met Alex's gaze, challenging her to break eye contact.

"What funk? I don't know what you're talking about." Alex felt awful lying to her best friend, so she changed the subject. "How's your salad?"

"Uh-uh. That doesn't work with me, missy. We've been friends too long. You'd tell me if something were wrong, wouldn't you?" Brittany exhaled and tilted her head toward the young woman who had been her best bud since second grade.

"Of course," Alex said, allowing another fib to roll off her tongue more easily than it should.

She hated to do it, but she had no choice. The shame and guilt from what had happened to her were too much to speak of out loud. She couldn't even bring herself to tell her best friend of her recent speculations. Alex had a sinking feeling everyone would know soon enough.

"Good," Brittany said, brightening. She'd polished off her salad and couldn't wait to get to the movie theater.

"I'll be ready in just a sec," Alex said, excusing herself as she made a bee line for the ladies' room, leaving Brittany to clear their trash from the table.

Worried she might not make it, Alex rushed into the stall, slammed the door behind her, and heaved what little salad she had eaten.

This wasn't good.

❦ ❦ ❦

Alex's focus wandered everywhere except the plot of the sappy romantic comedy. In the dark theatre, she stared unseeing at the screen as her imagination played its own macabre scene in her head. All the swirling thoughts brought her no closer to a solution. Alex, overwhelmed by the enormity of the problems facing her, felt the hot sting of tears.

Allowing them to flow unchecked, Alex realized the movie was at the stereotypical break-up scene. She sneaked a glance at Brittany, whose tears were out of sympathy for the poor girl who had been jilted at the altar. Brittany giggled self-consciously and handed Alex a tissue from her purse.

"We're so pathetic," she whispered, blowing her nose with a resounding honk.

Alex accepted the tissue, blotted her eyes, and tried not to fall apart. She had to get it together before the lights came up and they were in the car, again. Alex left her seat to splash some water on her face and try to compose herself, letting Brittany know she'd be right back. A distracted and transfixed Brittany just raised her hand at Alex, engrossed in the story unfolding on the screen.

As Alex emerged from the dark theater, something across the parking lot caught her eye that gave her a crazy, but brilliant, idea. She glanced at her watch as she approached one of the teenage ushers.

"Excuse me, could you tell me what time the movie in theater 6B will be over?"

He consulted his schedule. "It's still got like 25 minutes left, ma'am."

"Thank you. And, if I have my ticket stub, can I leave and re-enter?" She gave him her sweetest smile.

"Well, I guess so. I'm kinda new here, but I don't think that would be a problem," he said.

Alex had plenty of time. She'd dash to the drug store across the parking lot, make her purchase, and hurry back to her seat before Brittany ever missed her. This task would be impossible in Woodvale. Everyone there knew her. It was now or never.

She pushed open the theater door and strode across the parking lot. Concern mounted as she noticed the threatening clouds looming in the sky. The volatile spring weather in North Carolina, notorious for pop-up cloudbursts, could work against her. Alex quickened her pace.

Once inside the drugstore, she quickly located the home pregnancy test section, but her head spun at the overwhelming number of choices. She felt self-conscious, as if everyone were staring as she inspected the various packages. Exasperated, she snatched one off the shelf and headed to the checkout counter, where the cashier was a guy. A cute guy! *Could this day get any worse?*

She put the box on the counter, label side facing down, and refused to make eye contact with the cute cashier. He turned the box over several times and, after what seemed an eternity to Alex, held it up and asked her, "Do you know how much this is?" Yep, today just got worse.

"No, um, I…it…uh." Alex's less-than-intelligent stutter drew a curious look from cute cashier guy.

"Price check at the front register," the guy announced into the store's PA system. Alex wished she could dissolve into a million pieces. When she checked her watch, she gasped to see twelve minutes had already elapsed since leaving the theater. If she didn't hurry back Brittany would start to worry. Or worse, she may come looking for her.

When her purchase was finally complete, she had a scant eight minutes to make it back to her seat before the movie was over. She shoved the test into her purse and was halfway across the parking lot when she heard an ominous rumble. Two seconds later, the bottom fell out of the heavens, and Alex sprinted the rest of the distance in a drenching downpour.

The icy blast of the air-conditioned theater met her rain-soaked skin, making her shiver uncontrollably. A stern-faced usher, not the nice teenager she had conversed with a few minutes ago, held up a hand to stop her.

"Where do you think you're going, young lady?" he demanded.

A frantic search of her pockets proved fruitless. Her ticket must have fallen out of her pocket when she paid at the store. Alex's words tumbled out as she tried to explain she'd been in the movie, ran over to the drugstore, and now needed to rejoin her friend.

It sounded lame to her own ears as she stood there looking like a drowned rat, and she could tell the usher didn't buy it. His arms crossed and his brows knitted into a tight V, he gave all indications he might be considering tossing her back out into the storm at any moment.

Just when Alex was ready to tuck her tail and walk outside to wait on Brittany in the pouring rain, the movie dismissed. Brittany ran out of the theater looking from side to side as if she had lost something.

Alex tilted her head toward her friend and said to the usher, "You may want to call her over here."

Once the two friends were reunited, Alex launched into the explanation of her disappearance, minus, of course, the true reason for her shopping excursion. Brittany examined her with narrowed eyes.

"Alex, are you feeling all right?" she asked.

"I'm fine. Let's go." This line of questioning could get uncomfortable. Alex wanted to switch gears. They strolled toward the car under beautiful blue skies. "Where are we having dinner?" Alex asked, feeling the ill effects of not eating any lunch.

"That's a little bit of a secret," came the cryptic reply. Brittany didn't say another word or look in Alex's direction until she pulled into the parking lot of a McDonald's on the way home.

Alex turned to her, unable to believe her eyes. "Are you serious? You're taking me to Mickey D's for my birthday?" The pitch of her voice rose with each word.

Brittany doubled over laughing as she turned off the car and collected their clothes from the back seat, imploring Alex to relax and follow her.

The girls went into the restaurant where Brittany waved at the manager, a friend of hers. She grabbed Alex's hand and pulled her toward the ladies' restroom, where they changed into their dinner outfits. Confusion clouded Alex's brain. After a quick hair fluff and makeup refresh, Britt stuffed all their clothes into a large duffel bag she had brought, and out they went.

As Alex reached for the car door, Brittany put a hand out to stop her. Still confused, Alex met her eyes, trying to figure out what was happening.

"I'm sorry I have to do this, but it's the best way to keep this secret a complete surprise," Brittany said, wrapping a scarf around Alex's eyes, rendering her sightless.

"What are you doing?" Alex said, struggling against the blindfolding process. Britt couldn't be serious.

"We're going to dinner," came the calm reply. Brittany eased her friend into the passenger seat and helped get her seatbelt fastened. Alex heard the car start and felt the familiar rumble of the engine. She assumed a sulking posture, arms crossed and head turned toward the window.

"You could at least tell me how long we're going to be travelling in this ridiculous fashion," Alex demanded.

"Not much longer now. How 'bout some music?"

"Hmm."

Soon the two of them were singing along to their favorite songs, Alex's sour mood forgotten for the time being. She felt the car slow, then turn, then drive slowly for a short distance. Brittany turned the car off.

"Here we are," Brittany announced. Alex reached up to remove the scarf, sending Brittany into spasms.

"Alex, no! What are you doing? Do you want to ruin everything after all I've done?" This elicited a small smile from Alex. Brittany swatted at Alex's arm. "You did that on purpose, didn't you?"

"Just wanted to see how serious you are about this whole 'secrecy' thing."

"Wait there. No peeking!" came the command as she exited the car and hurried around to get Alex out of the car.

Brittany succeeded in maneuvering Alex down the garden path, through the gate and into the spacious backyard-turned-dreamland.

🖋 🖋 🖋

Brittany found herself reluctant to end her wonderful one-on-one time with her best friend. She'd known something wasn't right with Alex. She couldn't quite put her finger on what it was, though, and Alex denied any problem whenever Brittany asked. However, today's outing confirmed something was amiss.

Brittany would smile for the sake of the party. But, just for tonight.

Karen had instructed Brittany to wait for her cue to remove Alex's blindfold so the guests could yell the obligatory greeting of surprise at her friend. But as she reached up to lift the scarf from Alex's eyes, she determined to get to the bottom of whatever was bothering her friend as soon as this party was over.

Chapter 4
The Party and the Plan

The crunch of gravel underfoot and the unmistakable aroma of a charcoal grill told Alex this was an outside event. The further they walked Alex smelled the familiar scent of her mother's perfume underlying all the other wonderful smells. *That's weird*, Alex thought. *Had they driven long enough to be back at the Wickham home? Why would Brittany bring her home before taking her to dinner?* Confusion reigned in Alex's mind as she felt Brittany untie the scarf. She whispered in Alex's ear as she did, "They did this."

As Alex opened her eyes, what met her gaze overwhelmed her, eliciting a small gasp. The backyard was unrecognizable after the dramatic transformation. Karen had outdone herself. As the scarf dropped, at least a hundred people yelled, "Surprise!" at the top of their lungs. Alex experienced a complete sensory onslaught.

Her hands flew to her mouth, tears welled up in her eyes, and she tried to decide if what she felt was a result of happiness, fear, anger, or a combination of emotions. Her heart was leaning toward anger, but she smiled for the crowd. Karen, standing at her daughter's side, interpreted Alex's reaction as nothing less than elation.

"Happy birthday and happy graduation, darling," Karen said, her voice dripping with the sweetness she reserved for clients as she kissed the air beside each of Alex's cheeks. "Isn't it just divine? Now go run a comb through your hair and touch up your lipstick so you can greet your guests." Ever the Southern lady, Karen believed in the empowerment a fresh coat of lipstick gave a lady.

"Mom, I'm pretty hungry. I didn't have much lunch," Alex replied, noticing the grill loaded with burgers, hot dogs, and veggie skewers. Karen rolled her eyes and sighed.

"Oh, Alex. I'll fix you a plate while you start mingling. If you're going to take over J.T.'s business, you simply must start rubbing elbows with the right people. Don't hang out with just your own little friends tonight. Understand? Chat with some of our friends, too."

As Karen issued her orders, Alex scrutinized the crowd. True, many of her own friends from school were there, but there was also an older crowd, several of whom she recognized from the black-tie business affairs she attended with her mom and J.T. mingled among the teenagers.

Of all the nerve! They'd used her birthday and graduation as an excuse for throwing a huge shindig for their business associates. She wondered if they would write the event off on their taxes as a business expense.

Once the initial shock of the surprise waned, Alex gazed at the elaborate decorations and the mountains of mouth-watering food. Having always been the second priority in her mother's life, Alex deluded herself into believing for tonight she could pretend Karen had gone to all this effort for her own daughter.

Alex could imagine herself as Karen's top priority. Alex's heart knew she would never be as important or interesting as Karen's beloved career, but for one evening she'd pretend she was. It wouldn't even be difficult to do. Her mother in full-on hostess mode doted on the guest of honor as she always did. This time, however, the guest of honor was Alex.

Tomorrow, reality would crash in when things returned to normal, but tonight Alex decided to relax and indulge in the festivities. She mingled with the guests, wistful envy welling up as she watched her friends enjoy the pool while she carried on small talk about where she would attend school and how far away California was.

At one point in the evening, Alex got cornered by an eccentric geologist who worked for J.T. His long-winded explanation of the subsurface geology in California had Alex biting the inside of her mouth to stay conscious. She'd never been so happy to see her mother as when Karen came to her social rescue.

"If you'll excuse the birthday girl for a few minutes. She's been out shopping all day and worked up quite an appetite. I've got a hamburger calling her name."

Karen hooked her elbow in Alex's and began walking as she talked, making no further apology to the rock man.

"Mother, thank you. Does anybody ever listen to him?" Alex asked, plopping into a folding chair at one of the white linen-covered round tables dotting the back yard.

"Of course not. Why do you think he was so excited to have an attentive audience?" Karen dismissed him with a wave of her hand. "Now, eat up. It'll soon be time to sing and cut the cake."

"Uh, Mom, I'm not three years old. You don't have to sing to me."

The idea of everyone standing around looking at her, singing to her, and expecting her to blow out a bunch of candles made her squirm and sent her stomach into knots.

"We'll see." Karen pivoted on her heel and walked away.

Alex knew what that meant. It meant Karen was going to get her way. It always had and always would.

Taking her first bite of the burger, Alex closed her eyes and sighed with appreciation. She'd wolfed down almost half of it when Brittany ran over and occupied the seat next to her.

"So, were you surprised?" she asked. Her flushed face was evidence of how much she was enjoying herself.

"Mm hm," Alex nodded with her mouth stuffed, trying not to be too rude. When she finally swallowed, she said, "I can't believe you kept this a secret. I know you. You're a terrible secret-keeper." Alex glanced sideways at her best friend.

Placing the back of her hand to her forehead, Brittany feigned a hurt expression. "You wound me, my friend. Of course, I'm good with secrets. At least, the important ones."

She reached over, snatched a chip from Alex's plate and hurried off to join the line dance in full swing on the dance floor near the pool house. She motioned for Alex to join her.

Alex took one more colossal bite, gulped a swig of her soda and sprinted to join her favorite line dance. For a few brief minutes, she put aside the concerns that plagued her. After a few songs, she and Britt abandoned the dancing to find something cool to drink. The lull in activity provided Alex the opportunity to remember her purse, with her secret drug store purchase, remained in her friend's car.

Alex suggested they move her purse, shopping purchases, and the clothes she'd changed from to the house so they didn't forget in all the excitement. A quick glance toward the punch bowl assured them

Karen was occupied with a guest and wouldn't miss them, so the girls walked to the driveway.

They grabbed Alex's stuff, headed inside, and ran up the stairs. Opening the door to her room, Alex said, "Let's just toss this stuff on my bed. I'll organize it later."

Without thinking, Alex launched her satchel purse toward the bed, regretting her decision almost at once. It landed on the edge of the bed, tumbling off and spilling the contents across the hardwood floor of her bedroom. Alex watched in what seemed like slow motion as the pregnancy test box rolled over, label up and facing directly toward them. She scrambled to grab the box and stuff it back into her bag, but she knew Britt had seen the whole scene unfold. Alex had no choice but to come clean with her friend.

"Alex?" Brittany asked, her voice barely a whisper. "What's going on?"

"I wanted to tell you about this so many times, Britt. I haven't told anyone. I don't even know if it's true yet." She inclined her head toward the test kit on this last statement. The explanation tumbled out of Alex, who actually felt a great unburdening to share her secret.

"But how...?" Brittany asked.

Alex didn't even have a boyfriend, so she could understand how this revelation shattered everything Britt thought she knew about Alex.

"Alex." Karen annoyed voice carried from downstairs. "Where on earth are you? You have guests. For heaven's sake, get down here and act like a decent hostess."

Alex rolled her eyes and shoved her purse under her bed, hugging Brittany and promising to explain everything to her as soon as the party ended. Brittany's eyes held so much hurt Alex wanted nothing more than to climb under the bed, too, and make everything and everyone just go away.

∅ ∅ ∅

Both girls pasted smiles on their faces and cast many furtive glances at their watches while the party seemed to stretch into eternity. Of course, Karen focused on Alex, watching her like a hawk stalking prey. Right before the cake cutting, Karen grabbed Alex by the arm, yanked her away from the crowd, and whispered through clenched teeth.

"What is going on with you? You've been sulky and moody almost from the time you got here. Aren't you enjoying yourself?" She asked it with more accusation than question in her tone. *How dare someone not enjoy themselves at one of Karen Wickham's parties.*

"Of course, I am, Mother," Alex's response rolled off her tongue, the reflex of years of appeasing Karen.

The encounter with her mother served as a reminder to put on a better mask for the remainder of the evening. Otherwise, more interrogation was inevitable. Alex addressed Karen, deflecting the focus from herself.

"You wouldn't believe how Brittany wore me out shopping today. Man, are we beat! What a power shopper!"

Alex covered both hers and Brittany's tracks with this little fib. Her mother eyed her with suspicion but conceded a day of girl time could indeed take its toll. Convinced Alex was enjoying herself, Karen whisked her over to the cake table and whispered to the DJ.

As Alex's discomfort grew under the guests' focused stares, Karen gushed how the opulent three-tiered cake featured a different decadent flavor on every tier, each flavor more delicious than the previous one. Alex tried to zone Karen out by carefully inspecting the creation before her.

Elegant pink and white icing roses cascaded down and around the entire sugary concoction. And to top it all off, eighteen spaghetti-thin candles sprouted from the centers of more roses. The effect was nothing short of dazzling. Alex would have been happy with a homemade chocolate cake, but homemade had never been Karen's style.

Having dispensed with blowing out the candles, Alex breathed her relief when the caterer stepped in to cut and serve. The birthday girl received the first slice, but she found cake didn't hold the temptation for her it normally did. Once the older guests enjoyed their dessert, they congratulated Alex on her graduation, wished her happy birthday, and headed for their cars. Aware of her mother's watchful stare, Alex did her best to be cordial and thank each guest as they departed.

Night had fallen and the paper lanterns' glow transformed the backyard into a cozy, intimate oasis in a cavern of darkness. The cool evening temperature forced even the hardiest of teens to change out of swimsuits and back into dry clothes. The glass-like surface of the

35

pool reflected the shimmer of those little floating lotus-shaped candles Karen used at most of her parties. Several of Alex's friends slow danced to a popular boy band song.

Brittany hooked her arm with Alex's, and together they took the whole scene in. Alex wanted to remember every detail about tonight. Her home. Her friends. This perfect North Carolina evening. Then, loud tapping on the DJ's microphone shattered her reverie.

"May I have your attention, please?" *What was J.T. doing?* Alex's stomach clenched as he continued. "We're here tonight to honor Alex, our birthday girl and graduate."

He looked right at her while he spoke. She tried to tear her gaze away. She'd avoided him for almost two months. But some morbid curiosity forced her to listen to what he had to say. She remained rooted to the spot, still holding on to Brittany for support. Alex knew her friend had no idea Alex's heart beat so fast she felt faint.

"So, I just wanted to say, Alex, I hope you know how proud your mother and I are of you and how much we're going to miss you. You may not be my daughter by blood, but you're my daughter in my heart," J.T. said, pointing at his chest as he finished.

On these last words, his voice caught in his throat as if stifling a sob. Alex wondered what people would think if she screamed, vomited, or threw something at him. The vile liar! Throughout his saccharin diatribe, her mother stood beside him, smiling and nodding as he spoke. *Did she know the truth? Or had he lied to her, too?* The events of the evening and the last few months swam in her head until, in a flash of insight, everything became crystal clear to Alex.

J.T. had orchestrated this party for his own selfish purposes, his precious untarnished reputation. How would anyone believe her now if she voiced her allegations? The people of Woodvale would unite in his camp, finding him incapable of such. He said himself he loved her like his own daughter. No. No one would believe he'd done such a thing.

Alex endured the rest of the party in a fog of hurt. Disbelief. And uncertainty.

⚕ ⚕ ⚕

Later, as they waited in Alex's room for the little stick to reveal its answer, Alex told Brittany the whole story, starting with J.T.'s apology

36

for her mother's absence on prom night. The girls took turns snatching a tissue from the box on the bed whenever a T-shirt sleeve no longer controlled the tears. Being able to talk about the whole ordeal unburdened Alex in a way she'd not expected, and she admitted for the first time how ashamed she felt.

"Alex," Brittany's jaw dropped as she shook her head, "you have nothing to be ashamed of. Nothing, do you understand? I can't believe you haven't already told somebody about this. Should you go to the police?"

Mortified, Alex answered, "Of course not. Do you know what kind of scandal that would cause? My mother would freak out! And besides, Britt, do you think anyone would believe me?"

Alex launched into her theory about the party being J.T.'s attempt to protect his reputation around Woodvale. She reminded Brittany how attentive J.T. had been to his clients at the party. And why *had* his clients been invited to a party for Alex anyway? Sure, they all knew Alex through her position in J.T.'s business, but Alex stressed how odd to invite a bunch of adults to an eighteenth birthday party. With each finger Alex raised to count off the reasons her theory was sound, she watched Brittany grow angrier.

A loud knock at Alex's bedroom door made both girls jump and stare at each other as if caught doing something they shouldn't. Alex jerked opened her nightstand drawer, threw the test stick inside, then slammed it closed before addressing the interruption.

"Come in," Alex said, trying to look and sound much more relaxed than she felt. She arched her brows in question at Brittany as Karen struggled to open the door under the weight of a huge, gift-wrapped box and about half a dozen gift bags.

"A little help here, please," Karen said. Annoyance dripped from her voice.

Alex jumped up and hurried to her mother at the door, relieving her of some of her burden.

"Have you girls been crying? I just threw a birthday party for the record books, and y'all are crying?" She asked, at once both incredulous and miffed.

"We were just thinking about not being together in the fall, Mrs. Wickham," Brittany answered, her cover so smooth Karen didn't even question it.

"Mother, what in the world is all of this?" Alex asked, rerouting the conversation as she gestured toward the load Karen dumped on Alex's bed.

"Seriously? These are your gifts, silly. You don't think everyone came to a birthday and graduation party and didn't bring you at least a little something? Now, I arranged for all of the guests to sign in when they arrived and include their mailing addresses so you don't have to go to the trouble of looking them all up when you write your 'thank you' notes." As Karen spoke, she arranged the gift bags on the window seat and removed the lid from the large, wrapped box with a flourish.

Alex mentally calculated that with only a few gift bags and one large box, she could polish off thank you notes in no time. Then she peeked over the edge of the box and saw forty or fifty envelopes inside! The guests' generosity rendered Alex speechless. Brittany, on the other hand, was never at a loss for words.

"Oooh, can she start opening them now?" she asked Karen clapping her hands with excitement.

"Good idea. Brittany, you get a sheet of paper and keep track of what each guest gave her. That'll make her thank you notes a piece of cake." Karen's adherence to the rules of proper etiquette elevated her to the equivalent of a manners drill sergeant.

Alex had long ago learned to properly acknowledge gifts, but she'd never had to write so many at one time. With Brittany as her encourager, she felt sure she could get through it. The news awaiting her in the nightstand drawer was a bit of a distraction right now, though. She longed to focus on that important bit of business first, and then she could dive into the cards and gift bags.

Karen, however, had other plans. "I think I'll stay and find out what you got. I don't ever get to share in your fun times anymore." Alex groaned inwardly. *Why would Mother choose tonight of all nights to share in these things?*

Karen relocated some of the bags to the bed to make space for herself on the window seat. She curled her legs underneath her and got comfortable, smiling at her daughter.

Alex pasted on the most natural-looking smile she could muster.

"Great, Mom. Let's get started."

She handed Brittany a notebook and pencil, shooting her another questioning look as she did so. Alex got down to the business of opening gifts, which would have been a much more enjoyable experience if her mind and eyes didn't constantly wander to the drawer.

If someone spent time selecting a card, Alex believed she should at least take the time to read the sentiment within, especially if a handwritten message had been added. After about twenty cards, her technique met with resistance from Karen and Brittany, who were tiring of the whole operation. Nevertheless, Alex forged ahead, reminding them she would neither turn eighteen nor graduate from high school again.

After almost an hour, Alex sat on the floor, shocked and overwhelmed at the generosity of her party guests. Coupled with her substantial savings from years of working for J.T., she now had not only enough to buy her new car, but plenty left over for a tidy rainy-day nest egg as well.

Karen rose to leave, but she paused with her hand on the doorknob. "I almost forgot about your gift from J.T. and me," she said, turning to face Alex.

"What? I thought the party was my gift from y'all," Alex said.

"Well, sure, but we wanted to get you something special you could keep. You won't be able to take it to school with you, because it won't fit in a dorm, but we got you your own set of professional-grade tools. There are hand tools, a few power tools, a beautiful tool chest. It's all in the garage. You can use them during your summers at home, then when you graduate and take over J.T.'s business, you'll be well on your way to being outfitted for whatever you need."

Alex thought back to the summer she turned twelve, when her desire to take over J.T.'s business was born. Karen and J.T. had decided to add the pool house in their back yard, the exact one that had been used for her party tonight, to have a space for teenage get-togethers that would accommodate a boisterous crowd. Alex had begged to be included on the construction crew.

She'd accompanied J.T. to build sites ever since she was in first grade, when they began stopping after school to check on a few of his projects before heading home to start homework. When she got her own beginner's tool set at the age of eight, her creativity soared. She built bird houses, bookends, decorative boxes, and whatever else she could fashion out of the scraps on the trash heap. By the time the pool house build started, Alex needed a bigger project to challenge her.

Alex had convinced a reluctant J.T. both she and the equipment would be fine in her capable hands. In Alex's time on job sites, she'd seen the scary toll of a single second of inattentiveness. Severed fingers, gaping wounds, or damaged vision could result from the slightest lapse in focus. J.T. trusted Alex to remain alert, just as she trusted him to teach her the secrets of the trade. Each evening that summer, J.T. wrapped up his regular workday and arrived home to find Alex waiting in the driveway, hardhat on and ready to learn the new skill of the day.

It turned out Alex was a natural talent. By summer's end, she could operate a backhoe, frame a building, blow in insulation, hang drywall, shingle a roof, paint, and even do a little brick and stone masonry. She accompanied her mom to select curtains, a sofa, rugs, and accessories. Alex saw first-hand what it took to make a home beautiful and inviting from the ground up. She'd found her calling, and now she intended to turn it into her ticket out of an impossible situation.

"Mom, I don't know what to say. It's all too much," Alex said, as tears welled up in her eyes. Never one to seek attention, such extravagance being heaped on her in one day was overwhelming.

It crossed Alex's mind to ask her mother if she knew the truth. *Did she know her husband, while in a drunken stupor, had assaulted her daughter?* But she stopped herself. Maybe her mother did know. Maybe all of the gifts, the party, the sudden out-of-character interest in her daughter was Karen's way of assuaging her own guilt at not having protected her. These suppositions caused anger to brew in Alex. She recalled the absences, the slights, the times when she'd landed far down the list of her mother's priorities.

Alex knew making a scene was pointless, accomplishing nothing more than putting her mother on the defensive. Besides, confrontation made Alex break out in a sweat. All she wanted was for Karen to leave. Alex and Brittany needed to move on to more important things, like checking the result on the test stick. With slow, burning resentment still simmering within her, Alex recognized one thing for certain. She needed to break free. The thought was at once liberating and terrifying.

The warmth of the tear slipping down Alex's cheek snapped her back to the present. She jerked her head toward her mother, worried Karen could read her thoughts. Karen smiled at her, hand still on the doorknob, ready to make her escape and return to something more pressing in her hectic schedule.

"Thank you, Mother," Alex choked out.

"Well, you're welcome, dear. Don't forget to thank J.T., too. He's the one who picked out the tool set. You know I have no idea about those things," she said with a flick of her hand. "Now, I'm heading off first thing in the morning to do some shopping for our cruise. Have you got everything you need for your beach trip?" she asked.

"Yes, ma'am."

"Good. You girls can get back to having fun doing whatever you were doing before I got here." Alex and Brittany exchanged a glance that spoke volumes, but neither said a word.

🕊 🕊 🕊

Once they knew Karen and J.T. were otherwise occupied, the girls cleared the gifts off the bed and Brittany locked the door.

"Just for good measure," she assured Alex.

They sat cross-legged on the bed facing each other. Alex reached into the nightstand drawer, wrapped her hand around the piece of plastic that would determine her life's path, and pulled it out without looking. She told Brittany to close her eyes, and she did the same. They agreed that on the count of three, Alex would open her hand and they would open their eyes and find out together.

"One, two, three."

Alex turned her hand palm up and opened her fingers, clearly exposing the plus sign in the test stick window for both girls to see. They stared in disbelief. Brittany hazarded a cautious glance at her friend. But instead of tears or anger, quite the opposite met Britt's gaze. Stoic and quiet, Alex drew in a deep breath and exhaled through pursed lips.

"Now what?" Brittany whispered. She looked scared, and this wasn't even her trial to face. Alex knew she had Britt's unwavering support.

"I don't know yet, Britt. I've got a whole lot of thinking to do. This isn't how I planned for things to go."

On this last word, Alex lost her voice and her composure, collapsing in sobs into her friend's arms. Brittany whispered soothing

41

words and stroked Alex's long brown hair, giving her the time she needed to process the news.

The two of them had always supported each other during times of boyfriend breakups, test stress, mean girl bullying, or any other normal girl drama. They'd planned their future to include each other. But this current scenario had never even crossed their minds.

Pragmatic almost to a fault but reeling from the shock, Alex dried her tears, blew her nose and issued orders to Brittany.

"My hands are shaking too much to take notes, so I'm going to need some help making a list of the pros and cons of my alternatives. I can search for stuff on the Internet, but if you can write things down, I'd really appreciate it. I know we've had a busy day, but do you mind staying up a little bit later?"

"I'm here for you. Just tell me what you need me to do." Alex knew she'd never forget the depth of sadness in her friend's voice as she pledged her assistance.

"Okay," Alex said, taking another deep breath and attempting to regain some control over her circumstances. "Here are my options as I see them."

Thus, their all-night research, discussion, and planning began. By dawn, Alex felt more informed, even if the uncertain future ahead still terrified her. Now, she just had to put her elaborate plan into action. Still, she felt confident she could pull it off.

Chapter 5
Departure

The late-morning sun bore down on the graduates, parents, and friends, forcing everyone to seek respite in their air-conditioned cars. The commencement ceremony had concluded and all the goodbyes had been said. Alex slipped the mortar board off her head, unzipped her graduation gown, and walked toward Brittany's car, trying to evade her mother's stare. Everyone in the large crowd would soon be sitting in a long line of people eager to depart from one of the two stadium exits, while Woodvale's finest directed traffic along the highway.

How Alex longed to escape, and it wouldn't be long now. She had almost reached Brittany's car when her mother spotted her from across the parking lot. Karen waved, motioning Alex to join her and J.T.

"Alex, dear. We're parked over here," Karen called.

Alex had ridden to the stadium with Brittany, arriving early with the other graduates to line up for the processional. She had no intention of hanging out with Karen and J.T. today. Most of her time over the past week had been spent at her computer preparing to carry out her plan, and time was now at a premium.

"Can you wait just a minute?" Alex asked Brittany.

"I don't think I'm going anywhere anytime soon," Brittany watched the long lines snaking toward the exits. "Besides, I already told my folks we'd meet up at home. You go do what you need to do."

Alex couldn't think about how she was going to make it without her trusted best friend by her side. She tried to push the thought to the back of her mind as she made it to Karen's red two-seater sports car. Karen embraced her daughter and kissed the air by both cheeks.

"Honey, your speech was wonderful. I can't believe you're a graduate!" Karen yelled her congratulatory remarks as if Alex were still across the parking lot.

Alex tried to gracefully accept her mother's accolades, but she couldn't be certain if they were sincere or for the benefit of those standing around them. Several people walking by stopped to congratulate Alex on her excellent speech, and Karen reveled in accepting their praise. J.T. stood silently in the background.

"J.T., aren't you even going to congratulate our girl?" Karen motioned for him to join them.

J.T. stepped up and reached forward as though to hug Alex. Without thinking, Alex shrunk back from his attempted embrace. She cleared her throat to break the awkward tension and slipped her long brown hair behind her ear.

"Well, Britt and I are going to grab a burger, and then I'll be home." All she wanted was to get away. Now and forever.

"I thought we could go out somewhere nice for dinner," Karen said, pouting.

"We can go when y'all get back from your cruise. Then I can hear all about your trip, and you can hear about my beach trip. I'm sure you've got a lot of packing to do." Alex felt uncomfortable lying to them, but her ruse seemed to mollify Karen, who waved goodbye and dismissed Alex to go and have fun with her friend.

Back at Brittany's car, Alex ticked off a long list in her head of all the things she had to do. In reality, there would be no beach trip for her. Unless, of course, she counted the beach in California. That trip would begin way before school started in the fall.

Alex and Brittany had planned Alex's exodus from Woodvale to California down to the last detail. Before she left, Alex would purchase a dependable used vehicle, preferably a sport utility vehicle. She had a lot of luggage and tools to haul and needed the space. She'd deal with all the paperwork by mail once she settled into her new life.

Next, they'd mapped out an obscure route across the country. Instead of heading directly west, she planned to travel down through South Carolina, across Georgia and Alabama, then westward from there. Although Karen and J.T. would be in Alaska during Alex's getaway, Alex wanted to be as unpredictable as possible, in case the couple decided to try to find her. In the back of her mind, Alex doubted they would care enough to go to that much trouble.

Another part of the plan involved Alex getting a job until school began. With her new tools, she was counting on being able to find some kind of construction work near the school. She even considered speaking to the dean about doing maintenance at the school in exchange for moving into the dorm early. This part concerned her a bit, but Alex knew her skills were top-notch and would serve her well.

The one decision she hadn't yet made was the most important. And, the most difficult. What would she do about the tiny life inside her? The easiest thing to do would be to end it, make a fresh start in California and never look back. She knew from her research that abortion clinics abounded all over the country. But every time such thoughts entered her mind, a horrible feeling in the pit of her stomach threatened to make her sick. This decision wouldn't wait forever, though. She needed to make up her mind, and she needed to do it soon.

"I can't believe we'll be apart forever in just a few days," Brittany said, the tone of her voice betraying emotions she dared not discuss. She started her car, the air conditioning blast relieving the sweltering sauna of a Southern summer day.

"Don't."

If Alex allowed herself to get sucked into Brittany's sorrow-fest, she might lose her nerve. She couldn't be distracted by the fact her dearest friend since as long as she could remember would no longer be by her side. She had a task to complete. She needed to focus.

Alex planned never to set foot in Woodvale again. And if her friend ventured out to California, it wouldn't be often. Instead, Britt would soon be making the trek to New York City where a spot in the freshman class at NYU awaited her. Alex had no idea what she was going to do without Brittany's steadying support, sense of humor, and voice of reason.

None of that mattered right now.

"You're right," Brittany said. "We're going to enjoy our time together these last couple of days. Let's go get a burger. We can go through your checklist again and make sure you're not forgetting anything." She edged her car forward into the line of cars, leaving behind the last vestiges of high school life.

Yeah, Alex thought, *phone calls and e-mails aren't going to be the same as having my best friend by my side.* Losing Britt would leave a gaping hole in Alex's life and heart.

Ø Ø Ø

Alex woke early on her birthday, dressed in nice pants and a conservative blouse before fixing a light breakfast. She wanted to be ready to buy her first car, but she had no idea what to expect. She had enough in her savings to allow her to afford the purchase. Exhibiting her typical fierce independence, she long ago decided to wait until the day she turned eighteen, the day after graduation, to make the cash purchase with no help from her mom or stepdad. Alex guessed her mother would say something about her making such a major decision by herself, but, after all, where did her mom think Alex's headstrong, independent, determined attitude came from anyway?

She'd been feeling a bit queasy for a few days and didn't know whether to attribute it to the pregnancy or nerves. In the kitchen she spotted an envelope bearing her name in her mother's familiar flowing script propped up beside the coffeepot. Had she left the house already? It wasn't even 8:30, yet.

Tamping down her irritation, she opened the birthday card. In it, her mother explained she'd be working in Charlotte most of the day, but expected to be home in time for the family to go to dinner for her birthday. Alex took some minor consolation in knowing she'd never have to take a back seat to Karen's other commitments after today.

Still, it hurt.

Halfway through a glass of orange juice and a piece of toast, Alex's senses went on full alert when J.T. walked into the kitchen, still rubbing the sleep from his eyes. She stared at him, a wariness in her eyes belying the confidence she attempted to exude.

"Good morning. And, happy birthday," he said, stopping in his tracks on his approach toward the coffee.

Alex lost her appetite. She snatched up her plate and glass and put them in the sink. "Thank you," she muttered, avoiding eye contact and maintaining her distance.

"So, are you still planning on looking at cars today?"

"No. I'm going to buy a car today," she clarified, determination and defiance clear in her voice.

"Don't be too hasty. Car dealers love to take advantage of young girls." As soon as he said it, J.T. winced at the comment.

"Well, you should know, right, J.T.?" she spat out as she turned from her position by the sink. Weeks of living like a prisoner, knowing she'd soon leave everything she'd ever known behind, and now facing

46

her attacker alone, a man she had trusted all of her life, gave her an uncharacteristic fearlessness.

"Alex," he said, hands extended, palms up in surrender. "I've apologized, we threw you an amazing party, I picked out the best tools money could buy. How else can I tell you how sorry I am for what happened?"

"You don't get it, do you, J.T.? Do you know I could go to the authorities and press charges? You committed a crime. You raped me." Alex punctuated her argument by pointing her finger at J.T. and jabbing at the air toward him. "Do you realize how serious this is?" By the time she finished, she was shrieking, her face flushed.

As suddenly as the emotions escalated, the fight drained out of her like so much water out of a bathtub. Of course, he didn't get it. Besides, nobody would believe her, and he knew it. She needed to stick to her plan and let J.T. and Karen live their lives without her. They deserved each other.

A horn honked in front of the house. Alex grabbed her purse and headed toward the front door. Brittany was taking her car shopping. She wondered for the millionth time how she could survive without her best friend.

"I'm outta here." She brushed past him and slammed the front door as she left. It gave her some small level of satisfaction to do so.

𝄐 𝄐 𝄐

Driving her two-year-old, new-to-her sport utility vehicle home from the dealership with a smile on her face she couldn't seem to suppress, Alex realized it might have been to her advantage to have a huge confrontation with J.T. right before buying a car. She was primed for battle and in no mood to take any trouble from a car salesman. In fact, she marched right out of the first dealership.

Her smile turned into a chuckle remembering this morning. She'd walked into the showroom resolutely, heels clicking on the polished tile, Brittany struggling to keep up. When the salesman asked if he could help her, she told him she wanted to purchase a used vehicle and handed him her list of specifications.

With a condescending smile, he had patted her shoulder and asked if she'd like to come back later when her dad could help her pick out "something sporty." Without so much as a "Good day," Alex and

Brittany had turned around and walked out, taking the salesman's commission with them.

The next two dealerships were only a bit more welcoming, but on the fourth try, just as a deflated Alex was prepared to admit defeat, the situation turned around. She found Lisa, an attentive and helpful saleswoman. When Alex explained what she wanted, what she intended to use it for, and what her budget was, Lisa smiled before showing Alex three different SUVs to suit her needs. The result was Alex driving home in her very own pewter gray beauty.

A few details still needed to be wrapped up, but Lisa assured her everything could be done through the mail or e-mail. Brittany and Alex exchanged glances, knowing it might be quite some time before Alex had a permanent mailing address. She tried not to worry about those details. She had enough to worry about without adding something else to the list.

Alex pulled into the driveway a little after five and observed neither her mother's car nor J.T.'s truck in their normal locations in the three-car garage. Breathing a sigh of relief, she parked her car, locked it, and went inside to finish packing. Both Karen and J.T. believed she was packing for a beach trip. Neither suspected she'd be gone forever soon after they departed for their cruise.

It made for a convenient ruse, but it left her in a quandary over what to do with her boxes of mementos, those trinkets of life she had collected growing up. Now that she knew how much space she had in her SUV, she could decide what went and what stayed. She needed space for her computer, tools, and luggage.

All her other possessions amounted to nothing more than luxuries that required prioritization. Alex knew she neither needed nor wanted to take a carload of memories of this old life with her on her fresh start. She kept reminding herself of the whole point of this clandestine departure: to break free once and for all and never look back.

She strolled around her bedroom looking at the keepsakes from her life. The elegance and excess of her surroundings spoke of her privileged upbringing. She'd never wanted for any material possession. Though she would miss Brittany fiercely, she had few qualms about embarking on this new chapter, which would likely bring with it a meagerness she'd never known.

Alex ran her hand across her still-flat belly and the sinking, queasy feeling returned, threatening to buckle her knees. For a moment Alex allowed herself to forget her hasty departure meant escaping her stepfather's vicious theft of her innocence, her future, and her dreams. She imagined embarking on the journey she'd been planning for so long. But those plans had changed. She pressed a bit harder against her taut abdomen.

What did the future hold for the baby growing inside her? By asking herself that single question, she knew she made her decision even harder. She already thought of it as a baby, a human life. Did she have it in her to end another life? She'd always had a difficult time understanding how people could justify killing others who'd wronged them.

This little person growing inside her had done nothing wrong. It may have been conceived through a horrible wrong committed by another, but this tiny being embodied the definition of the term "innocent bystander." What justification did she have to end this baby's life before it even had a chance to live? For her own convenience? To chase her own dreams?

The front door slamming cut short her introspection. She jumped when she heard her mother calling her name. With a sigh and a swipe of lipstick, Alex gathered her purse and went to endure one last meal with Karen and J.T., not the least bit sad about never having to do so again.

$$\mathscr{G} \ \mathscr{G} \ \mathscr{G}$$

Clouds filled the sky the morning of everyone's departure, but the radio weatherman spouted his heartiest assurances for a sunny day ahead. Karen fretted. What if their flight out of Charlotte experienced weather delays? A quick call to the airline assured her all flights were on schedule, and everything at the Wickham household proceeded according to plan.

The previous night, J.T. had loaded the majority of their luggage into the Suburban he used for work to avoid a frantic early morning scramble—to no avail. Karen kept thinking of things she'd forgotten—their camera...how could someone take an Alaskan cruise without a camera? She hadn't thought of her wool gloves when she began packing in the eighty-degree North Carolina late spring heat, but she might need them. As a rule, she didn't get seasick, but there was no use taking any chances, so she grabbed some Dramamine.

By the time they were loaded and ready to leave for the airport, Alex felt she'd run a marathon with them on her back. Karen almost forgot Alex and her friends were scheduled to leave the same day for their senior beach trip. As an afterthought, she handed Alex five crisp one hundred-dollar bills and asked her if it would be enough to cover her expenses for the week.

"Mother, I can handle this," Alex said, trying to give the cash back to Karen. But Karen wouldn't hear of it. Alex guessed it was another attempt to apply a balm to her guilty conscience. Shrugging, Alex tucked the bills into her jeans, hugged her mother goodbye as she climbed into the passenger seat, and waved to J.T.

Then, they were gone. She didn't know when or if she'd ever see them again, which suited Alex fine. Heaving a deep sigh of relief, Alex turned on one heel and set her steps toward the house.

Now the real work began. With the huge Suburban gone, Alex moved her much smaller SUV into the garage to pack all her things. It would be easier to load her enormous new tool set from the corner of the garage rather than having to haul it out to the driveway. Exhaling so hard her cheeks puffed out, she gathered her resolve from deep within, marched into the garage, and dove into the task at hand.

As she pushed the button to lower the garage door, she spotted Brittany's car pulling into the driveway. Smiling, she reversed the door's descent and jogged out to meet her friend.

"What a special surprise," she said, hugging Brittany as she got out of her car. "I thought you'd be on your way to the beach by now. We already said our goodbyes."

"I know, but I thought I'd swing by and see if you needed any last-minute help getting loaded before you left." Brittany paused a brief second before asking for the hundredth time, "Are you sure this is what you want to do, Alex?"

"I'm positive. And, as a matter of fact, there is something you can help with. You see that huge red tool chest in the corner? We need to get it into my car."

A mighty struggle ensued, but after taking some of the heavier things out of several of the drawers, they accomplished their mission. Alex secured the chest with rope so it didn't slide around the back of the vehicle, then she wrapped an old blanket around it before making her way back inside to retrieve the rest of her belongings. With Brittany's help, the job took much less time than Alex had expected, and she was soon ready to make her escape.

"Could you give me just a minute? I'd kind of like to, you know, look around the house one last time."

"Yeah, sure. I'm gonna go ahead and take off. Call me tonight and let me know how far you get." Tears streamed down Brittany's face.

They'd agreed there would be no sad farewell, but as the reality of the situation came crashing down around them, Britt obviously found it impossible to stick to their deal. Alex didn't trust her voice. All she could do was nod as she hugged her lifelong friend. Then Alex watched Brittany climb into her car and drive away. The hurt of her friend's departure cut deep...much deeper than when her own mother had breezed away. Karen's leaving occurred regularly. But leaving Brittany. Well, that was another thing altogether.

Alex wiped her eyes on her sleeve and reached for the doorknob. She opened the door and walked into the house without hurrying, scrutinizing the surroundings as if seeing them for the first time, knowing it could actually be the last. Wandering around each room, she touched reminders of significant times in her life, smiling at the memories certain items evoked. She made a pointed decision, however, to avoid the den where her life had been forever altered. She hadn't gone in there since that awful night.

At last, she took one long last look around her childhood bedroom, drawing in a deep breath before turning to leave. Hoping to avoid any unnecessary missing person's report, she had the genius idea at the last minute to leave a note telling her mother she'd decided to go to California early. She left the note on the kitchen counter, knowing Karen wouldn't find it for two weeks. Alex planned to be settled into her new life by then. Finally, she shut the door behind her for the last time.

She turned the key and felt the lock slam into place. Life as she knew it ended. Her adventure awaited her, just like she'd dreamed. However, dreams and reality, as Alex was discovering, didn't always look the same.

Chapter 6
Change of Plans

Alex made better time than she anticipated, considering she traveled only on country back roads. The quaint little towns she drove through were overflowing with lovely flowers and signs announcing upcoming festivals. Alex welcomed the distractions they provided as they encouraged her to keep her lead foot off the accelerator in the little speed trap communities.

Around one o'clock, hunger overtook the desire for progress, and Alex decided to stop at the next fast-food chain she found. A guilty twinge nagged at her about how she nourished the small life growing inside her. Deciding a sub or a salad might be healthier than a burger and fries, she checked out the choices in the town as she drove through.

A road-side sign indicated a sub shop in the strip mall just ahead, so Alex pulled in. Locking her car, she noticed she'd parked right in front of a beauty salon with a "Walk-ins Welcome" sign beckoning from the window. She fingered her long brown locks, a plan forming in her mind.

What better way to make a new start in life than with a drastic new hairstyle?

An hour later, Alex resumed her journey, her tummy full, her neck bare, and her face beaming. The stylist had assured her that her hair would be donated to a local charity specializing in wigs for cancer patients. Alex now sported a cute pixie style, requiring little more effort than some mousse and a bit of tousling.

She didn't care that short hair focused all attention on the big brown eyes in her heart-shaped face. She simply liked the feel of the sun shining on her neck and how weird it felt to look from side to side with nothing swishing across her back.

With the sun quickly sinking, Alex developed a serious case of driver's fatigue, which she later admitted might have contributed to her mishap. Or perhaps she simply belonged in the small town of

Burton, South Carolina. Either way, she didn't see the deer dart in front of her car as she navigated a twisting stretch of two-lane state highway leading into the town. She slammed on the brakes, managing to avoid a collision with the animal, but lost control of her car and ended up hitting a tree.

The silence settling in around her left Alex breathless, shaken, and terrified. She'd never been in an accident before, and she had no idea what to do. Tears of frustration or exhaustion, she wasn't sure which, rolled down her cheeks as an elderly lady cupped her hands around her eyes and peered in the driver's side window. A startled gasp escaped Alex, but glancing in her rearview mirror, she saw the woman had emerged from the car that had been behind her when the deer darted into the road. Alex rolled down her window.

"Are you all right, honey?" the lady asked, concern so evident in her voice she could have been Alex's own grandmother, if she'd had one.

"Yes, ma'am, I think so. Just shaken up. I'm not sure how bad my car's messed up, though," she replied.

This incident would put a huge dent in both her travel schedule and her budget. She unfastened her seatbelt, snatched the key out of the ignition, and got out to survey the damage. It didn't look too bad, but there was smoke and a suspicious hiss issuing from beneath the hood.

"My name's Matilda Gault, but everyone calls me Miss Matilda," the lady said she held out her delicate, crepe-skinned hand.

This tiny lady, barely reaching the five-foot mark, appeared to be in her mid-seventies. Alex reached for the older lady's hand, intending to be as gentle as she could with this frail looking woman, only to discover a rock-solid grip. Matilda smiled with a twinkle in her eye, apparently proud to have thrown Alex a bit off kilter.

"I'm Alex, ma'am. I'm pleased to meet you, although, I've got to tell you, I do wish it were under different circumstances," Alex admitted.

"Understood. Now, what do you say you hop in my car and we get you to the mechanic's shop in town so you can arrange for a tow truck to come get your car? You're in luck. Today's their late day." Matilda wobbled off as she talked, her purse dangling from her arm.

"Wait, Miss Matilda," Alex said, jumping out of her car and rushing to keep up with the older lady. "Everything I own is in my car. Is it safe to leave it parked here?"

"Grab your purse and an overnight bag, then lock it up. The boys'll be here to fetch it within the hour," Matilda promised. Alex hurried to do as she was told, grateful to have someone take charge in this stressful situation. Even a complete stranger.

They weren't far from town and Miss Matilda chatted the whole way, pointing out interesting landmarks such as the park where the Christmas parade started each year. She glanced over once or twice at Alex, who sat in the passenger seat staring out the window, arms folded across her mid-section. She provided polite responses to Matilda's questions, but she was in no state of mind to engage in witty banter.

Soon, the tank-sized Cadillac groaned as Matilda guided it into a packed-dirt lot in front of a mechanic's garage. All four bays had vehicles in them, either up on lifts with men at work underneath or on the ground with hoods lifted, The human legs that seemed to sprout from the engines were evidence of someone indeed attending to the vehicles. A few cars sat in the large lot off to the side, waiting their turn.

Alex followed Matilda into the reception area where a chaotic profusion of outdated dog-eared magazines lay strewn across a beat-up coffee table. This was stationed in front of a ratty sofa upholstered with long-ago unidentifiable fabric, now worn threadbare on the armrests. Despite the less-than-cozy surroundings, the young girl at the desk welcomed them with a warm smile and greeted Matilda by name. Alex surmised her elderly rescuer was a regular at the shop.

"Hello, Miss Matilda. What can I do for you today?"

"Hello, Jamie. Is Chad in? My friend Alex had a bit of a mishap out near the county line, and I need him to send someone to fetch her...um," Matilda turned to Alex, "What do you call that thing you drive, dear?"

"It's a pewter gray SUV," Alex said. She added the make and model, and Matilda filled in the details of the location. Chad White, who'd seen Matilda's Caddy rolling into the lot, chose that moment to stroll into the reception area.

Chad wiped his greasy hands on a shop towel as he smiled at his two customers. He was much younger than Alex had expected, twenty-five years old, but his strawberry blond hair and dimples lent him a boyish appearance. His fondness for Miss Matilda was evident in the way he hugged her.

"What seems to be the problem with Bertha today, Miss M.?" he asked. Appalled, Alex gasped.

Does he think that's my name?

"Oh, sweetie," Matilda said, chuckling as she patted Alex on the back. "He wasn't talking about you. My car's name is Bertha. She's a regular here."

When Chad understood Alex thought he'd called her Bertha, he turned a deep shade of red and lost his ability to form a complete sentence. Matilda smoothed over the awkward silence by filling him in on Alex's predicament with her vehicle. Within minutes, he'd dispatched one of his tow trucks to bring her SUV into the shop.

"How soon do you think you'll be able to get to it?" Alex asked, not wanting to seem too pushy. "I'm kind of on my way someplace."

Chad rubbed the back of his neck. "Well, ma'am, I'm not too busy right now. I might be able to squeeze you in tomorrow. I'll put a rush on your job, seein' how you're a friend of Miss M.'s."

"Thank you," Alex said. All she wanted to do was find someplace to curl up and cry. But Matilda had other plans for Alex's night in Burton.

"Well, then," Miss Matilda said as if everything was settled. She reached in her purse for her keys, "Alex will be staying with me," she waved Alex's protests away, "so, Chad, you know how to get in touch with her. You call as soon as you know what's wrong and how much it's going to cost. All right, then. Bye."

"Yes, ma'am. I'll be in touch," Chad assured her, waving goodbye as he watched them drive away.

※ ※ ※

Chad wondered how one guy could be a genius with cars and so stupid with beautiful girls. Something about this particular beautiful girl, though, told Chad she kept her distance. Not in a literal sense— she'd stood right next to him. But everything about her closed up as soon as he walked into the room. He felt it.

She was running from something. *Or someone.* He didn't know where she was going, but Chad felt sure Miss Matilda would know before she took off. He rubbed his neck again as he remembered the frightened look in her eyes.

He knew it might mean trouble, but he wanted to get to know Alex better. He hadn't thought about a girl like this in a long time, and he didn't dare tell Charmain.

✍ ✍ ✍

Matilda steered the ancient automobile into a driveway so long it was often mistaken for another road. A huge white two-story house appeared as they crested a knoll.

"Why is there a sign in your front yard?" Alex asked Matilda.

"Well, there's an interesting story." Matilda smiled, glancing at Alex to gauge her receptivity. "That house you see right there isn't technically my house. I live in the guest cottage out back. The big house is the home where the girls live. You see, dear, I run a home called Together for Good."

"What kind of home is it?"

Matilda sighed, considering how to best answer the question. She sensed in Alex the need for what this place had to offer. The way she wrapped her arms around her midsection without even seeming to realize it. The wary look she'd given Chad when he smiled at her. The way her car was packed to the gills. All these signs indicated a hurt girl trying to run away from something. Matilda had done this job long enough to recognize the signs.

"Sometimes, girls find themselves in situations they just can't handle by themselves. They need a little help, someone to encourage them, guide them. Together for Good is a home for girls who are facing a crisis pregnancy and have nowhere to turn. We counsel them, provide prenatal care, teach job skills, and offer adoption services."

Finishing her explanation, Matilda guided the car around the big house to the adorable little white guest cottage out back. Shifting the car into park, she looked over and saw tears streaming down Alex's face. She extended an arthritis-gnarled hand to stroke Alex's cheek.

"Do we need to go inside and have a long talk over a cup of tea?" she asked.

Alex nodded, the sobs racking her body. Paying no heed to the screaming pain in her hip, Matilda walked around to the passenger side, opened Alex's door, and gathered her into her arms. Guiding her

57

into the kitchen, she settled the girl at the table. While Matilda made tea, Alex unburdened her heart, sharing her story leading up to her flight from Woodvale. She took special care to avoid mentioning names, but otherwise, after an hour of confession, Matilda knew her whole story.

Matilda prayed another life could be spared.

℘ ℘ ℘

"Do you believe in fate," Alex asked Matilda, sniffing while she nibbled on a delicious homemade cookie.

"Oh, no, my dear." Alex looked taken aback at her response.

"Why?"

"Because the Lord is Sovereign; He's in control of everything. The baby growing in you is no accident. Your being here is no coincidence. God has a plan for everything. That's what this home was named for. The Bible tells us, *'All things work together for good for them who love God and are called according to His purpose.'*"

Alex looked at Matilda, doubt clear in her expression. She'd never thought much about God one way or another. Where had He been while J.T. assaulted her? How could any good come from such a despicable act? What was Matilda talking about being called? Alex had so many questions, but before she could ask Matilda any of them, the old lady rose from her chair and beckoned her to follow.

"Where are we going?" Alex asked.

"Just come with me. I've got something I want to show you."

They exited the cozy cottage through the front door and entered the main house. Alex saw a few other girls in varying stages of pregnancy. Miss Matilda greeted each by name with a warm hug, their love for her evident. She introduced Alex to each of them, and they all welcomed her.

The social pleasantries out of the way, Matilda ushered Alex into a room resembling a doctor's office, including an examining table, cabinets, and a large machine.

"Would you like to see your baby?" Matilda asked Alex, clapping her hands together.

"What?" Alex couldn't believe what she was hearing.

"This is an ultrasound machine. With it, we can see the baby inside you. I'm an ultrasound technician, and I do them for the girls

58

who come in here. Then they can make the decision to either carry to term or..." Alex knew what she implied without her having to say it. Alex still wrestled with the decision to abort or not.

As Miss Matilda spoke, she readied the exam table for Alex. Her hostess patted the table twice, indicating Alex should hop up and prepare to see her unborn baby. Alex hadn't been this nervous since the night she took the pregnancy test. Even preparing to leave home had brought her a certain peace.

But this...this terrified and excited her all at once.

With a warning about the cold gel, Matilda squirted some on Alex's abdomen, placed the probe on the girl's skin and began to move it back and forth with practiced precision while staring at the screen. She soon found the object of her search and, holding the probe still, turned the screen around so Alex could see. As Alex gazed at the rapid heartbeat and the tiny limbs moving about, a fierce protective instinct unlike any she'd ever known crushed her, rendering her speechless. Once she regained the use of her voice, she addressed Miss Matilda.

"Oh, my goodness. I had no idea. There's really a little person in there," Alex whispered, wiping away tears, a common occurrence of late.

"Well, of course there is, sweetie. I told you God doesn't make any mistakes. Now, here's a tissue. You get cleaned up, and we'll see what the girls are cooking for dinner." Matilda exited the room, closing the door behind her and leaving Alex to clean herself up while she composed her emotions.

Alex wiped the slippery goo off her belly, reflecting on what she had just witnessed. When she arrived here today, she thought of what was inside of her as an unidentifiable blob, an inconvenience in her life she needed to determine how to deal with and still be able to live with herself. True, she'd been having qualms about an abortion. But now, with one swipe of the sonogram wand, her role as the protector and sole provider for another human being became crystal clear.

The enormity of the situation slammed into Alex with hurricane force, enormous and overpowering, spinning her life out of control. How did things turn around so completely and with so little warning? A few short months ago, she'd been certain of the path she'd mapped out for her life, and now here she sat, contemplating becoming a single mother.

Had she lost her mind?

She was only eighteen years old. She had no job. No degree. No friends. No family. There was no way she was moving back to Woodvale. And, what about this child? It was the result of a crime that had changed Alex's life forever, altering her life's course. Could Alex love this baby as it needed to be loved? Her own mother was no pillar of maternal care. Her dreams of school in California floated in her mind as distant and vague clouds, almost as if from someone else's life.

Laughter from the kitchen interrupted her thoughts. Matilda came to the door to check on her.

"You all right?" she asked, concern etched in the lines on her face.

"Yes, ma'am. I may have a few questions for you after dinner. Would you have time to chat for a little while?"

"I thought you'd never ask," she answered. "Now, how 'bout you come help peel potatoes. I make the best mashed potatoes you've ever tasted, but with all these young hands around, my arthritic fingers don't do the peeling anymore."

They walked arm in arm to the large farmhouse-style kitchen, which had been recently renovated, Alex's trained eye noticed.

Alex had never had so much fun preparing a meal in her life. The other girls welcomed her as they would an old friend. They laughed and joked, sharing stories of their day while getting lessons from Miss Matilda on proper cooking techniques.

Katie was a girl about seven months along. When her baby kicked during the potato peeling, all of the girls placed their hands on her swollen belly and felt the little nudges, "oohs" and "aahs" echoing around the kitchen.

The meal smelled delicious as everyone sat around the dining room table. Miss Matilda asked who would like to pray. Several girls raised their hands and Matilda chose Katie. They all bowed their heads.

"Dear Lord," she said, "we thank You for bringing Alex to us. We know You work all things together for good for those who love You and are called according to Your purpose. We pray You would reveal Your purpose and will for Alex's life to her, and if we can help her fulfill Your will in her life, please help us do so. We thank You for this meal, but most of all we thank You for Jesus who died to take away our sin. It's in His name we pray. Amen."

The others echoed Katie's amen and passed the mouth-watering meatloaf, mashed potatoes, green beans, and homemade rolls. Miss

Matilda beamed, her beautiful smile lighting up the room. She reminded everyone to leave room for peach cobbler.

In unison with Miss Matilda, all of the girls chorused, "After all, you are eating for two." They dissolved into a fit of giggles.

"I guess I've said it a time or two," the older woman said, glancing at her plate to avoid looking at the girls.

Her admission made them all laugh so hard; they were wiping away tears before they could control their mirth.

𝄞 𝄞 𝄞

After dinner, Matilda settled into a porch rocker while the girls took clean up duty. The workload split among seven girls made the chore go quickly. The story of Alex's car trouble and how Miss Matilda got involved captivated their attention. They had the kitchen spotless before Alex finished the saga of how she came to be in Burton.

When the last dishtowel was hung up, the girls wandered off in different directions, some to watch TV, some to do homework, and others to check on the large garden. Alex saw her opportunity to seek out Matilda for some one-on-one time. Finding her on the porch in a rocking chair, she asked if it was a good time to talk.

"I've been waiting for you, hon. Come take a load off and tell me what's on your mind."

Alex curled her legs beneath her in the rocker beside the older lady and sighed. Where did she begin? This woman already knew her deepest pain, her darkest shame. Alex understood the other girls here had probably experienced some level of hurt or betrayal or were facing their own brand of regret.

And yet, Miss Matilda appeared to love every one of them. She treated each girl special and gave them a reason to hang on. More important than those things, she convinced each of the girls what a special gift each precious child was. Alex needed to know more.

"How do you do it, Miss Matilda?"

The question was beyond inadequate to divine answers to the need pounding in Alex's head and assailing her heart. But Matilda smiled and nodded, rocking as she stared at the sun setting on the horizon.

"I don't know if you've noticed, but I'm not a young woman anymore." She chuckled at herself. "When I was, though, the Lord got

61

ahold of my heart and gave me a love for little babies. Come to find out, it just wasn't in His plan for me to have any babies of my own."

Her voice broke a little and a tear slid down her wrinkled cheek. She wiped it away, sniffed, and continued, "Through all my struggles, I knew I needed to help save the babies who didn't have a voice. Sometimes the mamas make the right choice. Sometimes, the pressure from other influences in their lives is just too great. Together for Good helps many girls by meeting their needs. Yes, we provide education, job skills, and adoption counseling. But it's so much more."

"Well, why do you do it?" Alex asked.

She still didn't understand the motivation for dedicating one's life to girls facing unexpected pregnancies. Matilda appeared to weigh her words before speaking.

"Sometimes these girls can't grasp the gravity of their decision. It indeed is a tiny person living within them. Once I show them the indisputable evidence, it often opens their eyes. They don't want to end a baby's life. Often. But not always."

"It sounds expensive," Alex said. Her hope of staying there for a little while faded considering her limited finances.

"Oh, sweetie, it's totally free to the mother! We have generous donors and sponsors who support us. Some of the girls do housekeeping for some of the patrons until late in their term, we sell our produce, we give internet classes for the town's senior citizens. Everybody works, but nobody pays." Matilda turned to look at Alex. Twice Alex saw her start to speak before stopping herself. She finally summoned the courage to ask, "Alex, do you have anywhere to go?"

Alex shook her head. She explained about the engineering scholarship waiting for her in California.

"Somehow, it doesn't feel right anymore," Alex said.

"What feels right?"

"This does," Alex replied, looking around her at the peaceful home she'd found because of an errant deer.

"Then, stay."

And, again, the course of Alex's life changed in a moment.

❦ ❦ ❦

The phone in the cottage rang early the next morning. Both Alex and Matilda were dressed and sitting at the table enjoying a cup of tea and a bowl of oatmeal. Matilda answered on the third ring and greeted Chad, a smile spreading over her face. The conversation, however, soon had her frowning and shaking her head, causing Alex to bolt from the table and rush to her side, mouthing questions and gesturing with her hands.

"Okay, Chad, we'll be there with Bessie in about an hour. Thank you." She hung up the phone.

"What? Who's Bessie? And why is she going with us to the mechanic's?" Alex ran her hands through her cropped hair, making it stand on end and giving the effect of a baby doll that some little girl has loved on a bit too much. Matilda laughed at the spiky results, frustrating Alex even more.

"Now, settle down. Bessie is my pickup. We need to go into town and get your things out of your car. It's going to be awhile before they can fix it. The part they need had to be ordered, and it's going to take a few days to come in. Chad was very apologetic."

Alex knew Chad couldn't do anything about the availability of the car part, but this turn of events put her in a foul temper. She slammed her hand on the table and stormed out the door to wait on Miss Matilda.

Unfortunately, Alex had gone out the front door and Bessie was parked in the shed out back. It took some time for Matilda to retrieve her keys, go to the shed, and drive to the front of the cottage. When Alex got in, her frustration had almost run its course.

"I apologize for my little pity party back there. I should be so grateful to you and Chad for taking care of things for me. I don't know what came over me." Regret sparkled in her eyes as clearly as the tears pooling there. Matilda reached over and patted her shoulder.

"Think nothing of it, dear. We're going to get you all squared away and settled in before you know it."

In the parking lot at Chad's shop, fewer vehicles occupied the space than the previous day. He asked one of his mechanics to move Alex's belongings to Matilda's truck while they waited. Alex scanned the shabby decor in the waiting area again while Chad and Matilda chatted, an inspired plan brewing in her mind.

"Chad," she said at a break in their conversation, "how much is my car repair going to cost?"

The total he quoted almost made her knees buckle, but it also made her more determined to suggest her plan. She hoped he'd see it as a win-win idea.

"I've got a business proposition for you," she said.

"What kind of deal?" he asked. Matilda looked on with interest.

"It's been a while since you've spruced up this place. Why don't you let me remodel in here and on the outside? Like a make-over. I'll even set up a website for you. In six months, if my bill hasn't been paid off by the increase in your business, I'll pay you in full."

Chad seemed to consider the idea, looking around as if seeing the space for the first time. Alex knew from her conversation with Miss Matilda Chad had inherited the business after his dad passed away following a brief battle with cancer a couple of years earlier.

"I *have* been meaning to make a few changes. What do you have in mind?" His question let Alex know she'd piqued his interest. Now she had to close the deal.

"You're missing a huge demographic without even knowing it. I can make this place more attractive to ladies. If you target their business, you can increase your customer base fast. Think about it," Alex said, raising a finger for each item she pointed out. "You can reach the single ladies, married ladies, and widows." She crossed her arms before she finished, "*And,* I can get this place looking nice enough that a lady won't mind spending a little time in here."

"It's that bad?" Chad asked, looking around and wrinkling his nose at the worn-out decor as if seeing it for the first time.

"It's not that it's bad; it's just not what a woman would call… comfortable," Alex explained, trying to be diplomatic as Matilda camouflaged her chuckle with a cough. Chad rubbed his neck, then ran a hand through his reddish blond hair.

"What do you think, Miss M.?" he asked.

"I don't think she totes all those tools around with her for her health," the woman replied. "She must know what she's doing. I say give her a shot and see what she can do with the place."

"You've got a deal," he said, thrusting his greasy hand toward Alex to seal the bargain. Without hesitating, Alex grasped it and shook.

"Can I start today? I saw a few pallets out back I'd like to use before they get carted off to the dump. Besides, there's no use taking my tools to Miss Matilda's place if I'm going to be using them here."

Alex's eagerness elicited laughter from Chad and Matilda. Matilda arranged for a ride home with a friend who'd come in to retrieve her newly repaired car. Alex would drive Matilda's truck back to the home when she was done for the day. Alex waved goodbye to her new friend, then sought her gear.

Chad set aside an area in a shed behind the garage where she could work and gave her a budget for materials and supplies. The local home improvement store was only a couple of blocks away. Otherwise, he promised to leave the entire project up to her. The undertaking would sink or swim based solely on Alex's skills. The prospect both terrified and thrilled her. This kind of work was her comfort zone in a strange, unfamiliar place. She relaxed somewhat, feeling at ease doing what she knew.

Lost in her work, Alek looked up in surprise when Chad approached her little work shed to announce quitting time. Alex had transformed the old pallets destined for the dump into a new coffee table and matching end tables.

She couldn't decide whether to stain or paint the new pieces, launching into a comparison of the virtues and short-comings of each. Chad listened mutely, staring at her as if she spoke a foreign language. She packed up a pad of paper with sketches and measurements into a beat-up backpack.

"See you tomorrow, Chad," she called as she climbed into the cab of the truck.

"No way, missy," he said, shaking his head. "Tomorrow's Saturday. We're closed on Saturday and Sunday. I'll see you Monday," Chad started his own car and drove away.

Alex pondered the business Chad lost every Saturday as she drove to Miss Matilda's house. Having dealt with the construction workers in J.T.'s business, though, she knew nobody wanted to work six days a week. She'd have to give this problem some consideration and see if she could come up with something to benefit Chad's business and keep the employees happy.

Chapter 7
Eternal Implications

The next day, the girls had finished their chores in the house when one of Matilda's friends from church came by with a huge van. Saturdays meant a trip into town to visit yard sales, flea markets, and craft shows. A couple of the later term girls stayed behind to rest, but the others piled into the van, eager for a change of scenery.

Alex had never shopped at a yard sale, but she soon discovered the siren's song of bargain shopping. With a keen eye for finding treasures among the junk heaps, she picked up several items to make into one-of-a-kind functional pieces for Chad's waiting area. The best part was the minimal dent her purchases put in the budget Chad had given her.

Back at the house, Alex set to work assembling a lamp out of an old oilcan and funnel. She'd need a few more pieces from the home improvement store, but she liked the way it was coming together. She didn't hear Matilda approach until the older lady cleared her throat. Alex almost jumped out of her skin.

"I'm sorry, dear. I didn't mean to startle you. What's that you're making?"

"Oh, it's fine. I got pretty caught up in my lamp project. I have a few other things to make. I hope Chad likes them." She looked around at her new work area, set up in a corner of the barn, and was again overcome with gratefulness to this precious lady who barely knew her. "Miss Matilda, how can I ever thank you for taking me in and letting me set up shop? You've done more for me in the past week than my own mother has in my whole life."

It seemed everything Alex said, did, or heard made her cry these days. Whether from the pain of a lifetime of inattention or from missing her familiar world, the floodgates burst again. Mortified at being unable to control her own emotions, she turned from Matilda in shame, murmuring her apologies as she covered her face with both hands. Matilda turned Alex to face her.

"Have you ever been to church?" she asked, wrapping her arms around this child-becoming-a-woman. Alex relaxed in the embrace for a moment. Then pulling away, she sniffled and shook her head, confused by what church had to do with Matilda's generosity.

"I want you ready to go tomorrow morning at 8:30. Things are going to change for you after tomorrow."

∅ ∅ ∅

Walking back to the house, Matilda considered the exchange she'd had with Alex. A seasoned veteran in dealing with young pregnant women, she'd delivered her share of pep talks and lectures. But the brokenness she'd seen in Alex's chocolate brown eyes caught Matilda off guard.

This girl had grown up among incredible privilege, true, but at what cost? And, to endure such utter devastation and betrayal by the one she trusted most in the world. How would she ever learn to trust again? How could she ever learn to feel loved? Matilda prayed Alex could open her heart to the Truth.

∅ ∅ ∅

Sunday morning at Together for Good resembled something between a three-ring circus and a train wreck. Multiple expectant mothers and an elderly lady trying to have breakfast, fix hair, do makeup, reach their shoes, and rush out the door on time qualified as nothing short of a divine miracle. Somehow, though, they managed to pile into the van on time every Sunday.

Alex couldn't remember the last time she'd been to church. She didn't understand all the fuss the girls and Miss Matilda made. Why would a bunch of people get up early every Sunday, sit in a stuffy auditorium and listen to a boring man drone on for an hour when there were more important things to do? Alex considered how and when to tell Miss Matilda this would be her only time accompanying the group.

The church van arrived at Mis Matilda's place precisely at 8:30. The ladies stood on the front porch steps eagerly awaiting its arrival.

68

"Good morning, Miss Matilda. Ladies!" the cheery driver called as he parked the van and hurried around to assist everyone, a true Southern gentleman to the core.

"Good morning, Paul. How are you this beautiful Lord's Day?" Matilda inquired as she grabbed the handle beside the door to pull her short frame into the seat.

"Couldn't be better, ma'am. I get to spend it with all these lovely ladies." A relaxed camaraderie flowed between the middle-aged man and the girls. But something else – something deeper Alex couldn't quite place – hovered around them.

The girls settled into their seats and Paul shifted the van into gear, wheels crunching in the gravel as they departed. Alex's stomach knotted as she anxiously anticipated the upcoming experience. What would they do? Would she be singled out and judged? She hated having attention called to her. She whispered her concerns to Miss Matilda, who patted her knee and reassured her.

"Don't worry, dear. Nobody will make you feel uncomfortable. We'll sing some songs, hear a message from Reverend Drummond, pray, and then be dismissed. Just like any other church service." Matilda recognized the look of fear in Alex's eyes. "Haven't you ever been to church?"

"I... I, that is, um, maybe once." Alex dodged the question.

"It'll be fine, honey. You sit next to me. There's nothing to be afraid of."

While they talked, the other girls chattered about what songs they hoped to sing. Without warning, they started singing a song about love and hope. Even Miss Matilda and Paul joined in. Alex's trepidation mounted. She didn't belong to this exclusive club and doubted she ever could.

Self-pity, however, had no time to gain a foothold in Alex's heart. Paul expertly guided the van under a covered portico for the ladies to disembark, and a distinguished-looking white-haired gentleman emerged from inside the church to offer his hand as each girl stepped down.

Alex's mind spun at the kindness extended to these girls. She remembered hearing somewhere about Christians looking down on people who made bad decisions or did bad things. Didn't they call that sin? If so, why were Matilda, Paul and the white-haired man so nice?

Things didn't add up in Alex's mind as her list of questions grew steadily longer.

Matilda found a pew. The girls filed in behind her and took their seats. Within minutes, piano music filled the space. As the strains of an unfamiliar tune carried on the air, Alex drank in her surroundings, examining every detail with a critical but appreciative eye. The wooden pews gleamed, as did the pine floors, accounting for the lingering fragrance of lemon oil heavy in the air.

Dark green velvet cushions and a dark green runner down the center aisle relieved the starkness of the wood and muted the acoustics. At the front of the church, a raised area held several rows of padded chairs, in front of which was an elaborate podium. Overhead, the white vaulted ceiling soared to a grand height of at least twenty-five feet, giving the whole space an open, airy feeling. Alex understood the craftsmanship displayed in this place, and she stared in wonder at these beautiful, but foreign, architectural elements.

The choir entered and filled the padded seats up front. Captivated, Alex lost herself in the flow of the service: singing a song she had never heard, greeting those nearby, participating in a responsive reading, listening to the choir sing a song so beautiful it gave her goose bumps. As if on cue, everyone rustled pages and focused their attention on the podium. The white-haired man who'd greeted them earlier stepped behind the podium, opened a book and spoke, his voice reaching the highest beam in the ceiling.

"Would you open up God's Word with me this morning? Let's ask the Spirit for insight as we come before the Lord. Please bow your heads."

Alex looked around, confused by the pastor's instructions. God's Word? What was he talking about? She glanced at her new friends, who had their heads bowed and eyes closed and books opened in their laps.

Bibles! They had Bibles opened in their laps.

She'd never thought of the Bible as God's Word. She just thought it was a bunch of outdated, boring old stuff no one read anymore. But now, everybody had a Bible opened and was ready to read from it. Everybody except Alex.

After the "Amen," Matilda sensed Alex's confusion and discomfort, pulled a Bible from the pew rack, found the sermon reference, and handed it to her. Alex shot her a look of gratefulness before focusing her attention on the white-haired man.

"We're continuing our journey through the Gospel of John. We'll be in John 14 this morning. One of Jesus' seven 'I Am' statements comes from this passage of Scripture. Let's take a look, shall we?"

Reverend Drummond began to urge listeners to free their hearts of trouble, to trust in God, and to look forward to the mansion in Heaven Jesus had gone to prepare. Alex followed the preacher's words until he got to the part where Jesus said, *"I am the Way and the Truth and the Life. No one comes to the Father except through me."* This statement sent uncertainty crashing over Alex. Reverend Drummond couldn't mean there was only a single way into Heaven. She scribbled the question onto her bulletin to ask Miss Matilda later on—but she didn't have to wait for an answer.

Closing his sermon, Reverend Drummond reached out once more to those who might not grasp Jesus' meaning in the morning's Scripture verses.

"Friends, some folks have a hard time understanding this passage. Was Jesus saying He was the <u>only</u> way to salvation? Let me make it easy for you…yes, yes, He was! He came to Earth to die for our sins, to provide the atonement we couldn't provide for ourselves. You may think you're a good person, but as Paul said in the book of Romans, *'All have sinned and fall short of the glory of God.'*

"Now, maybe you're thinking you're not a good person at all, and you don't deserve the amazing gift of salvation God offers. I'm here to tell you, though, it's offered for every man, woman, and child, no matter what you've ever done. All you have to do is admit you're a sinner in need of a Savior, believe Jesus Christ is God's own Son, and confess Him as the Lord of your life. It's that simple and that life-altering."

After he spoke these words, the first notes of another song began. Two of the girls from Together for Good, Haley and Simone, slipped out of the pew and walked down front to the pastor. He shook their hands and embraced each one. They turned to take a seat on the front pew, and Alex could see they were crying and smiling at the same time. Matilda slipped out to join the girls down front.

As the final note faded, the congregation took their seats and a beaming Reverend Drummond addressed them once more.

"It's not every Sunday I have the pleasure of introducing two special ladies from our partner in growth, Together for Good. Our church has supported this worthy organization since its inception in the 1950s. And today, two of the lovely residents, Haley and Simone, have accepted Jesus as their Lord and Savior!"

At this announcement, the people erupted into applause, punctuated by shouts of "hallelujah!" and "Amen!" Joy filled the place. Reverend Drummond motioned for the congregation to settle down so he could make an announcement.

"These young ladies will be down front for you to extend the hand of fellowship after the service. Welcome them into the family of Jesus. And now, go in service to our Lord as led by the Holy Spirit. And all God's children said…"

The congregation followed with a hearty, "Amen!"

The next few minutes passed in a blur of hand shaking and introductions Alex knew she'd never remember. Chad appeared and whisked her away, whispering in her ear something about rescuing her for a campus tour. He told Matilda where they were going, then off they went to the Sunday school rooms, fellowship hall, and gym.

"Thanks," she said, gratitude evident in her voice.

"No problem. We've got some pretty nice facilities for a smaller church," Chad said, avoiding eye contact.

"That's not what I meant," she said, smiling. "I meant thanks for saving me from the crowd. I get a little freaked out around so many people I don't know."

Out of habit, she tucked a stray wisp of now-short hair behind her ear. She looked up at him through her lashes, an innocent yet unintentionally captivating gesture. Alex noticed Chad fidgeting, looking nervous and uncomfortable. Strange behavior for someone who'd seemed to be in complete control in his shop.

"Well, we should probably be getting back," Chad almost shouted.

Alex shot him a questioning look and wondered why he was yelling in a deserted room. Shrugging, she followed him back to the worship center. Most of the people had left, so Alex easily spotted Miss Matilda talking with Reverend Drummond and a middle-aged couple. Chad strode toward them, said a quick goodbye, and bolted out the side door.

What an odd man, Alex thought. *Nice, but strange.*

"Alex, I'm so glad you're back. I'd like you to meet Reverend Drummond, our pastor, and Terry and Gail Lovell, my nephew and his wife," Matilda placed a hand on each shoulder as she introduced them. Alex shook hands with each one, her mother's endless etiquette lessons serving her well.

"Well, Aunt Tilley, what's for lunch?" Terry inquired after they told the pastor goodbye and were walking toward the exit. Paul had the van waiting.

"Oh, the usual...fried chicken, fresh corn, green beans, and biscuits. Y'all will be joining us?" Matilda had looped her arm through Terry's as she walked toward the van. He took her elbow and helped her in.

"Yes, ma'am. We'll be right out. Don't wait on us, though. Gail has a few calls she needs to make, so it may be a few minutes before we can head to your place."

Alex noticed a look of displeasure cross Miss Matilda's face when Terry mentioned Gail making calls. Alex questioned her about it once they were settled and moving.

"She has six days a week to make those real estate deals. You'd think it would be enough. *But, no!* She's got to work as soon as she's out of church on Sunday!"

Matilda's feathers were ruffled, no doubt about it. In the short time Alex had seen their interaction, it was clear Terry and his aunt shared a special bond. How his wife Gail fit into the equation wasn't so obvious.

In some ways, Gail reminded Alex of her mother. Their physical appearance couldn't have been more different. While Karen was tall with dark hair and a slim build, Gail was petite, blond, and curvy. But they both had an icy glint in their eyes that sent a clear message not to cross them, telling the competition to back off. Alex recognized it the minute she met Gail and made a mental note to stay out of her way.

⚑ ⚑ ⚑

The girls scrambled with last-minute Sunday dinner preparations, stopping only when the phone rang. Miss Matilda picked it up, a smile initially lighting her face, but disappointment soon drew her features into a scowl. Terry couldn't make it after all. Despite her bravest efforts to act happy during the spiritual birthday celebrations for Haley

73

and Simone, the girls knew her nephew's absence hurt her deeply. Alex, the one person at the table in the dark concerning the family dynamic, considered asking one of the other girls about the situation. Her more pressing concern, however, was this morning's sermon.

She had so many questions, but she didn't know who could answer them. Did she need to go to Reverend Drummond for this information or could Miss Matilda fill her in. Once dishes were washed and dried, she sought out the older woman and found her walking through the large garden with a basket.

"Hello, dear. Did you enjoy your lunch?" Dear Miss Matilda. Always concerned about everyone else.

"Yes, ma'am. It was delicious. But I have some questions about what I heard this morning." Alex honed in on her doubts and the difficulties she had. "I just don't get it. Why is there only one way to Heaven? Where are these mansions? My heart *is* troubled, so how do I stop it from being troubled? And how does the Bible fit into all of this? What would I do with one if I had one?"

Question after question tumbled out, so great her thirst to find answers. Matilda handed the basket to Alex and beckoned her to follow as she walked to the barn that housed Alex's workshop. In one corner stood a tall, narrow, dust-encrusted cardboard box.

Matilda asked Alex to help her rescue it from behind the other odds and ends that had accumulated in the barn over time. They placed it flat on the floor before Miss Matilda opened it. Alex saw an unassembled shelving unit and looked at the older woman, more questions running through her head.

"Why haven't you put it together?"

"Because I bought it at a yard sale. I thought I'd gotten a super bargain. The problem is, I didn't realize until I got it home it didn't come with any of the hardware or instructions. So, you see, it's useless to me the way it is."

Alex knew the older lady was trying to teach a profound life lesson, but she couldn't make the connection between her own myriad questions and Matilda's random story of a bargain purchase gone wrong. She stared at Miss Matilda, waiting for the revelation.

"Don't you see?" Matilda asked. "The Bible is our set of instructions God has given us to help build our lives. He equips us with all of the tools and talents we need to do His work so we don't end up like this shelf. It could have been so useful, but it just sits in a corner collecting dust."

The truth Miss Matilda spoke, put in terms that resonated with Alex's heart, made perfect sense. An idea flashed in her mind.

"Miss Matilda, where can I get a Bible?" she asked, excitement bubbling up in the question.

The lady again beckoned Alex to follow her. Inside the little cottage, Matilda opened a bookcase stocked full of Bibles. Alex's jaw dropped in disbelief.

"This is part of our ministry. Many of the girls who come here don't have one. We make sure they do. Now, I want you to start by reading the Gospel of John. That's what the Reverend was preaching from today. When you're finished, come back to me and we'll talk."

Homework!

Miss Matilda was giving her homework. Fine. Alex hadn't earned the title of salutatorian by being a slacker. She'd attack this task with the same tenacity she had every school and work assignment in her life. What she didn't know was the assignment Matilda charged her with carried eternal implications unlike any she'd ever known.

🕊 🕊 🕊

Once Alex received her Bible, she found it difficult to concentrate on anything else. She ate very little at dinner. She didn't sleep. She read the gospel of John twice, and then she read the other gospels. She came to understand she was dying of thirst and had been offered the sweetest, purest, most abundant source of life-giving Water.

At 2 a.m., unable to stand it any longer, she padded into Miss Matilda's room, glad her transition to the other house wouldn't happen until sometime next week. Right now, she needed to know how to have this Living Water, this Bread of Life.

She wanted Jesus as her Savior, and she wanted Him now. She remembered some of the words the pastor had prayed at Sunday's service, but, ever the perfectionist, she didn't want to botch this. She knew the stakes were too high to make a mistake now.

Alex tiptoed to Miss Matilda's bed by the glow of the nightlight in the corner of the room. A soft touch on the older lady's shoulder caused her to bolt upright in the bed. Alex guessed that years of running a home for expectant young mothers made Matilda accustomed to waking at all hours of the night. The lady's first question confirmed Alex's suspicion.

"Is one of the girls in labor?" she asked, blinking as she swung her legs from under the sheet.

"No, ma'am. I'm so sorry for waking you. This could probably have waited until the morning, but I need to know about the prayer the girls prayed. You know. When they asked Jesus to be their Savior."

Alex would not be deterred until she completed this transaction and had the peace of knowing things were right between her and the Lord. Matilda turned on the bedside lamp, they knelt together, and Matilda led her in the sinner's prayer.

Before the sound of their amen died on the stillness of the early morning, Alex knew why Haley and Simone wept during the church service. Feelings unlike any she'd ever known overwhelmed her: joy, contrition, thankfulness, but most of all, an inexplicable peace.

She thanked Matilda, hugged her goodnight, and went back to bed. Her heart and mind now at ease, Alex fell asleep as soon as her head touched the pillow.

Chapter 8
The Bookshelf

Monday morning, Alex jumped into Matilda's truck and drove to Chad's shop to continue working. The route to church had taken them by the home improvement store, so she knew where to get paint, lumber, and other supplies. Her excitement at showing Chad the lamp created from reclaimed objects grew the closer she got to the garage.

Alex found a parking spot out of the way of Chad's customers and began unloading her supplies. Despite not going to sleep until the wee morning hours, she'd awakened refreshed. She glanced at the cloudless sky, her mood mirroring the sunny weather...until she rounded the corner of the building to occupy her appointed spot, and saw Chad kissing a beautiful girl on the cheek. The simple greeting, so normal between acquaintances in the South, sent a pang of an unfamiliar feeling straight to her heart. Her gut reaction disturbed her on so many levels.

First, she didn't know the guy. At least, not very well. He seemed nice enough, and he was being more than fair about fixing her car. But she had no right to feelings of jealousy. Second, he seemed a good bit older than Alex. She hadn't dated many guys in high school, but the one or two guys who had taken her out had been around her age. Chad had to be at least six or seven years older.

And, finally, and this was the big one...she was pregnant! Having feelings for a guy, any guy, could not happen now. No matter how nice. No matter how old. No guy. Her primary focus consisted of getting her life in order for her baby and herself. She wondered if she'd ever be able to trust a guy enough to have a real relationship after what she'd been through.

A thought popped into her mind, changing the way she looked at her life. Everything she did, every decision she made, every aspect of her life from now on would shape and be shaped by her baby. The prospect didn't scare Alex. Instead, she rolled options around in her mind as she worked. Her tools, creating beautiful things with her hands, this was her solace, where she found comfort and relaxation. If she could make a living this way, what a blessing it would be.

Alex refocused her attention on the project at hand. To stay within Chad's budget, Alex decided to freshen up the woodwork on the existing furniture with a coat of white paint and recover the cushions with a bright but durable, washable fabric instead of replacing them. Of course, she'd incorporate the pallet tables she'd built last week.

The beautiful weather allowed for outside work, so she finished the painting in the well-ventilated shed. There had been enough pallet lumber left over to build planters to place by the front door. If she stretched the budget far enough, she hoped to be able to get flowers to plant in them before the big re-opening.

She'd been working for a couple of hours before Chad noticed her. He ambled over to her workspace to check on her progress, bring her a bottled water, and see if she needed anything. After seeing him with another girl, Alex remained polite but detached. She could tell the lamp impressed him and, while she wanted to share his enthusiasm, she simply accepted his compliment and the water and continued working. When he didn't leave, Alex looked up at him.

"Is something wrong?" she asked.

"No, no. Nothing's wrong. Everything's great. I mean, everything looks great. You weren't kidding when you said you knew what you were doing." He looked uncomfortable as he shuffled his feet.

"Well, I've been doing this kind of thing for a long time. Sort of like you and cars. Listen, I'll be finished building the furniture by this week. I'll sew the cushion covers next week. I'd like to find a good sturdy rug and some accessories. Then we'll be done with the decorating." As she said this, Chad's smile fell until she continued. "But we've got to get you a basic website set up before you'll be ready for a grand re-opening."

This made his previous smile pale in comparison.

"A grand re-opening? I hadn't even thought about that! What would we do?"

"Well, you could put up a sign on the road advertising the date. Then, you could serve refreshments, something simple like cookies and iced tea. This can all help you capture the female demographic."

"Whoa," Chad put his hands up to slow Alex's fast-paced sales pitch. "I was with you until the last part. Do what?"

Alex's laughter reverberated off the walls of the shed like an echo in a canyon, sweet and clear.

Alex had thought about Chad's business structure for days. It was time to let Chad in on her ideas. She took out her notebook full of notes for his re-opening and shared her thoughts with him. Together they finalized an early fall date for the re-opening and came up with some innovative ways to capture the attention of the busy moms and businesswomen in town who needed car repair and maintenance work. Alex believed it could be a large untapped market share for Chad, who admitted that most of his customer base, outside of Miss Matilda, was men.

"I think this is going to be good for you, Chad," Alex said, continuing to take notes.

"Yeah, I think so, too," he replied, paying no attention to the notebook, but instead staring in amazement at this girl who had swooped in and turned his business, his thoughts, and his life topsy-turvy.

∅ ∅ ∅

The week passed in a blur, with Matilda assisting Alex acknowledged she'd never have gotten settled in her new room, set up her first doctor's appointment, or gotten registered for summer classes at the local community college without Miss Matilda's expertise. The business curriculum she'd soon be starting had been inspired from working at Chad's.

"Business is a far cry from engineering. Isn't that what you'd planned on doing out in California?" Miss Matilda asked Alex when she heard what the girl planned to do. Matilda had volunteered to drive Alex the thirty minutes to the campus, giving them time to chat.

"Yes, ma'am, it is. But my life now isn't the same as when I thought I was going out west. I want to learn how to be a savvy businesswoman. I picked up a lot watching my mom and stepdad." She turned away from Matilda and gazed out the window at the thought of J.T. "But I'd really like to know the best strategies, learn about the latest technologies in management and marketing. Maybe I could get my contractor's license someday." Alex ended with a shrug.

Matilda almost wrecked the Cadillac. Who had ever heard of a little tiny thing like Alex as a contractor? Her look of disbelief and dismay showed on her face, making Alex chuckle.

"Miss Matilda, I can drive a backhoe better than most guys. And, I can figure the amount of lumber, sheet rock, and shingles a job will take without even using a calculator. I'll make a great contractor."

Matilda shook her head, muttering to herself about being a die-hard, old-fashioned, uncompromising old woman. Alex just smiled and patted her soft arm. They rode the rest of the way in silence, each lost in her own thoughts.

𝄢 𝄢 𝄢

A few weeks after Matilda showed Alex the useless bookshelf pieces in the barn, a large, bulky envelope arrived in the mail for Alex. Since mail was rare for the girls, this strange package sparked conversation and the girls' imaginations. It sat on the kitchen table, the girls speculating on the contents, until Alex arrived home from Chad's shop.

Alex knew what was inside the envelope at once, and her face broke into a huge grin as she hurried to find Miss Matilda. The older lady enjoyed sipping tea in a porch rocker on nice afternoons, which is exactly where Alex found her. Alex grabbed her hand and tugged her down the porch steps.

"My word, Alex! Where in the world are you taking me?" she asked.

"You'll see. Just come with me." Alex could hardly contain her excitement as they made their way past the garden and into the barn, where Alex opened the envelope.

"Hold out your hands, please," she instructed Miss Matilda, who complied even though she shook her head and made a face that announced her confusion. Alex emptied the contents of the envelope into her hands: a clear plastic bag filled with various nuts, bolts, washers, and screws; and a thin pamphlet in several languages with the diagram of a bookshelf on the cover.

"What is all this?" Matilda's brow furrowed.

"I looked up the serial number of your shelving unit online. It's pretty old, so the only way to get the instructions was to have them snail mailed. And, the company sent you a set of hardware for free.

Now we can put your shelf together!" Alex's joy at being able to do something for this lady who had done so much for her bubbled over.

"I don't know what to say," Matilda whispered as her eyes misted over. "This is one of the sweetest things anyone's ever done for me."

"How 'bout if we start tomorrow? I'll teach the other girls how to build and paint a piece of furniture?" Alex asked. "And you can share your lesson about the instructions for our lives."

"It's a deal," Matilda replied as they shook on it.

🜊 🜊 🜊

Chad had Alex's vehicle repaired just in time. Her first day of summer classes at the community college fell on the same day as her first doctor's appointment. She thanked him and waved goodbye, noting her jeans were beginning to feel a bit snug.

A wardrobe update might be in order, she thought.

Classes lasted several hours a day, so she only enrolled in two classes for the first session. All day in class and all evening studying left little time for a job. Alex began to re-think attending the second summer session, hoping she could find a part-time job. Although her expenses weren't too extreme right now, having another person to provide for would be a different story. She'd feel better knowing she had a little bigger nest egg saved up for things like a place to live, diapers, food...luxuries like that.

The girls at Together for Good were under the care of Dr. Rose Sheffield, a kind and talented young OB/GYN who viewed her practice as her mission field. Alex liked the doctor the moment they met. Dr. Sheffield could have stepped out of the pages of a magazine, with her coffee-colored skin, jet-black hair, and piercing green eyes. She made Alex feel at ease, even in the awkward and unnerving situation of having to be examined for the first time.

"Have you ever had a pelvic exam?" Dr. Sheffield asked as Alex lay on the table, the nurse holding her hand while the doctor prepared to perform the exam.

"No, ma'am," Alex said, trying to be brave, though her voice faltered.

"It's okay. I'll tell you everything I'm going to do before I do it. No surprises. And, when we're done, we'll have an idea of how far along you are and if everything is progressing normally. Let's get started, shall we?"

When she was finished, Dr. Sheffield instructed Alex to get dressed and meet her in the adjoining office. Alex settled into the comfortable chair and the doctor smiled across the desk at her.

"Everything looks just fine, Alex. You're a very fit and healthy girl, which is in your favor. Your blood work, urine, and weight are all normal for this stage of your pregnancy. Based on the copy of the ultrasound image Miss Matilda sent over, my exam, and the date of your last period, I calculate your due date to be January eighth. We'll get you set up on a regular schedule of appointments, and I'd like you to take these vitamins." She scribbled something illegible on a prescription pad and handed the sheet to Alex.

"Do you have any questions?" she asked.

Did she have any questions? Why was this happening to her? How did she get her life back? How do you raise a baby? Would she be able to make it through pregnancy and childbirth?

And, only a million others.

"No, ma'am. Not right now," Alex lied. Dr. Sheffield smiled.

"Very good. I'll see you in a month. If you have any problems, call the office any time, day or night. Miss Matilda knows the drill. She's got some great books you may want to read to help you learn what's going on with your body." The nurse ushered her out the door.

And, so, the journey into pregnancy, prenatal care and, ultimately, parenthood began.

⏀ ⏀ ⏀

The sweltering summer days dragged on. Several girls at the home gave birth. New girls came to live with them. Miss Matilda's love remained the one constant through all of the changes. As they sipped iced tea in the kitchen one afternoon, Alex asked her how she could love so unconditionally, even when some of the girls tried her patience. Matilda smiled before answering.

"Sweetie, I've seen a lot of girls come and go through these doors. The Lord hasn't called me to tell them what's right and what's wrong. He's called me to love 'em, show 'em the truth, and pray like crazy they'll make the right decision. A lot of the time they do. Sometimes they don't. Sometimes, even after I show a girl that beautiful little heartbeat, she still decides there's no way she can go through with the pregnancy." A tear escaped the corner of her eye. "It's all in the Lord's hands."

"So, you're saying you just love and pray? But how do you have the strength to do it after all these years?"

Alex knew Miss Matilda had been doing this for a long time based on the photos scattered around both the home and the cottage.

"It's not my own strength, child. I draw my strength from the Lord. You'll need to be doing the same. Pray every morning when you rise. Ask for His strength to face the day, for His guidance to lead you, for His protection from the evil one."

Talking about such things seemed as natural as breathing for Miss Matilda. But Alex didn't get it, and the bewildered look on her face must have been telling. The older woman tottered to one of the kitchen cabinet drawers and pawed through the contents until she found what she was looking for. Returning to her seat, she handed Alex a small booklet.

"This devotional book will be a good start for you. It has a Scripture verse and a few paragraphs to help you apply the verse to everyday life. Try reading one every morning when you wake up."

Alex thanked her as she slipped the booklet into her back pocket. She wondered if it would help alleviate the growing anxiety invading her every waking moment. Worries about her finances, her living situation after the baby was born, and what would happen when her parents discovered she wasn't in California.

She'd alerted Brittany of her true whereabouts, but had sworn her to total secrecy. She called the university in California and withdrew from school. Thinking about doing it had been worse than actually doing it. Making the call had been empowering, like she was the one in control of her life for once. Ending the call, she felt as if one of the weights that had been sitting on her shoulders had been lifted off.

Now, if she could just shake the rest of them!

⌀ ⌀ ⌀

Their cruise now a distant memory, Karen and J.T. still didn't agree on how to handle what they now referred to as the "Alex situation." Upon arriving home and reading her note, which told them she was leaving and would be in touch when she was settled, Karen went ballistic.

"Can you believe this? She just took off without so much as a goodbye," she fumed. J.T. dared not point out how many times Karen had done the same thing to Alex and him when she left on business trips.

"I'm sure she's busy getting settled in, finding a job, making friends. You know Alex," he said, trying to placate his wife. Just when J.T. thought things were going so well, they come home to this lingering source of discontent.

The cruise had been exactly what they needed. Time away from Woodvale and all of its prying eyes, snooping ears, and chatty mouths. Before the trip, J.T. wondered if he'd ever feel comfortable in his hometown again. Guilt gnawed at him, plain and simple. He had outrun it before, and he could do it again. Lounging on one of the ship's deck chairs, wrapped in a warm blanket in the middle of the summer while floating past a glacier, he believed all could be right with his world again.

Then, they arrived home and found the note. Karen wanted to hire a private investigator to go find her. J.T. thought he'd squelched her idea by reasoning Alex was, after all, an adult now, capable of making wise decisions. Shouldn't they trust her? Deep down, though, he couldn't believe his good fortune!

On one hand, he had to convince Karen that Alex would be fine in California, and he hoped she would be. But on the other hand, the only person who could incriminate him now lived on the opposite coast of the United States. It seemed almost too good to be true.

After he felt certain he'd swayed Karen to his way of thinking, J.T. kissed his wife goodbye as she left for work. He wanted to use this opportunity to take a closer look through Alex's room to see if she'd left any clues regarding her hasty departure. He noticed many of her favorite photos of her and Brittany were gone, but those of their family together remained behind, gathering dust.

Checking her dresser, he saw most of her clothes were gone, but her swimsuits were still in their drawer. It crossed his mind that leaving them behind was strange, since she was going to one of the sunniest locations in America.

J.T. wandered into her bathroom, now devoid of toiletries...no, make that almost devoid. He saw her feminine hygiene products remained in the little box she had built. His stomach clenched. Looking in the cabinet under the sink, he found more, confirming his guess that she had taken with her everything she thought she would need. Apparently, she didn't believe she needed these items right now.

He made it to the toilet with no time to spare before he threw up.

Chapter 9
The Deal

Alex gave herself a mental pat on the back as she placed her final exam paper on the professor's desk and stepped out of the air-conditioned classroom. The scorching heat and unbearable humidity of Burton in late July nearly suffocated her. One thing she missed about Woodvale was the temperate summer weather in the North Carolina mountains. And, now that her baby bump was a real thing, she couldn't deny the need for clothes with a bit more stretch than those in her current wardrobe. Her old cut-off jeans wouldn't make it much longer.

Miss Matilda had asked her to pick up some fruit, milk, and bread at the grocery store on her way home. The second-hand shop in the heart of downtown would be a quick detour, giving Alex a chance to check out the clothing section. Matilda had honed Alex's bargain shopper skills.

Alex knew many of the other girls found some cute things for their early months at this particular shop without having to shell out a fortune, an important criterion considering she'd be wearing them only a short time.

A parking place on the crowded downtown street rarely opened up. The merchant's association had spent many long hours and hundreds of thousands of dollars revitalizing the historic buildings, maintaining the town's charm while providing trendy clothing stores, upscale dining and quaint antique shops.

Tucked away in an alley near the end of the street, the secondhand store enjoyed a steady stream of both faithful shoppers and curious newcomers. Alex felt fortunate to snag one of the last parking spots left during the busy lunchtime rush.

She locked the door of her SUV and hurried toward her destination, sandals flapping with each step. The bright new sign over the café across the street caught her attention, and she never saw the woman intent on a stack of papers coming out of the office building Alex was passing. She didn't see her, that is, until the moment they collided. They bounced off one another and landed on the sidewalk, scattering the woman's papers in the wind.

"Why don't you watch where you're going?" The woman's shrill voice in Alex's ear sent a shock wave coursing through her body. Her stilettos and pencil skirt seriously complicated her attempt to stand. Alex recognized Gail Lovell, Miss Matilda's nephew's wife, from church. Alex apologized, though, in truth, neither of them had been watching where they were going.

"Well, are you just going to sit there, or are you going to help me clean up this mess you made?" Gail demanded. Alex felt her blood begin to boil, and this time not because of the sizzling temperature outside.

"Ma'am, I'll be glad to help you if you'll give me just a moment." Alex placed a protective hand on her abdomen before attempting to retrieve the errant papers. Crawling toward a page as it skittered away in the wind, Alex placed her hand on an expensive black wing tip shoe. She looked up and saw it belonged to Terry, Gail's husband.

"Hello, dear," he greeted his wife with a kiss. "Did you have a run-in with a stranger?"

"I think she's one of your aunt's girls," Gail answered, derision clear in her response, as if Alex couldn't hear her. Terry cleared his throat.

"Don't worry about those papers, ma'am. Gail will have her secretary get them for her," he said, offering his hand to help Alex up from her collection efforts. She handed what she had been able to gather to Gail before the woman vanished back into the office building to summon her secretary.

"So, what brings you downtown?" Terry asked Alex.

Though his eyes were a cool blue, his smile was warm and engaging. His dark brown hair had just the slightest hint of white at the temples, and Alex could tell he was fit and took good care of himself. His well-tailored suit accentuated his muscular shoulders; and it had been a soft hand extended to assist her, not the calloused hands of one accustomed to manual labor.

"I was going shopping at the secondhand store before picking up some groceries for Miss Matilda, but I think I'll just skip the shopping for today. Not really in the mood anymore." She turned to go when he touched her shoulder.

"Don't hold one unfortunate encounter against Gail. She's not so bad when you get to know her."

"Whatever," Alex said over her shoulder while she unlocked her door and got in the SUV.

"Give Aunt Tilley my love," he shouted as her door slammed.

There was something vaguely familiar about Terry, but she couldn't put her finger on it. At least now she had a reason to ask someone about these two mysterious people who held such an important place in Miss Matilda's life.

🂠 🂠 🂠

Alex didn't have to wait long to find the answers she sought. After dinner that evening, Miss Matilda retreated to the porch rocker while the girls cleaned up. Alex washed dishes, pretending to be intent on scrubbing a stubborn pan, as she set up the conversation with some girls who had been around for a while.

"So, I ran into Gail Lovell downtown today," Alex began, leaving the true meaning of the statement open ended.

"Ooh. How did it go? Did she realize you were a resident here?" Lauren asked.

Lauren was due in less than two months, and she didn't want to shirk her household duties even though the girls were excused from chores in the third trimester. Everyone knew all the good girl talk happened during dinner cleanup, and she had no intention of missing anything.

"Um, I'm pretty sure she did. Why?"

"Well, you know, Gail's never been a big fan of this place," Lauren whispered, not wanting Miss Matilda to overhear them.

"Why not?"

Lauren and some of the other girls exchanged uncomfortable glances.

"She's gonna find out somehow anyway," Haley said.

"I guess so," Lauren sighed, not totally convinced but swayed by the argument. "Let's finish up here. Then, we'll take a walk, pick the vegetables, gather the eggs. I'll tell you what I know," she promised.

They hurried through the last of the dishes, hung up their dishtowels and aprons, and grabbed the baskets for gathering produce and eggs. At the door, Lauren held up her hand, halting the group's progress.

"Wait a minute. This looks suspicious. Normally Miss Matilda has to almost beg us to get the veggies on a hot summer night. She'll know something's up if we're all tromping outside."

They agreed that a few of the girls would stay in the house, some would head out the back door for the chicken coop, and Lauren and Alex would go straight to the garden, which was the furthest away and the most likely to be out of earshot.

Miss Matilda was getting up in years, but she still had exceptional hearing. Through all of the clandestine planning, Alex was about to pop to know what kind of secret could be so important to require such stealthy maneuvers.

In the muggy evening shade of the garden, Lauren recounted all she knew as the two girls gathered the vegetables. According to the word passed down as the girls rotated through, and from what Lauren had gleaned from the ladies at church, Miss Matilda was indeed Terry's aunt.

Matilda's sister and her husband had run the home years ago. Terry's daddy had been a preacher, and one night when Terry was about ten years old, the couple lost control of their car on the way home from a revival in a neighboring town. They hit a semi head-on and died instantly.

The whole town had been devastated, but none more than Terry Lovell. He adored his parents, admired them for the work they did, and wanted to be like them someday. Matilda was already living in the guest cottage, after having earned her master's degree in psychology and traveling to Africa to study the birthing practices of native tribes. Although as different as night and day, she and her sister had been inseparable.

Matilda and Terry had somehow known they would help each other through the inevitable grief and pain after their horrific loss, and they did.

Terry grew up to be strong, tall, and handsome.

Whatever Matilda needed done around the place, Terry had a knack for doing it. He taught himself to build and fix things. If the chicken coop latch was broken or a new swing needed to be built, he figured it out.

He decided he could help people, like his parents had done, by becoming an architect and designing better, more affordable housing systems. Big dreams of making a difference in the world slowly dulled his grief.

"So, where does Gail fit into the picture?" Alex wondered aloud. Something didn't add up. She wasn't the altruistic type.

"Hold your horses. I'm getting to the good part," Lauren answered, placing a tomato in the basket.

A baseball scholarship and the architecture program at Georgia Tech delivered the one-two punch Terry needed when trying to decide where to go to school. Focused and driven, Terry strove to excel both in the classroom and on the field. Gail Benson, an Atlanta socialite, ran with an elite crowd and attended school only to appease her father and kill time until she found a husband. Apparently, Terry Lovell was the man she'd been looking for. And, when Gail Benson wanted something, nobody stood in her way. Alex nodded as Lauren continued the story because she'd learned this truth the hard way.

According to Lauren's sources, Terry's commitment to his studies and the team tested Gail's best moves. She persisted in her pursuit, learning both his class schedule and the team's practice schedule. Their paths crossed, occasionally at first, with a friendly wave or a casual twist of her hair on her finger.

Terry eventually introduced himself, and they were soon inseparable. They married at the end of Terry's junior year in an elaborate ceremony in Atlanta. Gail decided to stay in school and earn her business degree. Terry quit the baseball team to concentrate on his new wife, his final year of school, and the big design required to graduate. As expected, Terry graduated among the top of his class.

The marital problems began soon after graduation. Gail wanted Terry to work for a big firm in Atlanta, fulfilling her dream of becoming a socialite wife. Terry had other plans. Four years was too long away from the woman who'd sacrificed everything for him and those girls who needed so much. He'd already made up his mind to move to Burton and make their life there, but small-town life appalled Gail.

"What changed her mind?" Alex asked Lauren, riveted by the story.

"Well, Terry promised her a huge house, her own business, and as many trips back to Atlanta as she wanted. She started her real estate business when Terry opened his architecture firm." The storyteller wrapped up her tale as they reached the end of the garden row, the back porch in sight.

Miss Matilda had company, and when the girls saw who it was, they stared at each other, eyes wide and mouths open. Terry and Matilda sat on the porch, rocking and sipping iced tea. They looked relaxed, talking with a camaraderie born of mutual love and respect. Matilda saw the girls approaching and motioned them over to the porch.

"Uh oh. Do you think they know what we've been talking about?" Lauren whispered between clenched teeth.

"Of course not," Alex answered in the same style. "We were a hundred yards away."

"You just don't know," Lauren responded. "She has supersonic hearing!" Alex giggled, nudging Lauren as they climbed the steps.

Everyone greeted one another with welcoming hugs before Miss Matilda announced Terry had some business to discuss with Alex. She and Lauren excused themselves while Alex and Terry re-occupied the rockers. They sat in silence for a few moments listening to the music of the croaking frogs in the nearby pond before Terry spoke.

"I took my car to Chad's place for an oil change today," he stated. Alex didn't know how to respond, since it wasn't a question.

"Okay," was the only reply she could think to give.

"Alex, where did you get those great ideas for re-doing his waiting area? It looks like a whole new place. Chad said you did all the work yourself?" His questions came at her like buckshot – fast and scattered, affording her little time to consider which one to answer first.

"Well, we're not done yet. We're going to do a grand re-opening to try to bring in more female clients. When I first walked in there, I knew he was missing out. I believed I could help him." She finished her explanation with a slight lift of one shoulder, trying to minimize her contribution to the success of the makeover.

Terry scooted his rocker to face her, excitement etched on his face.

"I've got a business deal I'd like to throw out there. You see things that aren't there."

"What?"

"I mean, the way you made a lamp out of the oilcan and funnel. Brilliant. And tables and planters made out of pallets. Genius. Do you have more ideas where those came from? Because if you do, I've got a market for them in the homes and businesses I build." His excitement was bubbling over and becoming contagious.

"You said this was a business deal?" she asked, eyes narrowing as she considered the possibility of someone she didn't know trying to take advantage of her. Always playing in the back of her mind was the thought of the new person she'd be supporting soon. Terry might be Miss Matilda's nephew, but she had to trust him before she agreed to work with him.

Terry laid out the terms of the deal, which seemed more than fair to Alex. He offered the up-front cash for supplies, reimbursable in six months. She asked to make it three, realizing she'd be shelling out a lot of cash in about six months when she was providing for two people. They agreed she'd receive sixty percent of the profits of commissioned pieces, and for pieces she made on speculation, she'd get seventy percent.

"I understand this isn't the norm for you, so we can revisit these terms when I pay you back for supplies," Alex offered as they shook on it.

"Sounds good," Terry agreed, his broad smile exposing beautiful white teeth. "I've got a feeling we're both going to do great. I'll leave the artistic control up to you. Have Aunt Tilley give me a call when you have about half a dozen pieces finished. Here's some cash to get started." He handed over several hundred dollars as he rose, helped her up, and guided her toward the back door.

Terry bade his aunt goodbye, wrapping her in a tender hug before leaving. She waved until his car was out of sight. It wasn't long, though, before Matilda's curiosity got the better of her, and Alex heard her rapping at her bedroom door asking to come in.

"Did you and Terry have a good talk, dear?" Matilda asked, leaning against the bed.

"Yes, ma'am. Did he tell you what he wants me to do?"

Matilda shook her head. "All he said was he had business to discuss with you. I found it a bit strange."

Alex explained the plan to Miss Matilda. Alex added her own plans for scouring yard sales and thrift shops for treasures she could use as the building blocks for her new creations.

"Well, you know what they say. 'One man's trash is another man's treasure.' I guess you're going to prove that to be true," Miss Matilda predicted as she patted Alex's hand.

"Miss Matilda, you know, I've prayed for weeks I would find a job to help provide for my baby and me. I wanted to do what I enjoy, but I didn't see how."

Here came those unbidden tears, again.

"That's the Lord's provision, child. Proverbs 3:5 says, '*Trust in the Lord with all your heart and lean not on your own understanding.*' When we trust the Lord, He'll take care of us, even when times are hard. Have you thanked Him for this unexpected blessing?" Alex shook her head. "Well," Miss Matilda suggested, "how about we do that right now."

They bowed their heads.

Chapter 10
A Blowup and a Birth

Try as she might, Alex couldn't squelch the rush of pride as she loaded her final piece into her vehicle, preparing to take them to Terry's office. She'd learned pride was sinful if not kept in check, but she also understood artists needed a critical eye and confidence in their work to produce excellent results. She believed she'd created beautifully unique items for homes in Burton and beyond. All that remained was to see if Terry agreed.

Each piece in the group she loaded today was on the small side: a couple of lamps, a few end tables, a coffee table, and some wall-mounted shelves. Regardless of size, each piece bore Alex's inimitable style and impeccable craftsmanship. Except for Chad's waiting area, she'd never had her work on display for strangers before, and she'd never considered getting paid to do something she loved so much.

Following Miss Matilda's directions, Alex found Terry's office easily. A tiny brick house under a stand of long-needle pines greeted her when she steered into the circular drive. She saw a small pond a few hundred feet beyond the back of the house.

This looks more like a home than an office, she thought.

Alex opened her car door to see a smiling Terry emerge from the front door. Gail stood slightly behind him, stone-faced and arms crossed. Alex's stomach clenched. Terry hadn't said anything about Gail being here. Since the unfortunate collision downtown, Gail had regarded Alex with coolness at church, and the couple had never made it out to Miss Matilda's for Sunday lunch. It devastated Miss Matilda. Alex hoped she could make amends today.

"Alex, thank you so much for getting your first group done and delivered. We can't wait to see them. Right, honey?" he addressed his wife, placing his hand on her back. She twisted her shoulder, dismissing Terry's gesture.

"I've told you. I don't think I'll be able to put any arts and crafts projects into the high-end homes I sell, Terry. Could we just get this over with so I can get back to work?"

Alex saw Terry flinch, but she remained unshaken. She'd dealt with her mother for a long time. Although Gail intimidated Alex, the girl felt confident in her work and in her ability to handle difficult people. Alex drew in a deep breath and began her subtle sales job.

"I understand, Gail." Alex locked eyes with the woman, leaving no mistake regarding the target of her comment. "Your clients expect exceptional quality, and you aren't going to disappoint them. But your clients also want a particular vibe, different for each one, I would guess. That's why you need unique, distinctive, top quality, hand-made pieces you can offer to set their new home apart and truly make it theirs."

As she spoke, Alex removed her handcrafted items from her vehicle, setting the tables on the driveway and placing the other pieces on them. Gail feigned disinterest at first, but her eyes lit up a bit more with each piece Alex brought out. Terry made a mighty attempt not to grin at Gail being beaten at her own game.

"Well," Gail said, inspecting each piece, "I suppose we can try this out and see how it goes. But," she spun around to face Alex, "if I see the slightest decrease in quality, reduced turnover of merchandise, anything reflecting on my reputation in a negative way, this deal is over. Understood?" Gail had abandoned her crossed arm posture, drawing herself to her full five feet and two inches.

"Yes, ma'am." Actually, Alex didn't understand how she'd entered into a deal with Terry and ended up finalizing the transaction with Gail. She thought she would have been better off if it had been the other way around, but the prospect of a source of income pushed all misgivings from her mind.

Alex watched in silence as Gail announced she was late for a meeting, slammed the door of her convertible, and drove away with a squeal of tires. Alex bent over to pick up the coffee table, but Terry stopped her.

"Let me get the tables, and you get the other things. I know you're feeling strong, but you don't want to take any chances."

"Thanks."

It was nice to have someone other than Miss Matilda be concerned about her well-being. Despite the traditional-looking exterior of the little brick house, inside was open, modern, and bright. Terry had cleared a space in the entry for Alex to place her work, maximizing visibility when clients walked in the door. She arranged and re-arranged, adding a few extra touches like vases, books, and frames until finally she declared she was ready for the world to see her work.

"Hey, I'm sorry about what Gail said earlier," Terry apologized as he walked with Alex back toward her SUV.

"Don't worry about it. I'm going to have to develop pretty thick skin if I want people to take me seriously as an artist and a contractor."

"Yeah, Aunt Tilley said you want to get your license. That's great. If you decide to stay in Burton, give me a call when you're licensed. I'm always looking for reliable contractors." They shook on it, and she was off.

She'd now officially launched her business.

℮ ℮ ℮

After church on Sunday, Alex held Miss Matilda's elbow, helping her into the van, when Terry rushed toward them. Matilda's face lit up at the sight of her nephew. After hugging her, he finished getting her settled into the front seat while Alex and the other girls climbed in the back.

"Where's Gail?" his aunt asked as she surveyed the sidewalk behind Terry.

"She's at the office trying to land a big deal. Is a lunch invitation open for just one?"

"You know it. We'll see you there."

The two new girls hadn't met Terry yet, and Alex knew Miss Matilda would take this opportunity to introduce her favorite, and only, family member to "her" girls.

The kitchen bustled with activity as soon as the girls poured out of the van. Everyone had a job to do, and Alex marveled at the well-oiled machine they became at mealtime. Soon, the girls had set the table, dished up the food in serving bowls, and transferred the heaping steamy bowls to the dining room. Everyone prepared to sit down and enjoy.

Then, Terry walked in with Gail, and in seconds the mood changed from festive to funereal. The girls exchanged furtive glances, but Matilda, a true Southern lady to the core, welcomed Gail with open arms. She hugged both of them as they walked in the door and invited them to sit down so lunch could commence while it was hot.

Gail looked appalled and disgusted. Lauren had told Alex this place had never appealed to Gail as it had Terry. She'd always looked down on the girls with a judgmental scowl. Terry tried to joke with Gail that she'd have to forget about her salad and protein shakes today. Gail's frown deepened as she surveyed the delicious Sunday dinner of fried chicken, green beans, and biscuits. But Terry and the girls took their cue from their mentor, taking their seats and bowing their heads for the blessing.

Immediately, the clinks of spoons against the bowls and requests to pass the plate of biscuits echoed in the dining room. When all plates were served and everyone's attention became directed at eating the delicious lunch, Terry addressed Alex sitting across the table from him.

"I've got some great news about your line of home décor pieces."

"I'd hardly call them a line," Gail corrected, rolling her eyes. "She's made a few tables and lamps. It's more of a hobby at this point."

"I don't think so," Terry said, undeterred by his wife's pessimism. "All but one of the lamps you brought last week are sold, and I've got two clients who would like to talk to you about commissioning a few pieces. What do you think? Do you have the time?"

The girls watched the conversation like the action at a tennis match. Alex had mentioned taking a few things out to Terry's place, but she didn't realize her work would be so popular. Radiant, Miss Matilda's expression exuded pride in her nephew and this talented girl.

"Well, of course she doesn't have time, Terry!" Gail shrieked, slamming her fork down so hard it shattered the plate. A collective gasp resonated around the dining room. "You know she's in school to get an education to take care of the illegitimate child she has to support. She'll be lucky to make ends meet in some dead-end job, much less have time to waste on trivialities like those knickknacks she brought to your office." Her voice was a shrill two octaves higher by the time she finished.

The entire assembly sat stunned, mute, and flabbergasted by Gail's unwarranted attack.

"Could we talk about this some other time, Terry?" Alex excused herself with the last shred of dignity she could muster and fled up the stairs.

⌀ ⌀ ⌀

This was the final straw. Matilda didn't care if Gail was Terry's wife, this woman would no longer degrade her girls.

"Gail Lovell," Matilda's voice shook, though it was barely louder than a whisper, "Never again are you to speak to any of the girls in my home in such a manner. You are not welcome here until you can conduct yourself in the way you were raised. I feel quite certain the display we all just witnessed is not a testament to what your momma taught you." She turned her gaze to her nephew, her eyes shining with unshed tears. "You are welcome here any time, Terry, dear. Alone."

Matilda's chair scraped across the hardwood floor as she stood, indicating Gail's welcome had been overstayed and she needed to leave at once. Terry rose too, breaking the icy, uncomfortable silence.

"I apologize for my wife's unforgivable outburst." He didn't look at Gail as he spoke. "We'll leave now so y'all can finish your lunch in peace. Aunt Tilley, please give Alex my heartfelt apologies, and let her know I'll be in touch."

Gail's head whipped around to protest, but Terry ignored her. He folded his napkin, threw it on the table, and stalked past her and out the door with a resounding slam. The residents remained seated, gawking at a furious and humiliated Gail Lovell. Nobody would forget this incident any time soon.

With a noise similar to a dog's growl issuing from her throat, Gail stomped to the door and gave it her own hearty heave. Her pricey designer heels punctuated her trip across the front porch and down the steps. Everyone left in the dining room heard gravel flying as Terry slammed on the brakes of his convertible BMW in front of the steps.

A huge collective sigh of relief escaped Miss Matilda and the residents in one great whoosh. They'd long since lost their appetites, and the food was cold anyway. Matilda watched as the girls rose to begin the task of clearing the lunch dishes and putting away the leftovers to have for supper.

There was no shortage of cleanup chatter about everything from Gail's outburst to Terry's slamming of the door. Matilda made sure their attention was fully focused on their task and their conversation before she folded her napkin, set it on the table and went to comfort

Alex. She ascended the stairs, on a mission to attempt to undo some of the cruel hurt inflicted on an innocent girl.

Again!

A few minutes later, all conversation in the kitchen ceased as soon as Miss Matilda walked in looking drained, sad, worn out. Lauren rushed to the kind lady in an effort to give back some measure of the comfort the older woman heaped on them.

"What can we do?" Lauren asked as she embraced Miss Matilda.

"I don't know. Alex is hurting and embarrassed. She needs affirmation. Chad's re-opening is next week. I sure do hope it goes well. For both of them."

With the mood in the kitchen a bit more somber, the cleanup continued. Matilda listened to the girls' voices singing the praise song they'd learned in church that morning. Matilda's heart warmed knowing these girls understood God carried them through both the good times and the tough times.

They needed to make sure Alex understood this fact, too.

$$\emptyset \ \emptyset \ \emptyset$$

With Chad's grand re-opening a little more than a week away, Alex had time to consider Gail's hurtful words, read the Bible about how to deal with unlovable people, and pray. Wednesday night at church, she spoke to Reverend Drummond about her problem, without revealing Gail's name. She told him how she felt hurt, wronged, belittled and asked how she should proceed.

"Well, now, that's a tricky subject, Alex," the preacher said. "The Lord Jesus told us we're to forgive seventy times seven. It doesn't mean a literal seventy times seven, but, rather, we should continue to forgive those who wrong us. Believe me, it's a lot easier said than done." He chuckled as he patted her shoulder.

"But, Reverend, how am I supposed to just forgive this person after all of the horrible things she said about me? I'm pretty sure she hates me, and I've never done anything..."

Alex trailed off as she spoke, remembering bumping into Gail on the sidewalk. Had one unfortunate incident caused such a strong dislike, even hatred, for Alex in Gail's heart? Coming out of her reverie, she heard Reverend Drummond talking to her.

"...have to find ways to mend the relationship," he concluded.

Uh oh!

Alex had no idea what he said before wrapping up, and she was too embarrassed to ask. She thanked him for the godly counsel and went in search of Miss Matilda and the two other girls who'd come with them to the mid-week service. The group was walking to Alex's vehicle in the parking lot when a young woman came running toward them, waving her arms to flag them down.

"Miss Matilda, I'm so glad I caught you before you left. The girls from the home just called my cell phone. It's Lauren."

"What about her, Casey? Is anything wrong?" Matilda asked, concern etched in every line on her face.

"No, ma'am, nothing's wrong. But she's gone into labor, and the contractions are coming fast. They don't think there's time for you to get home and take her to the hospital, so they called an ambulance. She wants you to meet her there." The words tumbled out of the girl.

"Let's go, Miss Matilda," Alex said, slipping behind the wheel and starting her car. Lauren was her best friend at the home, and she wasn't going to let her face this birth alone and scared.

Casey offered to take the other two girls back to the home, allowing Matilda and Alex to stay as long as necessary at the hospital. Before Matilda got in the car to leave, she calmed the group by reminding them Who was in control.

"Can we take a minute to pray? Heavenly Father and Sovereign Lord, You are not surprised at all by this. Help us to trust in You with all our hearts. We ask You to grant Your peace to Lauren, give her comfort in the delivery, and keep both her and the baby safe and healthy. You are powerful and mighty, and we praise You. In Jesus' name we lift our prayer. Amen."

Before the "Amen" died on the night breeze, Matilda had fastened her seatbelt and they were off.

✻ ✻ ✻

Alex watched her friend hold her beautiful little boy, more emotions than she'd ever experienced at once overwhelming her. Joy oozed from Lauren, bringing smiles to all who saw her. How could you not love the perfect innocence of a newborn baby? Alex recalled how privileged she'd been to witness the miraculous entry of this perfect little human into the world.

Driving faster than the law allowed, Alex had wheeled into the Emergency Room parking lot, glad when more than two tires stayed on the ground as she turned sharply. Once parked, Miss Matilda released her iron grip on the handle above her, and they hurried up to labor and delivery.

Lauren's contractions had been about three minutes apart when her friends arrived, and she made it clear she wanted Alex with her for the birth. Alex was objecting that she didn't have the necessary training when Dr. Sheffield walked in.

"Hello, Alex. Are you Lauren's birth coach?" she asked.

"I don't know. I've never done this before," Alex answered, overwhelmed by the situation.

"Don't worry. Lauren and I are going to do most of the work. Besides, you'll be on the pushing end in a few months, so you may as well see how this goes."

Another contraction consumed Lauren's attention, the nurses hooked her up to several monitors, and they gave Alex a crash course in being an encourager. Miss Matilda hugged Alex, promised to pray, and went out to the waiting room. It was sink or swim for Alex.

Time took on a strange quality in the delivery room. It seemed to creep along at a snail's pace during Lauren's labor, but when Dr. Sheffield checked her and said it was time to push, all medical personnel went into high speed. Alex stood still and watched as everyone moved around the room like a finely tuned machine with the goal of delivering a healthy baby.

Lauren locked eyes with Alex. "Thank you for staying with me."

"Are you kidding me? I wouldn't miss this for the world," she grinned. "Now, let's have a baby." Lauren smiled back and seemed to relax a bit. Two pushes later, she was a mom.

Tears poured unbidden down both girls' faces as they caressed the tiny boy, lying squirming and bloody on Lauren's abdomen. The nurse gave him a little shake, and he emitted a healthy, ear-splitting cry, eliciting a smile from the nurse before she scooped him up.

"You did a great job, Lauren," Dr. Sheffield said, peeling off her gloves.

"Thank you. For everything."

Lauren leaned back against the pillows, sweaty and exhausted. Alex didn't think she'd ever seen her look prettier. She slipped out and let Miss Matilda know Lauren and the baby were both fine.

"And, how 'bout you?" Matilda inquired.

"What? What about me?"

"You made it through your first delivery without a hitch?"

"Yes, ma'am, I did. What a miracle it is to see a life come into the world." Again, the protective hand went to her belly, now obviously swollen.

"I agree, dear. It's why I've done what I do for all these years." Matilda patted Alex's shoulder. "Let's go to the cafeteria for a cup of tea. They should have Lauren in her room by the time we return. After we stop by to check on her, we can go home."

"I say that sounds like a wonderful plan. I'm exhausted."

After a quick trip to the cafeteria, they were bidding Lauren goodbye when the nurse brought the baby to Lauren. They stuck around a few minutes longer to learn all the details of weight, length, and time of birth to share with the others back at the home.

In bed later that night, Alex reminisced on the events of the last few hours and allowed worry to creep into her heart and mind. Lauren had been in so much pain, but her labor was relatively fast. Alex had heard horror stories of labor lasting for hours and hours.

How would she make it? Had she made the right choice? As she tossed and turned throughout the night, her sleep-deprived, hormone-fueled, irrational thoughts seemed valid and logical in a weird way.

Alex finally made a concerted effort to turn off the negative voices in her mind. She had more important things to think about. Chad's grand re-opening was one week from tomorrow. Alex looked at the clock by her bed. Three o'clock.

Nope, she thought, *Chad's grand re-opening is one week from today!* Great!

Chapter 11
The Grand Re- Opening

The morning air in Burton held a hint of unseasonable coolness on grand re-opening day, with not a cloud in the sky. The sweltering summer temperatures had tried the patience, wardrobes, and air conditioners of the town's citizens. Labor Day weekend had arrived, and everyone was grateful for a little relief from the heat.

Frazzled and nervous, Alex rushed to get ready for the event. Her hands shook so much she dropped her brush and smudged her mascara. She was so excited for the town to see Chad's updated place and new website, and, while she shunned the limelight, she still wanted to look her best.

Some of Karen's ingrained training couldn't be shaken. She chose a flowy cornflower blue dress to camouflage her growing tummy and finished off the outfit with a simple pair of pearl earrings and comfortable dressy flat sandals. A quick glance in the mirror confirmed the understated look she'd hoped to achieve.

After all, this remodel was what got her new trash-to-treasure business started in the first place. She never knew when new prospective clients could be waiting, and she needed to look professional and polished at all times.

Hurrying down the stairs, Alex heard Miss Matilda's methodical gait as she moved through the kitchen. Alex headed in the direction of the sound to check on the older lady and see if they could speed up their exit. They needed to be leaving now. Alex hated to be late, and by late, she meant on time.

Prepared to deliver a speech on the virtues of punctuality, Alex took a deep breath as she entered the large kitchen, only to be greeted by a sight she could scarcely believe. Miss Matilda, surrounded by the other ladies, stood in front of a stunning arrangement of roses, lilies and peonies. Someone had made a heaping stack of pancakes, a pile of bacon, and a huge "Congratulations, Alex!" sign.

"Wow!" was all she could manage in a whisper. Her eyes puddled, her hands began to shake, and her knees felt like jelly. She didn't deserve this. "Y'all, I don't deserve all this." She might as well just put her thoughts into words because she no longer had the mental capacity for an eloquent speech.

"Nonsense," Miss Matilda fussed, as she began to fix a plate of pancakes. When she saw Alex glance at her watch, Matilda transferred her breakfast to a paper plate. "I think I'll take mine to go."

Alex smiled gratefully as she wrapped a slice of bacon in a pancake and escorted the older lady out the door. She had butterflies in her stomach from the excitement. Alex stopped in her tracks, her pancake halfway to her mouth, her hand almost on the doorknob. Miss Matilda was chattering away, but she trailed off when she noticed Alex's strange behavior.

There went those butterflies again. Only, Alex didn't think it was excitement or stress or even the Mexican food she'd eaten for dinner last night.

"Miss Matilda, I've got butterflies," she said, thunderstruck.

"Well, of course, dear. It's only natural. This is a big day, and you're excited. Maybe even a little nervous…" But as Miss Matilda turned to look at her, Alex had her hand on her tummy. She took Miss Matilda's and placed it there.

"Can you feel it?" she asked.

Matilda nodded.

It was her turn for the tears to puddle as she asked, "Is this the first time?" Alex nodded.

"Well, what a day! Let's get going, shall we?" Miss Matilda led the way out the door.

Alex hoped she could pull this off. Was she in over her head?

Ø Ø Ø

To Alex's delight, everything went according to plan. At first.

Chad proudly toured people around the remodeled waiting area, explaining how much more comfortable they'd be. He unveiled the new coffee bar, where guests could help themselves to a freshly brewed cup of coffee and a pastry while they waited.

He demonstrated the new website, showing folks how to schedule an appointment online or check their wait time. The whole presentation garnered enthusiastic applause and whistles, led by Alex. Chad's obvious pride in the upgrade warmed her heart.

"I'm glad you were able to get the mayor and the newspaper reporter here," Alex handed Chad a cup of lemonade after the official ribbon-cutting ceremony.

"I didn't call Mayor Carlisle or the newspaper. I thought you did," Chad said as he and Alex sipped their homemade lemonade in silence and pondered why these folks would choose to come to this event. They didn't have to wonder for long. Terry strolled over, mayor in tow.

"Alex, Chad, I don't know if you've been properly introduced to my friend, Sonny Carlisle. Sonny, this is Alex Powell and Chad White. They're the brains and brawn behind this transformation today."

Terry's smooth introduction bespoke a practiced ease of dealing with people. And, as Alex had noted when she'd seen him interact with everyone today, his body language—the way he rested his hand on the mayor's shoulder, leaned in to catch the important parts of conversations, or threw his head back to laugh at the punch line of a joke—made it clear he enjoyed being with people.

"Alex, I've been telling Sonny all of these pieces in the waiting area are your original ideas. He'd like to see more of your work for his office." Terry stood behind the mayor and, with a slight nod, raised one eyebrow at Alex, indicating the ball was now in her court.

"Yes, sir, of course. I can call your office and make an appointment to bring in some photos and some samples of my other work. Maybe we could take a look at the space you have in mind so I can get an idea of what would be appropriate." Alex went into business mode as she'd often done while working for J.T.

"Fine, fine," Mayor Carlisle responded warmly. "Give my assistant a call next week, and we can get started. I love to have the work of local artists in the office."

He gave her his card and shook her hand in parting, then he shook Chad's hand and congratulated him on a successful day. They watched him wander off to the refreshment table. Alex stared into the distance, dazed and unsure if the entire day had been a dream.

She ticked off in her mind one by one the events that had taken place since she'd awakened that morning. The celebratory breakfast, feeling the baby, the successful re-opening, free advertising from the newspaper, a new job opportunity, being called a local artist...could this day get any better?

As if answering her question and bringing her back from her dreamland, Gail Lovell walked in. Alex saw her as soon as her posh stilettos crossed the threshold. Alex gripped Chad's hand for support to prevent herself from collapsing since her knees had taken on the same texture as the car-shaped Jell-O mold sitting on the refreshment table. What was Gail doing here? Shouldn't she be showing houses? Was there no limit to the humiliation one woman could inflict on another human being?

It turned out, the answer was *no* to that question, too.

$$\mathscr{G} \ \mathscr{G} \ \mathscr{G}$$

Even though Chad had spent his entire life at the shop, working at it and running it had proven to be two entirely different things. Over the past few months, he'd made progress on the business side of things, but looking around the place now he had to admit, the girl knew what she was talking about. It had looked sad in here. He couldn't remember the last time his dad had done anything to spruce up the place.

Chad smiled when Alex interlaced her fingers with his, but when he glanced down at her, he noticed she'd gone ghostly white. She'd reached out for his strength. Chad's fiercely protective streak took over. He knew most folks around town had heard at least some version of Gail's outburst at Miss Matilda's place a few weeks back.

He'd heard crazy rumors about Gail flinging knives and Alex ripping the tablecloth off the table. But Chad had gotten the story straight from Miss Matilda, and he understood why Alex might feel like she'd been punched. He placed his hand over Alex's and steered her away from the door, shielding her from Gail's line of sight.

Chad kept an eye on Gail as she strutted over to Terry, hooked her arm in his, and proceeded to hijack his conversation with one of his business associates. By the time Chad found a quiet spot with a comfy chair in the back for Alex, Miss Matilda joined them, bringing Alex a glass of water. Alex thanked Miss Matilda as she took it, sipping as she listened to Miss Matilda and Chad.

"She won't stay long, once she sees none of her high-profile friends are here," Matilda said.

"What about the mayor? Isn't she trying to put a bug in his ear about building some fancy residential development?" Chad asked.

"Well, maybe she'll just chat and then leave."

"But I've still got the schedule change to announce," Chad reminded her.

"Better hold off for now. Let's see how this plays out."

Matilda had barely gotten the words out of her mouth when the trio at the back watched Gail motion for people to gather around her as if she planned on making some kind of announcement herself. Chad looked to Matilda for advice, and she nudged him toward the front in case he needed to go into damage control mode.

Chad noticed Terry stood well off to the side, arms crossed, legs planted apart, mouth fixed in a solid line across his face. Not the genial persona he'd projected just minutes before. Chad almost made it to Gail's side before she began to speak.

"Well, hello, my fellow Burton residents. How are you this fine day?" Gail addressed the assembled crowd, who looked confused as to why she would be speaking to them. "I'm here as a Chamber of Commerce representative, and I just want to congratulate Mr. White on the fine remodel of his shop. This is something he and I have been discussing for quite some time, and I'm so happy to say, when he decided to go ahead with this project, I was thrilled he finally took my advice!"

Chad's stomach lurched. This whole thing – the remodel, the website, the grand re-opening – it had all been Alex's idea, hatched the day a wayward deer had brought her to his shop. Now, Gail was taking credit for all of Alex's hard work.

First, she demeaned and belittled Alex for what she did, and now she was taking credit for it. What a sick, messed up woman. Chad looked at Terry, who had turned so he wouldn't have to look at Alex. Even from far away, Chad saw tears pool in her big brown eyes and threaten to overflow.

Alex sat in the chair, spine stiff and face composed in a disinterested mask. She accepted the tissue Miss Matilda offered, dabbed the moisture from her eyes, and blew her nose quietly. The fiasco continued next to Chad.

Gail opened her mouth and drew a deep breath, obviously prepared to spew more lies. But Chad raised his hand and silenced her. He took an almost imperceptible step forward, but it sufficed to place him in front of Gail as he addressed his customers and friends.

He knew he needed to smooth over the confusion and untruths Gail had spouted, but he had to portray a professional demeanor in doing so. It was a delicate balance. What he really wanted to do was heave Gail Lovell out the door by the scruff of her expensive blazer.

"I, too, want to thank y'all for coming out today," Chad said, looking around the waiting area with a forced smile. "I never thought the shop could look so nice. My daddy would be really proud. I've got one very talented lady to thank for it." Gail prepared to receive Chad's accolades, but the simpering smile melted on her flawlessly made-up face at Chad's next words. "Alex Powell, if it weren't for you, I wouldn't have realized how awful this place looked," this drew a laugh from the crowd, "or known how to turn things around for this business. Come on up here, Alex."

As Alex walked to meet Chad, Gail fumed. She tried to scoot toward Terry and slip her arm through his, but he remained as stiff as a statue, never acknowledging her presence. Humiliated and attempting to salvage what shred of dignity she could muster, she turned on her four-inch spiked heel and stormed out the door. Nobody noticed her tantrum, though, because by then Alex had arrived at Chad's side.

"This is Alex Powell, the brains *and* the brawn behind this remodel. Today, at her suggestion, and with the go-ahead from my employees, we're announcing our new schedule. We're now open Tuesday through Saturday, and closed on Sundays and Mondays. Our updated hours are on the flyers on the refreshment table. Please feel free to take one. We hope these new business hours will give working parents, especially those who work out of town, the flexibility they need to get their car serviced without having to miss a lot of work time.

"And don't forget about the website. You can also find our new hours there, along with the appointment calendar. Well, that's all I had to say. I hope you enjoy the rest of your day."

Chad was talked out.

He'd never spoken so much in front of a crowd of people. But he needed these folks to know Alex was a genius in so many ways. He didn't have much time to think about it before people bombarded both him and Alex with congratulations and questions.

Chad knew he had a lot to think about when all the excitement of today had passed. It wasn't about his newly renovated business either.

∅ ∅ ∅

"I'm so sorry. I had no idea she would be here today."

Terry's voice rang in Alex's ear as he stood behind her. She turned to face him. The emotional roller coaster of the day had left Alex feeling like a limp dishrag.

"You need to figure out a way to stop having to apologize for Gail. She's a grown woman and should be held accountable for the people she hurts. Her casualties are not your fault, Terry, unless you make them your fault. And it appears you're doing exactly that."

Alex turned away so Terry couldn't see the hurt she knew showed in her eyes. Alex hoped Miss Matilda was standing far enough away that she couldn't hear the exchange, but the older lady's superb hearing once again served her well.

Alex had no way of knowing the words she spoke were the ones Matilda had wanted to say to her dear nephew for a very long time. A scared, hurt eighteen-year-old girl had managed to make Terry see the reality he'd avoided for years.

∅ ∅ ∅

When the last guest left, Chad flipped the shop sign to Closed. Alex promised to stick around and help clean up since she had, literally, gotten him into this mess. Matilda hurried home to prepare a room for the new girl scheduled to arrive tomorrow, a new recipient of her loving care and kindness. Chad agreed to take Alex home once cleanup duty was complete.

"Hey, I don't know how to thank you for all you've done," Chad said, his back to her as he tossed a paper cup into the trash bag. Alex thought she heard a tremor in his voice, but dismissed the idea almost as soon as it entered her mind.

"So, are we even on my car repair," Alex tossed over her shoulder, keeping her tone light. When Chad turned to face her, however, and she saw the seriousness in his expression, her heart skipped a beat.

"Alex," Chad said, his usually booming voice barely audible. "There's something I need to tell you..."

As he approached Alex, a beautiful woman appeared at the glass door, knocking insistently.

"I've got to talk to Charmain about her horrible timing," he mumbled, reaching the door in three long strides and flinging it open. He hugged her and kissed her cheek, then asked why she hadn't made it on time, chiding her for her chronic tardiness.

Alex watched the two of them banter with ease, and a sense of melancholy washed over her, though she wasn't exactly sure why. Charmain's beautiful blond hair reached halfway down her back in loose, beachy curls. Tall, fit, and stylish, she served as a stark contract to Alex's own expanding abdomen and swelling ankles. In a flash of memory, Alex recalled Chad kissing a girl's cheek in the parking lot a few weeks ago.

Charmain!

Alex felt like an idiot. She'd begun to believe maybe, not for certain, but just maybe, after the baby was born, and she settled into her new life, she might be able to trust Chad. She even allowed herself to consider the possibility of having feelings for Chad. And she'd thought the sentiment might be reciprocated.

How stupid she was. This clarified things in her heart and mind. The ability to trust again loomed a long way off. Shoulders hunched, Alex attempted to excuse herself to go to the ladies' room and have a good cry when Chad suddenly remembered his manners and his guest.

"Oh, my gosh! I'm so sorry, Alex," he smacked his forehead with the heel of his hand. "We're just carrying on as if you've lived here all your life. This is Charmain."

"I gathered," Alex said, reaching out her hand to shake Charmain's. Instead, Charmain grabbed Alex's hand and pulled her into a big bear hug.

"You don't know how much I appreciate you helping my brother get this place fixed up." Charmain was swaying Alex from side to side, but Alex was pretty sure the bear hug had nothing to do with why the room was spinning.

"Your what?"

"My dumb big brother, who had let this place start looking like a trash heap reject pile."

"Wait a minute," said Chad, a devilish twinkle in his green eyes. "You didn't think we were...?"

"What? No!" Alex heard the inflection in her own voice get higher. "Besides, it's none of my business," Alex answered, feeling her face redden and busying herself once again with gathering cups and plates and throwing them in the trash can.

Out of the corner of her eye, Alex saw Charmain raise one eyebrow at her brother in an unspoken question. A single shake of his head was the only response Chad offered. Alex felt sure they'd talk about this awkward moment in greater detail when they were alone.

"Well, I'd love to hang around and help clean up, but I'm late for another appointment..."

"Imagine," her brother quipped.

"...so, I'm out of here. Alex, I'll see you later? Congratulations, guys. Bye."

Charmain escaped cleanup duty as deftly as she'd breezed in.

"What's that little smile for?" Chad asked Alex as he glanced over at her.

"Your sister reminds me of my best friend from back home. I mean, they don't look anything alike, but she's so sure of herself and outgoing. I've always admired people who feel comfortable wherever they are."

"You know what I admire?" Chad dropped what he was doing and walked over to stand in front of Alex.

"What?"

It was all she could manage to stand still and face Chad, she was so flustered and more than a little bit frightened at how fast her heart was pounding. She'd never been this close to a guy. Well, she didn't count that one horrific night. Besides, this was so different.

"I admire someone who can leave everything they've ever known, start all over, and become a huge success. Seriously, Alex, you were brilliant today. You've given my place a new life. The way you handled yourself around all those people. It's like you've done it forever." She kind of had, of course, but she remained quiet.

He put one hand on her arm to punctuate his sincerity, but it only served to spook Alex, who still carried the scars of a stinging betrayal Chad knew nothing about. The problem was, she wasn't ready to share the details with him, not now. Maybe not ever. It was too intimate, too humiliating, too soul-baring. No. She needed some more practice in building her walls before she could let Chad near.

She shrunk away from his touch.

💋 💋 💋

Chad recognized those walls. His dad had built walls most of his life to shield himself from pain—until he learned he was sick. Cancer, or any major sickness, had a weird way of putting a new perspective on life. Once his dad realized he wouldn't be around much longer, he began to tear down his walls. Chad wouldn't allow Alex to wait until a life-threatening event forced her to take down her walls. Chad's dad had wasted so much precious time; he couldn't let Alex do the same.

He intended to be a one-man demolition crew.

Chapter 12
Worth the Effort

The girls at Together for Good decorated the house with dozens of pumpkins and cornucopias, preparing for the bountiful Thanksgiving Day meal Miss Matilda promised. They invited Lauren back with her little boy Brennan, and the girls who remembered her couldn't wait to see her again. Chad and Charmain were invited, as was Terry, but it remained a mystery whether he would show up without "her."

Nobody said Gail's name at the house anymore.

Matilda sent several of the girls to the grocery store to get supplies for the big day, but asked Alex and Haley to stay behind to bake pumpkin pies before putting them in the freezer. They rolled out piecrusts while the radio played the songs Alex had learned in church.

"Have you decided if you want to know the gender of your baby?" Matilda asked Alex.

"You mean before it's born?" She'd known some girls found out, but hadn't formed an opinion either way. "I guess it would be good to know. That way, I can pick out a name and buy some clothes."

Since the day she'd felt the first kick, she waited with anticipation for every nudge from this tiny person within her. Lately, she'd begun to feel rhythmic little bumps and was concerned at first. After talking to Dr. Sheffield, she was relieved to discover it was only her baby having hiccups.

"Well, then," Miss Matilda interrupted Alex's musings. "Why don't we go have a little peek?" The three of them washed their hands and walked across the hall to the sonogram room.

Within minutes, Alex's exposed belly was covered in slippery goo, and Miss Matilda was sliding the probe around, muttering to the child within.

"Aha. There we go," the older woman said with a broad smile. "Shall I tell you now?"

"Yes!" Alex and Haley said together. Matilda chuckled.

"Alex, you're having a girl!"

Tears stung Alex's eyes with thoughts of what her daughter would be like rolling around in her mind. *Her daughter.* To even think the words made her dizzy with fear, excitement, anticipation, and...what else was it? Love! She already loved this little person, and she hadn't even met her. How did she learn to do this? Not from Karen, who'd had no time for her own daughter.

Alex's precious little girl hadn't been created in ideal circumstances, but the baby was blameless in the whole complicated situation. Alex knew she was responsible for creating a loving environment where this blessing from God could grow and thrive.

"Thank you, Miss Matilda," Alex whispered, sitting up and wiping the gel off her tummy. "I'm going to try to be the best mommy ever."

"I'm sure you will be."

The three ladies were putting pies in the oven when the other girls arrived home from the grocery store. They sent Miss Matilda to her cottage with a cup of tea to put her feet up for a bit while they put away the groceries.

"Are you going to tell them your news?" Haley whispered to Alex.

"What news? Wait, are you finally dating Chad?" asked Skylar, the girl who'd moved in the day after Chad's re-opening.

"No! I'm seven months pregnant. I'm not dating anybody! My news is I'm having a girl," Alex told the others. They were thrilled for her; hugs and high fives were exchanged all around.

Wow, Alex had no idea her growing, albeit timid, feelings for Chad were so obvious. What must he think? She made a mental note to keep her guard up, especially when he and Charmain came for Thanksgiving.

⌀ ⌀ ⌀

True to her word, Miss Matilda's Thanksgiving meal was a feast unlike any other. Chad and Charmain brought their standard: green bean casserole. Terry's chocolate cake rivaled any ever seen on a magazine cover. He offered a brief explanation about Gail going to Atlanta to visit family, but nobody questioned him and the subject quickly changed to something else.

Alex marveled at how everybody pitched in to get the mountains of food from the kitchen to the table. When it came time to sit down, Alex found the only empty spot was next to Chad. Not wanting to be obvious about avoiding him, she took her seat, smiled at him, and bowed her head while Terry said the blessing. Her daughter chose the exact moment of the "Amen" to develop a case of the hiccups.

"Ooh!" Alex placed a hand on her bouncing belly.

"Are you okay?" Chad asked, concern showing on his face.

"I'm fine. When she gets hiccups, it still startles me."

"She? A girl? Yay! I can start buying pink and frills," exclaimed Charmain, waving her fork in the air.

Alex smiled at Charmain's unbridled enthusiasm. Over the last few weeks, the blond beauty had become one of Alex's best friends. She noticed Chad's amazed gaze focused on the visible movement each time her baby hiccupped. Never one to be the center of attention, Alex squirmed and tried to shift the focus away from herself.

"So, Terry, how's business going?" she asked.

"It's going well. Your home décor line has quite a following since Chad's re-opening and the mayor's office project. Do you plan to continue working once the baby is born?"

"I'd like to. This little girl is due at the very beginning of the next school semester, so I plan to take one semester off and then pick up with my classes again at the beginning of next summer. If I can work some while she sleeps, great. I'm just going to have to figure out this whole single mom thing."

"Good. Because once you finish your degree and get your contractor's license, I'll be ready to put you to work. I've got a contractor who'll be retiring in about four or five years, and I'd love for you to work with him and learn the ropes."

"That sounds fun," Alex said, scooping a forkful of sweet potatoes. She liked making plans. But she also knew things didn't always go according to even the most elaborately developed plans.

Everybody stuffed themselves, enjoyed good conversation, then wandered away from the table in a turkey-induced stupor. Despite Miss Matilda's vehement protests, the guests insisted on handling the cleanup since Matilda and her girls had prepared the majority of the delicious fare. Everyone was too full and sleepy to argue overmuch, so almost an hour after leaving the table, Chad, Charmain, and Terry dried and put away the final dish.

117

While much of the country spent the holiday buried under a blanket of snow, Terry joined his Aunt Tilley on this unseasonably pleasant November day on the porch rockers with a cup of coffee.

Alex wandered in the vegetable garden, while Chad and his sister put away the last of the silverware. She didn't see him watching her from the kitchen window. She also didn't see Charmain shoo Chad out of the kitchen, waving him in Alex's direction.

"Hey," Chad said, interrupting Alex's time alone.

She jumped, not having heard him approach. He'd make an excellent hunter. Or burglar. She filed away this new piece of information.

"My gosh! You scared me."

But she smiled in spite of herself as she saw the sun glinting off his strawberry blond hair, which was still stuck to his forehead from the heat of the kitchen.

"Oh, wow. I'm sorry. If you'd like to be alone, I can go back to the house."

Chad took a tentative step backward. Alex thought he didn't look like a man ready to retreat, but she believed he would if that's what she asked of him.

"Nah. I'm just walking off some of that enormous meal. You can join me if you'd like."

They strolled in companionable silence for a while, Chad with his hands in his pockets, Alex with one hand propped on her growing belly. Chad slowed to a stop and cleared his throat. Alex looked around, puzzled.

"What's the matter," she asked, seeing the serious expression on Chad's face. Was he not feeling well? She didn't think she could run all the way back up to the house for help.

"Alex, the first day you came in my shop, I thought you were crazy." Chad rubbed the back of his neck, an action Alex now recognized as a nervous quirk.

Alex's thoughts spun in all directions. Maybe she'd read him all wrong. Though her head told her to stay away from him, her heart cried out to let go and trust him. Had he sought her out to point out the many obstacles in a relationship with her? The least of which was her huge tummy protruding between them. When she tuned back into what Chad was saying, she heard something quite different than where her thoughts had led her.

"...turned everything in my world around for the better. And, I'm not just talking about my business. I see my relationship with God in a different light because of you. I'm kinder to my family and my employees. Alex, I don't know your story, but I'd like to if you'll give me the chance."

Chad's sincerity broke her heart as he took Alex's hand in both of his. She knew he couldn't want her. She was damaged, broken, used up. Maybe God could forgive her, but nobody else could, not even herself. Not a day went by that she didn't question why she hadn't walked past J.T.'s door and gone upstairs without checking on him. How different would things have been?

Looking into Chad's green eyes, the pain of losing what she could never have, the love of a good man, filled her to overflowing. He said he wanted to know her story, but no. She could never again share the details of the night her life had changed forever. To get close to Chad would mean exposing parts of her life she wasn't ready to reveal. Not now and maybe not ever. She pulled her hand from his.

"Chad," she choked out, "you don't know what you're asking. I'm not who or what you think I am. You don't want me. Please, just go!"

She turned her back to him as her body shook with sobs.

℘ ℘ ℘

He stood there for a moment, wishing he could take her in his arms and hold her until the pain pouring from her was gone. He knew Miss Matilda wouldn't share Alex's story. She took an oath of secrecy with all of her girls. Chad heaved a deep sigh, tears welling in his own eyes as he delivered a few parting words with the sun dipping below the tree line.

"I'll go for now," Chad said, not understanding the demons haunting this beautiful woman. "But you're not getting rid of me forever."

Chad trudged back to the house, determined to help Alex forgive herself so she could give him the chance he longed for. The chance he believed he deserved.

"Well, how did it go?"

Charmain's animated personality greeted him as she packed leftovers and their clean dishes into her car. Chad stomped past her with nothing more than a grunt on his way inside. She hurried to catch

119

up to see if she could glean any information about his encounter with Alex. Still, she kept her distance, just to be on the safe side. When Chad located their hostess relaxing in her rocking chair, he bent down and planted a gentle kiss on her soft cheek.

"Thank you for having us, Miss Matilda. We had a really nice time. Everything was delicious." Miss Matilda had a firm hold of Chad's hand. She motioned for him to move in closer, speaking softly in his ear to ensure no one else would hear the advice she gave.

"Don't give up on her," she said. "She's worth the effort."

Chad gave the older lady one last hug before shaking hands with Terry, while Charmain thanked their hostess. Loaded up and headed home, Charmain peppered Chad with the inevitable questions.

"What did Alex say? What did you say? What did Miss Matilda say?"

It was so comical Chad laughed at his little sister, despite his foul mood. This was met by a playful but lingering pout. Chad released a deep breath with a great whoosh.

"I don't think Alex is ready for a relationship," he said. "Think about it, Char. She's moved to a strange town, she'll soon be a single mom, she's having to figure out how to support herself and her child while going to school," he held up a finger for each point he made. "Plus, and this is a biggie, we have no idea about her circumstances. Why did she come to Together for Good? I know some of the girls are running away from abusive boyfriends or neglectful parents, but Alex seems different." He shook his head as Charmain drove into the darkening night.

"She may not think she's ready for a relationship," said Charmain with a twinkle in her eye, "but she doesn't know what a wonderful guy my big brother is. Maybe Alex and I need to have some girl time."

"Charmain!" Chad's deep voice held a warning tone Charmain knew well.

Charmain giggled. He didn't scare her. All she wanted was to see her brother happy, and if she got to play Cupid while making that happen, then all the better.

Chapter 13
Decorations and a Diary

As Christmas drew near, life around Miss Matilda's place grew more hectic. A sweet church member brought in a tree, and the girls decorated it with ornaments Miss Matilda had collected through the years. Even though it was winter, the delightful Southern climate afforded gardeners the opportunity for cooler weather crops, and the girls were happy to learn firsthand about fresh lettuce, kale, and carrots. After they enjoyed a healthy salad, the Christmas cookie baking began in earnest!

Miss Matilda sat sipping tea and thumbing through her recipes while the girls gathered ingredients for gingerbread cookies. Alex noticed their care-giver seemed uncharacteristically distant, lost in her own thoughts. Alex lowered her ever-expanding frame into the chair next to the lady and placed her own young hand over Matilda's soft, crepey one.

"Is everything all right?" Alex asked, concern shining in her eyes.

Matilda sighed and patted Alex's hand with her other one.

"I'm fine, dear," she responded. "I was just remembering another year a long time ago when all the girls were baking at the holidays. We had a girl go into labor in this kitchen." Alex noticed the pools in her eyes, as if she'd been crying. Around them, the merriment of holiday baking enveloped them like a cloud.

"Are you getting all sentimental on us, Miss Matilda? Thinking back on your other residents?" Alex tried to lighten Matilda's melancholy as she held her hands. "We're here with you now, so let's have some fun baking up a storm." Her words achieved the effect Alex hoped for, bringing a smile to the woman's face and lighting her up from within.

"You're exactly right, Alex," Matilda said, pulling one hand free from Alex's grip to give the table a resolute slap. She rose to her feet, issuing orders to all within the kitchen regarding cookie size (extra-large), musical selections (Christmas-themed), and health hazards (no eating raw dough). Within minutes, the unmistakable, irresistible, stomach-rumble-inducing aroma only multiple batches of Christmas cookies can produce permeated the entire house.

The cookies had been baked, divided, and packed for either gift giving or munching after dinner. The bowls and cookie sheets were washed and put away when Miss Matilda addressed her girls.

"Thank you, ladies. You have no idea how much I needed this today." Again, Alex noticed those eyes shone brightly as she spoke. "I've got a surprise for you."

All the girls began to speak at once, speculating what the surprise could be. The kitchen was soon filled with the din of delighted squeals while the girls tried to talk over one another and gesture wildly trying to guess Miss Matilda's surprise.

A piercing whistle interrupted the mayhem. Everyone stopped what they were doing and looked to the source of the sound. Chad stood at the kitchen door, the baseball cap he always wore now in his hands and his face turning pink.

"Excuse me, ladies. I didn't mean to interrupt the, uh...conversation, but Miss Matilda asked if I could stop by to help."

He scanned the room for his older friend, who had taken a seat at the table and was hidden behind the sea of pregnant ladies. Hearing his voice, Miss Matilda popped out of her chair and bustled around the others to welcome him.

She settled him at the table with a plate of freshly baked cookies and asked Alex to pour a glass of milk. Alex had the feeling this probably wasn't the first time he'd sat at Miss Matilda's table enjoying a treat. Miss Matilda turned back to the girls to reveal her surprise.

"I've divided up some of my Christmas decorations and have a box ready for Chad to take to each of your rooms. Please feel free to decorate your space, if you'd like.

"When Christmas is over, you may have the decorations you use. I'm trying to do a little downsizing, so you'll be doing me a favor. And, you'll have a head start on your preparations for years to come. Think of me when you use them." Alex noticed Matilda's gaze travel to rest on each girl as she spoke.

Matilda directed the ladies to the formal living room, which was seldom used except for large gatherings, where they'd find the boxes.

Chad was tasked with ensuring each box made it to the proper room, ensuring none of the ladies had to lift and carry anything.

⌀ ⌀ ⌀

The girls descended on the boxes in the living room like ants on sugar, exclaiming over each new discovery. Some of the boxes were the old cardboard variety, indicating the contents could be vintage decorations, while some were modern see-through plastic ones, revealing sparkling, contemporary items.

Alex stood in the doorway smiling as the other girls made their selections. During Alex's childhood, Karen's goal was always to make their home as splashy, flashy, and, in Alex's opinion, trashy as she could at Christmas. Looking back, Alex realized how odd it was that her mother would go so crazy decorating for a season she didn't truly understand.

But then, Karen always had one driving passion behind all of her decisions: business success. She used the family's annual Christmas party to woo and schmooze current and potential clients. The joy of giving was as foreign a concept for Karen as hopping on a Harley and biking cross-country would be for Miss Matilda!

Alex's heart soared to see how excited her new friends became over the simple, beautiful, and meaningful decorations Miss Matilda had given them. Resting one hand on her huge tummy, she waited for the others to choose their box. Chad joined her in the doorway, coffee cup in hand. It was the first time they'd spoken since Thanksgiving, and the tension was palpable.

"Hey," he said, color creeping into his face. Alex hadn't seen him this awkward and nervous since she first knew him.

She smiled.

"Hi yourself. Thanks for coming to help out." She didn't understand the loyalty and compassion this man showed to so many people, Miss Matilda being a chief recipient of his kindnesses.

"Aw, anything for Miss M.," he said, smiling as he sipped his coffee.

Could anyone be as caring, compassionate, and likable as Chad seemed to be? Was it really a cover for something darker? Alex hated that her past made her cynical and distrustful, and daily she asked the Lord for the strength to love others as He loved.

And it wouldn't take much effort to just let go and love Chad.

This unbidden thought made her breath catch in her throat, startling Chad, who in turn spilled his coffee. Setting his cup on a nearby table, he turned to Alex, whose face had reddened at first, but was now turning a pasty shade of white.

"Hey, are you all right?" he asked. "You sit here. I'm going to get something to clean up that spill."

Concern shadowed Chad's face and clouded his eyes. Taking Alex by the elbow, he led her to a nearby chair. When he returned, not only did he have a paper towel in hand, but a glass of water for Alex.

Unshed tears made her eyes shine as she thanked him and accepted his sweet gesture. She set the glass on a nearby table and massaged her lower back. It kept getting more difficult to stand for long periods of time, and Alex welcomed the opportunity to sit still for a little while.

By now, the other girls had marked their boxes with sticky notes and headed upstairs to begin planning their decorating strategy. Keeping his eyes averted while he cleaned up the spill, Chad asked how much longer until Alex's baby arrived.

"Dr. Sheffield says three or four weeks. First babies can be a bit stubborn about sticking to the due date." She sipped her water, still self-conscious about unbidden thoughts of feelings for Chad running through her head. Chad eyed her suspiciously.

He must think I've either lost my mind or I'm seriously sick, Alex thought.

"Will you be okay sitting here while I take these things to everyone?" Chad already had two boxes stacked in his arms, but he hesitated to leave her alone.

"Yeah, sure. You go ahead. I'm going to start looking through my box."

One lone, beat up old cardboard box sat in the corner of the room, no sticky note attached. Alex pulled the ottoman closer to the box, lowered herself onto it and opened the flaps. The dust assaulted her nose, eliciting a sneeze.

"Bless you," Chad said, entering for another delivery.

"Thank you," she replied, smiling at him as he turned to go. She wondered, could she ever let go and allow herself to feel comfortable with him?

She wanted safety and security for herself and her daughter, but could these things and a relationship go hand in hand? There was so much she didn't understand, having never seen a healthy, loving partnership modeled in her own life. Maybe J.T. and Karen loved each other, but Alex suspected the majority of their relationship was based on work.

How sad.

Thoughts of her previous life vanished as Alex explored the contents of her box of decorations. She'd hit the jackpot. The lovely old ornaments, nativity set, and ceramic figurines suited her style as if Miss Matilda had selected this box especially for her. She pulled out what appeared to be an ancient little stable to go with the holy family, noticing when she did a small book underneath it. The pages were yellowed with age, and the cover appeared to have mildewed.

Curious, she retrieved the book from the bottom of the box and slipped it into her cardigan pocket, intending to ask Miss Matilda about it. The thought was pushed to the back of her mind when Chad walked back in the room for his final load. Alex was surprised to notice Chad had made quick work of his task while she'd been lost in the perusal of her new treasures. Chad followed Alex up the stairs and placed her box on her desk before making a hasty retreat for the doorway, turning to speak before he headed back downstairs.

"Hey, Charmain and I are fixing dinner tonight and decorating our tree. Would you like to come over and help us?" He fidgeted with his cap in both hands, boots shuffling nervously on the hardwood floor.

Alex saw the kindness, the concern, the…what else was it? Hope? He looked hopeful. Her better judgment shouted at her to decline, but the prospect of spending an evening with these two people who'd come to mean so much to her in such a short time was too enticing. Also, that longing, hopeful look in Chad's eyes caused her to toss her better judgment out the window.

"That sounds nice. I'd love to. What can I bring?" Karen's insistence on proper etiquette was the only thing her mother had done for which Alex would always be grateful.

"Just yourself," he called over his shoulder with a smile as he headed down the stairs, tugging his cap back into place on his head. He pulled up short as he had a thought and called back up to her. "But if you want to sneak a few of those cookies over to our place, I won't complain. Charmain's a terrible baker!" He grinned and took off, leaving Alex with only the sound of his work boots echoing on the hardwood floor, a whistled Christmas song, and the slamming door.

🗝 🗝 🗝

Alex decided a little nap before heading over to Chad and Charmain's house would do her good and maybe even ease the aching in her back that had plagued her all day. Being on her feet baking for hours had taken its toll, but she looked forward to seeing where her friends lived. She'd learned their father had left their childhood home to both of them when he'd passed away, so they'd both left their respective cramped apartments for the comfort of their own home. Miss Matilda had told her after Alex met Charmain the pair got along great, as a rule. Remembering this statement made Alex smile as she recalled the times when this wasn't the case.

A "double C clash," as they so affectionately referred to their disagreements, resulted when the two strong-willed people found themselves at odds. Although each tiff involved a lot of clenched jaws, rolled eyes and crossed arms, the pair came out on the other side hugging and laughing. With no siblings of her own to compare their relationship to, Alex knew from hearing others talk of bitter rivalries, screaming matches and hurt feelings that Chad and Charmain shared a special bond.

Alex reclined on her bed and closed her eyes. All she needed was a short nap. As she rolled onto her side to avoid the sunlight streaming through the window, she felt something sharp and rigid poke her in the side. At first, she couldn't figure out what could be on her bed. Then, remembering the small book she'd placed in her sweater pocket, Alex bolted upright, all thoughts of rest forgotten. She pulled the book from her pocket and examined its cover.

Diary.

The word, embossed on the front cover in faded gold leaf, implied privacy was expected. Feeling ashamed for even considering opening it, Alex took a peek inside. *Carol Ann.* The name inscribed across the first page in beautiful penmanship allowed Alex to breathe a sigh of relief. At least this wasn't Miss Matilda's diary she was snooping into.

She flipped through the pages, noticing more than half of it wasn't filled. Alex understood. How many times had she too started a journal with the unwavering intention of writing in it every day, only to have those plans sidetracked by more pressing life concerns.

Miss Matilda had met a few ladies from church to Christmas shop and deliver goodies, but Alex made a mental note to mention her find to her older friend another time as she leaned back and opened the book to the first page.

April 2, 1963

Jimmy's everything I've ever dreamed of. Tall, muscular, and handsome, he's a senior who also has the good fortune of being smart and witty. With my straight brown hair and green eyes, I've always felt invisible, but Jimmy notices me. No boy has ever noticed me before.

For several weeks at the start of my junior year, he carried my books home from school, sat next to me at pep rallies and flirted with me across the cafeteria before ever working up the courage to ask me out on a double date. I worried my parents would say no, but since they'd known Jimmy's parents for most of their lives, they gave in to my pleading.

It was a double date, after all. Our relationship progressed, and our fondness for each other grew. But it's always been double dates, group dates, or hanging out at each other's house...until tonight.

Tonight, Jimmy announced he had a special surprise for me. It started as a double date, but then Jimmy dropped off our friends at the movie theater. I asked what we were going to see as the other couple climbed out of the back seat while Jimmy left the car running.

"I've got something else in mind." Jimmy slipped an arm around my shoulder and pulled me closer to him. I tried to calm my nerves by concentrating on how warm and secure he felt beside me. I took a deep breath, enjoying the scent of his fresh soap with just a hint of citrus. Never in my life had anything felt as right as my love for Jimmy. The nervousness I'd felt just a few moments before melted away. I asked again where we were going.

"You'll see," he said with a cryptic smile. "Just relax." He massaged my shoulder to reinforce his words. "You trust me, don't you?" he asked with a little wink.

"Yes." It was true. I'd grown to trust him more than anyone. Even more than my parents, if that was possible. He was my everything. Why shouldn't I trust him? He was all I'd ever known or wanted.

He'd stood up for me against the bullies at school who said I wasn't pretty enough to be dating him, given me his sweater when the weather had turned cool, held my hand when the movies got scary, and, of course, he'd been my first kiss.

As the springtime air blew through my hair, I could smell the promise of our relationship as clearly as I could smell the daffodils and tulips. Daffodils and tulips!

As Jimmy stopped the car and I climbed out, I realized we were far from town. It was early enough in the evening to see that we were in a beautiful, lush meadow at the foot of the mountains. Spring had always been my favorite season. Every living thing remembered it wasn't dead, it had life in it.

Time to wake up! And everything in this meadow had decided to do just that all at once! Jimmy knew how much I loved the new life of spring. As I soaked in the sights around me, he caressed my hair.

"It's beautiful here, but it doesn't compare to how beautiful you are," he told me, taking my hand but never taking his eyes off of me. "I know how much you love the outdoors this time of year, and this is the prettiest place I've ever been when it's in bloom like this. My family's owned this place for a long time," he admitted.

"Your family? I didn't know y'all had land out this way." I'm sure he could hear the surprise in my voice as I turned to face him.

Jimmy squeezed my hand, leading the way to a gorgeous old oak tree whose branches swooped toward the earth before reaching skyward again, creating perfect seats and tree-climbing footholds. The closer we got to the tree, the darker it grew under the dense shade of its boughs.

I sneaked a peek at Jimmy, who grinned at me. It was then I noticed that he held a picnic basket in his other hand. I looked at him, raising one eyebrow as I tipped my head toward the basket.

"Oh, this?" He feigned innocence and tried to pretend he'd forgotten he even had it in his hand. "I thought maybe we could have a romantic dinner here under the old oak tree. How does that sound?"

As he asked, he set down the basket and took me in his arms. Putting a finger under my chin, he gently turned my face up to look at him. The shadows danced across his face as his clear blue eyes searched mine.

"Carol Ann, there's something we need to talk about," he began, a serious tone replacing the previous playfulness.

My heart pounded. My mind raced. I knew immediately why we didn't go to the movies with our friends. He wanted to bring me out here to break up with me!

He didn't want everyone to see me fall apart. I was touched thinking about how considerate he was, but the thought of losing him broke my heart and I burst into tears without warning.

"What's the matter?" Jimmy asked, caught off-guard by my crying jag. He stepped back, ran his hand through his hair, and paced back and forth.

Through sniffles and a few stifled sobs, I managed to croak, "I understand. You're older and so handsome. You'll be graduating in a couple of months and going off to college when the summer's over, and there'll be lots of other girls there." At this point my voice disappeared completely, and I had to turn away to regain my composure. "So, I understand why you feel it's best that we break things off..."

"Break things off?" Jimmy grabbed me by the shoulders and spun me around so fast that bits of my ponytail stuck in my tear-streaked face. He gently wiped them away and kissed my forehead.

"Carol Ann, that's not what I wanted to tell you at all."

"It isn't?" Sniff.

"No." He sighed. I guess I'd kind of taken the wind out of his sails. He forged ahead anyway. "What I wanted to say is that I love you, and I'd like you to marry me after you finish high school."

It was a good thing Jimmy was holding me close because my knees felt just like the scuppernong jelly I'd made with my mother last fall. I searched his face for any signs that he was joking or insincere. I saw none.

"I don't know what to say," I whispered.

"Maybe this will help." He bent toward me and our lips met, tenderly at first. Soon, though, it was much more than the sweet, quick kisses we'd shared up to this point. Once again holding my face in his hands, he pulled back and stared into my eyes.

"So? What do you say?" He wanted an answer. Now.

I was confused. Of course, I love him. Of course, I want to marry him. Some day.

And, standing there encircled in his loving arms, I believed someday didn't have to be so very far away. Why couldn't I marry Jimmy when I'm done with high school? Although I've dreamed of it, this was the first time we'd spoken of our future together. In that moment, I knew with certainty there was nothing I wanted more.

"Yes, Jimmy. Yes, I love you, too," I said, my voice strong as I beamed up at him. "And, yes, I want to marry you. We'll have a wonderful life together after high school."

"Whew," he released the breath he'd been holding, "I was hoping you'd say that," he said with a shyness not there before. "I planned a sort of celebration."

As he spoke, he pulled an old quilt, a bottle of wine, and two Mason jars from the basket. I held my breath as he spread the quilt on the ground.

"Jimmy! Where did you get wine? We'll both be in huge trouble if we get caught."

What was he thinking?

"Just one little glass to toast our engagement. Well, unofficial engagement. We'll make it official after I get out of school in a couple of months and can get you a ring. I've been saving for a while already. But, tonight, I want just the two of us to celebrate."

He poured wine as he spoke, and he looked so excited I couldn't deny him this one little extravagance. That was the problem. I could never deny him anything he asked of me. I sniffed my drink, wrinkling my nose, the tart, pungent aroma invading my senses. I took a tiny sip of the sweet, dark red liquid as he watched me, anxious.

"Well?" he asked, as if trying to determine if I might disappear from in front of his eyes.

"Not bad," venturing a larger sip. It wasn't bad at all. I took another gulp. He warned me not to drink it too fast or I might get sick.

By now, a warmth unrelated to the spring temperatures had begun to seep into my fingers and toes, making my head feel all fuzzy. I felt so relaxed. Snuggling up next to Jimmy, we talked of our future and sipped our wine. He brought out sandwiches and apples, which we washed down with one more glass of wine.

Once the food and wine were gone, we leaned against the tree trunk to watch the beautiful mountain sunset with me curled up under Jimmy's arm. Jimmy tilted my chin and kissed me with an abandon unlike any I'd ever known.

Whether it was the wine or my love for him, I don't know, but I felt powerless to stop him. Gone was my ability to halt the advance of his hands as they began to explore parts of me no one had ever touched before. The part of my mind screaming how wrong it was simply wasn't strong enough to speak up for the rest of me.

130

When Jimmy surfaced for air, I gathered my wits enough to ask if what we were doing was okay. I was worried someone was going to find out.

"I mean, we aren't married yet. Could anything bad happen?"

He assured me nobody knew we were there and nothing was going to happen. It was just one time.

"Besides," he reasoned, "we love each other, Carol Ann. How could anything bad ever happen when two people love each other like we do?"

Alex wiped away a tear as she finished the first day's entry. How scandalous this must have seemed back then. She wondered what had happened to Carol Ann and Jimmy, and how the diary had ended up in the attic with Christmas decorations. She guessed Carol Ann had been a resident at the home many years ago. But why hadn't she taken her diary with her when she left?

Had she married Jimmy?

The questions didn't stop. But for now, sleep. Alex drifted off into a fitful slumber. She awoke drenched in sweat, disoriented, and dazed. She couldn't recall where she was; this tiny bedroom with the high ceilings wasn't her room at home. The past few months slammed into Alex like a wrecking ball. She thought of Carol Ann, and Karen, and J.T., and Miss Matilda, and Chad. Her head swam, but she checked her watch and realized she needed to get moving if she was going to see her friends tonight.

The sound of voices in the kitchen told her the others had made it back from their shopping excursion. Alex saw the next entry was short and decided to read it before placing the little diary in her nightstand drawer.

May 27, 1963

I swiped at the tears streaming from my eyes as Mother lifted my long hair off my neck and placed a cool washcloth on it. I knew I was going to heave again soon, and with nothing left in my stomach I leaned over the toilet, miserable, awaiting the inevitable.

Mother asked if there was a bug going around school, the concern evident in her voice.

I shook my head, the barely perceptible motion setting off the next wave of violent retching. My energy spent, I collapsed on the cool bathroom tile.

"How about I draw you a nice warm bath and get your favorite PJs? Then you can climb in bed, and I'll bring you a cup of tea and some Saltine crackers," Mother suggested, moving toward the bathtub without waiting for my answer.

Her suggestion didn't sound half bad.

When she left the bathroom, I removed my vomit-spattered clothing, checking my panties for the tell-tale dark spot. I'm really late now. Is it six weeks? Two months already? Some of my friends are irregular, but my cycles have been like clockwork ever since I started two years ago when I was fourteen.

A cold finger of dread crept up my spine as I remembered the single night with Jimmy back in April. He promised me nothing bad could happen just one time. And he also promised he loved me. I lingered in the warm bath water to dispel the chill of fear beginning to grip me.

Alex closed the book and placed it in the drawer before stepping across the hall to splash her face with some cool water. There was plenty of time to talk to Miss Matilda about the diary.

And, besides, Alex reasoned to herself, *it was so long ago that she probably doesn't remember Carol Ann.*

Assuaging her guilt with that thought, Alex dried her face, swished on some lipstick and headed down the stairs to inform Miss Matilda of her evening plans. She might even sneak a cookie while she was in the kitchen.

Chapter 14
Chad's Secret

Charmain ran down the front porch steps, shrugging into her coat and pulling her purse onto her shoulder as Alex got out of her car at the White's house. They lived on several acres of land in a sprawling two-story yellow Victorian with a huge wrap-around porch, lots of gingerbread millwork, and a brick chimney. Charmain had told Alex the little cottage out back had been built for their grandparents, who had since moved into assisted living.

"Charmain, where are you going? Did I misunderstand Chad this afternoon?" Alex was going to feel like a complete idiot if she showed up at their place uninvited and no one was home.

Or worse, only Chad was home!

"No, you're right on time. My crazy brother did the shopping for dinner. And, guess what? If you're making tacos for dinner, you need taco shells. Imagine! I'm off to the store, but I'll be right back."

The slamming car door punctuated the end of her sentence. Alex smiled as she carried the packed cookie tin up the porch steps and rang the doorbell. Within seconds, Chad, sporting a frilly pink apron and studying a cookbook, flung open the door.

"Look, Char, I know I messed up but if you'll just go get…" as he peeled his eyes away from the cookbook to the person standing at the door, his sentence trailed off. Looking down, Chad realized his current attire was a far cry from his normal daily uniform of grease-covered mechanic's coveralls. "Oh, hey, Alex. I thought Charmain forgot her keys. Sorry about the, well, um…" He indicated his ruffles, and Alex smiled as he ushered her inside.

"Oh, it's quite all right," she said, handing over the cookie tin and taking off her coat. "Pink is definitely your color." Her comment caused his face to turn the exact shade of pink he wore while they shared a good laugh.

"Something smells delicious," Alex said.

"Come on in the kitchen with me."

Alex's eye for architectural details recognized the home's historic charm, punctuated by a few well-placed modern renovations. The rustic kitchen was airy and spacious. Chad invited her to sit at the kitchen island while he finished preparing the taco toppings, and she offered to help.

Chad politely declined before attempting a bit of small talk.

"Charmain said your school semester's over?"

"Yeah." Alex replied, reluctant for the conversation to focus on her.

Looking around the kitchen, she saw a photo of a man and woman and asked Chad who they were. A sadness appeared in his eyes before he took a deep breath and answered.

"Our parents," he paused, his voice barely audible when he continued. "In happier times."

"Oh."

"Has anyone told you their story?"

"No, just that your dad left the business to you when he passed away a few years ago."

∅ ∅ ∅

They continued to work together in silence as emotions warred within Chad. Certain Alex felt his discomfort, he contemplated whether to open up to her. The truth was painful and messy. Yet, he wanted her truth, with all of its pain and mess. How could he expect from her what he wasn't willing to give? He knew, though, even if he did tell her the whole sordid story, it didn't guarantee she would share in return. He decided it was worth the risk and dove in before he could change his mind.

"Our mother wasn't well," he began. His voice took on a hollow, far-away quality, and Alex didn't interrupt or ask questions. "Oh, she had her good days. On those days, things were very good. But on the bad days, she would stay in bed and cry…or sleep. It could be days on end.

"Dad had the business to run, so he didn't see most of what we saw. I'd get us ready for school on those days. Fix Char's hair. Pack our lunches. Try to figure out how to work the washing machine so we could have clean clothes."

134

"How old were you?" Alex asked, concern in her voice and her eyes. The picture he painted of her two friends suffering as little children obviously touched her.

"I was eight and Char was six when it started getting bad. It went on for years. Then, when I was twelve, I came home from the last day of sixth grade looking for Mom. I'd made the honor roll for the year, and I was about to pop with excitement to tell her. Her bedroom door was shut. We knew that was her signal to leave her alone. Char was playing at a friend's house, but I just had to tell someone. I wasn't allowed to call Dad at work.

"Eventually, I decided to go upstairs, wake Mom up really quick, tell her my great news, and then let her go back to sleep. I told myself it wouldn't take but just a second, and maybe it would cheer her up a little bit."

When Chad's voice broke, he saw tears pooling in Alex's eyes.

"I opened the door to Mom's room. It was dark, but she always closed the blinds and curtains when she wanted to sleep, so that wasn't odd. I called Mom's name, but she didn't answer or even roll over."

Chad had a distant look in his eyes as he relived that fateful day, the pain fresh and searing, tears rolling down his cheeks unchecked. "I tiptoed over to her bed and touched her arm. She was cold. I was so confused because it was June and so warm in the house. I knew she shouldn't have been cold. I shook her, but nothing happened.

"By then, my eyes had adjusted to the dim light. I could see the empty pill bottle on her nightstand. I began to scream and ran from the room, but I don't remember much of what happened next. Cops came, the ambulance came. Dad and Char came home. People asked me all kinds of questions. They took Mom away on a stretcher with a sheet covering her whole body. Even her face."

Chad leaned on the counter and began to sob, as though a dam that had been threatening to burst for many years had finally given way. Alex slid off the stool and went to Chad, her own tears flowing in sympathy. Maneuvering around her large belly, she wrapped her arms around him and rubbed his back. He dropped his head to her shoulder, and she stroked his hair, trying to offer some measure of comfort.

"Dad was never the same," he choked out. "A few years ago, when he was dying of cancer, he told me he had blamed me for Mom's death. At the end of his life, he saw how wrong he'd been, but I always

135

knew he blamed me. And, to tell you the truth, I blamed myself, too." Bringing her hands to his shoulders, Alex pushed him back far enough that she could look into his eyes.

"How could you blame yourself? You were a child?" Alex looked horrified at the burden Chad carried for so long.

"I thought if I had gone to her immediately when I got home, maybe they could have saved her. But the coroner said she'd already been gone for several hours by the time they got to her. She probably told us goodbye for school and then…" He stopped, unable to complete the sentence.

"Miss Matilda was a huge help," he continued, taking a deep breath, trying to pull himself together.

The ironclad bond between Chad and Matilda remained strong. He felt indebted to her for rescuing him and Charmain at their darkest hour.

"She was my Sunday School teacher back then. She took me under her wing, taught me about Jesus and how to trust Him, even when things don't seem to make sense to us. It was a hard lesson. Honestly, I'm still working on it," Chad smiled.

"Yeah, me too," Alex agreed.

"Alex, thank you," Chad said as he moved to the sink, washed his hands, and wiped his face with a wet paper towel. He did not want Char seeing this scene. He wasn't prepared to answer all the questions she would have.

"I haven't talked about Mom's death in a very long time, and I've never cried about it. I realize now that I've always just held that pain inside." He let out a big breath in a rush. "I feel kind of free now."

"You know, I think we all have demons from our past we have to free ourselves from," Alex said, as they heard the front door open and Charmain come in with her incessant chatter.

"I'll be here to return the favor whenever you're ready to get rid of yours," he said, tucking a curl of hair behind her ear. As a tear found its way down her cheek, all she seemed to be able to do was nod.

℘ ℘ ℘

After polishing off a heap of delicious tacos, the three moved to the living room to decorate the fragrant Christmas tree. Charmain had already gone to the trouble of stringing hundreds of tiny white lights and elegant gold ribbon on it. The only thing left to do was hang the decorations. Chad opened the boxes and began to unwrap each delicate ornament, handing them to the girls.

"Aren't you going to hang any ornaments?" Alex asked Chad, causing the two siblings to burst into laughter. Perplexed, Alex wasn't sure what was so funny about decorating a Christmas tree.

"Whenever I try to put even one ornament on the tree, Char gets 'that look' and tells me I didn't do it right." It wasn't a malicious comment. It was just how this family did Christmas.

"Well...," Alex said, a little nervous the placement of the treasured family heirlooms she had hung would be questioned. Charmain saw her discomfort and responded.

"Don't let Chad fool you. He'd much rather just unwrap and pass each one. Honestly, I think he used to clump them all together with the intent of annoying me!" Charmain's comment brought on another round of laughter, with Alex joining in this time.

Once the tree was decorated, Chad fetched the cookie tin and three mugs of tea, and they all sat on the sofa and watched the lights twinkle among the branches. Had it not been for the heartburn from the tacos, Alex wasn't sure she had ever felt such contentment.

The heartburn was a common occurrence, and Dr. Sheffield assured her it was normal as the baby took up increasingly more space. Alex thought sitting would relieve the ache in her back, but no position seemed to be any more comfortable than the last.

To distract herself from the discomfort, Alex considered the differences between her life now and how it had been this time last year. She'd been applying to colleges, trying to find scholarships, working her construction job, and living the privileged life of the child of wealthy parents. Although she wouldn't want to go through the past year again, Alex felt satisfied with, even proud of, the person she'd become.

She now knew Jesus as her Lord and Savior...what else did she really need? She was about to become the mom of a precious baby girl. She had good friends who cared about her. As Miss Matilda had taught her, she said a quick prayer of thanks for all of the blessings in her life.

Her "Amen" was punctuated by the baby kicking a cookie off her belly, where she had placed it while she sipped her tea. As the baby grew, Alex used her expanding girth as a shelf for propping her cereal bowl, resting the TV remote, or holding a book; but she always ran the risk of whatever she placed there being launched with one swift kick. Charmain saw the cookie tumble off Alex's tummy, and Alex cringed.

"Oh, I'm so sorry. I'll clean up those crumbs," she apologized.

"Are you kidding?" Charmain said. "I live with Chad. We decorate in mid-century bachelor," she said. Chad looked a bit sheepish but didn't deny the accusation.

"Is she still moving? Can I feel her?" Charmain asked, excitement in her eyes.

Alex nodded as Charmain slipped off the sofa to kneel in front of Alex.

"Ooh! I felt her," Charmain squealed.

"You can feel her, too," Alex turned to Chad, who was sitting next to her. "I mean, if you want. You don't have to." He rested his hand on her abdomen and was answered by a playful bump.

Looking at Alex, he smiled. She returned his grin.

Once the baby settled down and they all returned to their places, Charmain asked Alex where she planned to live after the baby arrived. Alex had scoured the local paper, church bulletin board, and rental circulars for a clean, affordable apartment or house. She'd found some promising leads, but she hadn't made her final decision yet. Alex saw the siblings exchange a glance.

"Well," Charmain began, "we were thinking. What if you move in with us?" she asked, clapping her hands and beaming with excitement.

"What Char means," Chad clarified, "is the house out back is sitting empty. I started doing some renovations a few years back with thoughts of taking in a tenant, but, as you can imagine, I didn't get far." Alex smiled, remembering what his shop's waiting area had looked like the first time she entered it.

"So, how much would the rent be?" Alex asked, knowing expenses were going to be tight for some time.

"That's what we wanted to talk to you about. If you could work a little of your magic on the guesthouse like you did on Chad's waiting area, we'll waive rent for a year," Charmain explained. "I'll be around to help you when I'm not at work, and I can help take care of the baby. You wanna go see it?"

"Well, sure."

What did she have to lose by taking a look?

It was dark and cold in the little cottage, as they had turned off the power and water years ago. The light of Chad's powerful lantern showed Alex it was definitely habitable, despite needing some renovations and upgrades. Chad and Charmain saved the best surprise for the end of the tour. As they opened the kitchen door, Alex expected to walk into the wide-open space of the field behind the little house. Instead, she stepped into a small garage. Looking around, she saw it had insulated walls, a sink in one corner, a large workbench, and long fluorescent lights installed above. Incredulous, she turned to her friends.

"You can't even see this part from the front of the house." Her mind raced at the possibilities this space could mean for her.

"Yeah. When our dad built this place for Grandma and Grandpa, he wanted Grandpa to have a space to do his puttering. Grandpa was an excellent woodworker." More than a hint of pride crept into Chad's voice as he spoke of his grandparents.

"Y'all, I don't know. It seems so generous. It's just too much," Alex said. The people of this town had been so kind, so giving. How would she ever be able to repay them?

"Are you kidding? We're the ones being selfish asking you to stay. Please, Alex, say you'll do it?" Charmain begged.

Even in the lantern light, Alex could see her pleading eyes. It was probably her imagination, but it seemed even Chad's eyes urged her to agree. Was this wise? She would be near Chad every day. And, as she stood there vacillating on yet another life-impacting decision, she remembered Miss Matilda's advice.

Trust the Lord, don't lean on your own understanding. Well, maybe she didn't know if she should be around Chad every day, but she believed in her heart this little house was right, for her and her daughter. She would trust the Lord she was making the right decision for both of them.

"Okay. I'll do it. And, thank you," Alex agreed, extending her hand to seal the agreement with a handshake. As soon as the words left her lips, Alex felt an uncomfortable dampness. It only took a moment for her to discover her water had broken. She was about to have a baby.

The punch of the first contraction almost took her down.

Chapter 15
Delivered

Alex insisted she had plenty of time before the baby was born, but when Charmain called Dr. Sheffield, she instructed them to come right to the hospital where she would meet them at the Emergency Room. Since Alex's water had already broken, the doctor didn't want to risk infection to mother or baby. Chad called Miss Matilda to tell her about the turn of events.

"Oh, my goodness, Chad. Please don't let anything happen to her," she whispered.

"She and the baby will be fine, Miss M.," Chad reassured his dear friend. "You keep praying, and I'll keep you posted," he said, snapping his phone shut.

He'd never heard her get so upset about a girl going into labor. After all, this was everyday stuff for her. It was after dark, and Chad knew Matilda wasn't going to make the long drive to the hospital if Alex had reliable transportation and a trusted support group. Still, he heard the worry, tinged with a bit of fear, in her voice.

Chad ended the call while questions filled his mind, but they soon vanished when he stepped out onto the porch for the trip to the hospital. The two women were at the bottom of the steps, Alex doubled over, Charmain rubbing her back and whispering soothing words in her ear. The reality of the situation slammed into him, kicking into gear his instinct to act in a crisis.

He bounded down the steps two at a time until he was at Alex's other side. Once the pain subsided and she was breathing normally again, each sibling took one of her elbows and guided her toward the car. Chad asked her if there was anything she needed out of her car.

"Oh, my gosh!" she exclaimed. "I'm so glad you reminded me. My packed bag is in the back of my SUV, and my purse is on the front seat." Charmain took off to retrieve the requested items, while Chad and Alex continued their progress toward Charmain's car.

"Why did you bring a packed bag with you to our house?" he asked her as she settled into the back seat. Seeing humor in the situation, she smiled.

"I wasn't planning on a sleepover. I packed it a couple of weeks ago and stashed it in my vehicle. I figured I was going to be so busy with Christmas shopping, church, exams, and working, if I did go into labor somewhere other than the home, I'd at least have my stuff with me. Turns out, I was right. Uh oh, here comes another."

She grabbed Chad's hand and squeezed as the pain gripped her body. By the time the contraction had passed, Charmain had stowed Alex's belongings in the front seat, closed both back doors, started the car, and was barreling down the driveway. Famous in her family for her lead foot, Charmain made it her personal mission to get Alex to the hospital in record time.

During the twenty-minute drive, which took most people thirty minutes, Alex had two more contractions. Charmain squealed into the ER parking lot, screeching to a stop. As soon as Alex emerged from the car, a nurse with a wheelchair came out the doors and asked her name.

"Dr. Sheffield asked me to bring you right up to labor and delivery. Your friends can join you there." She whisked Alex away, leaving Chad and Charmain to stare at one another in the parking lot.

"Well, what do we do now?" Chad asked his sister.

"I think we should take her stuff up. It may have her comfort items in there."

"Her what?"

"You know, things that bring her comfort if labor goes on for a long time," Charmain answered. Chad knew almost everything there was to know about cars, but standing in the freezing cold discussing comfort items made him keenly aware how very little he knew about other things.

Such as... women.

After consulting the hospital directory, the two took the elevator to the third floor, suitcase and purse in tow. After letting the nurse on duty at the nurse's station know they were there for Alex and handing over her belongings, they took a seat in the waiting room.

Meager Christmas decorations had been scattered around the room: a tiny tree, garland that looked to have been hung up and pulled back out of storage at least a dozen times swagged around the ceiling, and ten or more tiny red felt drugstore stockings. The effect was a sort of haphazard yet festive look.

Chad found the coffeepot and poured them both a cup. He thought they might be in for a long night, and he knew he needed a jolt. He sat on the uncomfortable sofa, elbows on his knees, cup cradled in both hands, and head bowed.

Please, Lord, watch over Alex and the baby. Keep them safe, keep them healthy, and Lord, if you would, please keep Alex's pain at least bearable. Thank you, Lord. In Jesus' name. Amen.

"What did you pray for?" Charmain asked as he raised his head and took a sip of the bitter brew.

"How did you know I was praying?" Sometimes his sister scared him, she knew him so well.

"Because I was, too. I'm nervous, Chad," she whispered.

"Yeah, me too," he confessed.

He remembered the verse Miss Matilda had always quoted when he was growing up from Proverbs 3:5, "Trust in the Lord with all your heart and lean not on your own understanding."

Well, this whole situation, from the way he felt about Alex to the fact that she went into labor at his house, all qualified as something he absolutely didn't understand. Why had he told her about Mom? He hadn't opened up to anyone about her in…well, ever.

But even though none of these things made sense to him, he had to trust the Lord had a plan for bringing Alex into his life. Chad had known it the first day he'd seen her in his shop with Miss Matilda.

Now, if he could just get her to trust him, too.

"Excuse me, are y'all here with Miss Powell?" a nurse at the waiting room door asked.

"Yes!" they both jumped up from their seats and leaped toward the door. The nurse smiled.

"She's asking to see you," she said. Chad turned to sit back down. "Both of you."

"Really?" he asked.

He'd never been in a labor and delivery room; he considered it to be too intimate an experience for casual spectators. Of course, he

143

wasn't a casual spectator, but he also wasn't in the category of intimate, either.

"She's asking for you. Surely you aren't going to say no?" Charmain encouraged.

When she put it that way…

💋 💋 💋

The nurse in the parking lot quickly rolled Alex into a staff elevator, took her directly to the labor and delivery floor and deposited her in a room outfitted with a bed and all manner of monitors. Alex was instructed to change into the standard-issue hospital gown and then endured a battery of questions, during which another contraction pummeled her.

The nurse looked at her watch and poked at Alex's abdomen several times throughout the pain, and when it was over, she made some notes in Alex's chart. Once Alex was settled in the bed and hooked up to an IV and the fetal monitor, Dr. Sheffield arrived.

"So, Alex, your little girl doesn't want to wait for Christmas, eh?" she joked, but Alex heard the tension in her voice and saw it in her eyes. "What I'm concerned about is whether your baby's lungs are adequately developed at this stage of your pregnancy."

Fear gripped Alex, and she struggled to breathe.

Dr. Sheffield told Alex they'd administer some medicine to help get the baby's lungs ready. They would keep Alex overnight and try to delay her labor while the medicine took effect. Nurses came in and injected the necessary medications into her IV. The only thing left to do was wait for the lab results tomorrow morning.

Scared and lonely, Alex asked if her friends could come and wait with her. The nurse returned with a smiling Chad and Charmain; whose demeanors changed as soon as they saw Alex's tear-streaked face. Charmain rushed to the young mother-to-be, but Chad hung back.

"What's wrong?" Charmain asked, holding Alex's hand in one of her own and stroking her hair with her other, her innate ability to comfort people kicking in.

"Worried about lungs…too soon…medication…stop labor…admit me…"

144

This almost unintelligible jumble of words poured out between sobs, but it sufficed to let both of her friends know the situation was serious. Chad covered the distance between the door and Alex's side in three long strides, picking up her other hand.

By now, Alex knew he wasn't by nature the comforting, encouraging person his sister was, but he understood the power of prayer. And, if Alex ever needed prayer, it was now.

"Alex, may I pray for you and the baby?" He asked. Nodding, she calmed somewhat. They all bowed their heads and Chad's quiet voice made them forget the beeping monitors in the background. "Sovereign Lord, nothing surprises You, not even this circumstance, which is scary for us right now. We know Your Word says, 'The Lord is my light and my salvation; whom shall I fear?' Father, we trust You right now, even though we don't understand what's going on. Remove fear from our hearts, Lord, and replace it with Your peace. Please bring Alex and the baby through this delivery safe and healthy. In Your precious Son's name, Amen."

As they lifted their heads, they saw Dr. Sheffield saying her own "Amen." She addressed the three scared faces staring at her.

"We've administered the medicine to mature the baby's lungs. In order for the drug to have a chance to work, we need Alex's little girl to stay put for a little bit longer, so we're trying to delay Alex's labor."

She sat on the end of the bed and rubbed Alex's leg through the sheet as she spoke. Her layman's terminology and calm attitude helped to put Alex a bit more at ease. Her tears subsided and she relaxed her vise-like grip on Chad's and Charmain's hands.

"Our mama is going to need her strength tomorrow, so why don't y'all call it a night? You can come back in the morning when we know more about whether the treatment has worked," Dr. Sheffield told the White siblings.

Fear gripped Alex's heart again at the thought of being all alone in a strange hospital. Chad looked in her eyes, offering what little comfort he could. He took her hand and squeezed it, speaking reassuring words while Charmain conferred with the doctor.

"Will you stay? Please," she pleaded, locking eyes with Chad. "I'm scared, and I don't want to be alone."

The tears threatened again, pooling in her big, brown eyes. Chad looked at Dr. Sheffield, who nodded.

"It's not going to be the most comfortable night of your life. The chair in the corner opens out flat, but it's not the Ritz. I'll have a nurse bring you a pillow and blanket."

"Thank you, doctor," Chad said.

Dr. Sheffield exited to find a nurse, and Charmain hurried over to her brother and friend.

"I'm going to go home, call Miss Matilda, and try to get some sleep. I'll be back first thing in the morning. Chad, do you need me to bring you anything?"

On cue, a candy striper walked in carrying a pillow, a blanket, and a toothbrush. The friends laughed at the uncanny timing. Charmain hugged them both goodbye and slipped out the door. Alex looked at Chad, the apology written on her face even before she said the words.

"Chad, I'm sorry if I put you on the spot. If you don't want to stay, you can go catch Charmain before she leaves," she offered in a small voice.

"Hey, I'm right where I want to be. You let me know if you need anything, and I'll take care of it."

He spoke from the same place where Dr. Sheffield had perched, and he rubbed her blanketed leg as he'd seen the doctor do. Alex now felt awful for asking him to endure such an uncomfortable night. If she were in a different situation, maybe she'd examine why she asked Chad and not his sister.

But she had more important things to think about right now.

❦ ❦ ❦

Chad's heart soared when she asked him to stay. Maybe she did feel something for him. He had to think clearly, though. Alex was facing a crisis right now and needed a friend she could count on.

As Chad tried to get comfortable in the chair in the corner a few hours later, he smiled as he recalled the conversation he and Alex had just had about their childhoods after the lights had been turned off per the doctor's orders. He'd heard the fatigue creeping into her voice as they whispered stories of their hijinks and accomplishments. Chad steered the conversation away from painful subjects, and Alex gladly obliged.

A little after midnight, she'd drifted off mid-sentence while telling him about her prom. Chad considered their differences. His own prom

146

had been many years ago, and he hadn't gone. After hearing about her childhood, he realized their backgrounds couldn't be more dissimilar; but the fact remained that she'd left everything she knew to start a new life. He didn't know what made her leave, but he promised himself that he would, one day, discover her reason.

Dr. Sheffield hadn't exaggerated when she said it would be a long, uncomfortable night. Chad didn't care though. He woke up every time Alex moved or made the slightest sound, worried she'd need a nurse or, heaven forbid, was going into labor again. As the sky began to blush with the coming sunrise, he stood at Alex's bedside and watched her by the glow of the call light while she slept. He checked his watch, thinking he might be able to catch a quick nap before Charmain came back.

Settling back into the tortuous chair to await his sister, Chad drifted into a deep, dreamless sleep. An hour later Charmain awakened him by shaking his foot. *I've got to talk to that girl about her timing,* he thought, swimming up from the depths of his much-needed nap.

"My turn. Go home and get a shower," she whispered.

Alex still slept.

He didn't want to leave without saying goodbye, but he also didn't want to wake her. He nodded at Charmain, rising to go, his body screaming in protest from the uncomfortable night. He grabbed his coat and hugged his sister, reaching for the door.

"You're not even going to say goodbye?" Alex's teasing voice called from the bed. She smiled, but he still saw the anxiety in her eyes.

"I didn't want to wake you," he said, returning her smile. "I'm going to run home for a bit. I'll be back soon." He didn't want her to think he was deserting her.

She nodded, Charmain already by her side, rubbing her shoulders, chatting about baby clothes. Maybe this was for the best. He needed some space and time to think about the last twelve hours. Chad slipped out without another word.

∅ ∅ ∅

Chad heard the phone ringing as he stepped out of the shower, threw a towel around himself and raced to get to it before it stopped.

"Hello," he panted, dripping all over the floor in his bedroom.

147

"You sound like you've been running a marathon. Where have you been? This is the third time I've called." Charmain sounded at once irritated and relieved.

She talked a mile a minute, but her message came through crystal clear. He needed to get back to the hospital as soon as possible. Soon after he left, Alex's contractions had begun again. The doctor told her although she would have preferred to wait a few more hours, the medicine had been in her system long enough. Alex's labor would be allowed to progress, and she'd have a baby soon.

"I'll call Miss M.," Chad offered before he hung up, promising his sister he'd hurry. He also needed to call the shop and make sure they knew where he was. *What had people done before cell phones?* he wondered for probably the hundredth time since yesterday.

He dialed Miss Matilda's number while he hopped around trying to put on his socks and shoes. She answered on the third ring, and he explained Alex's situation as best he could, considering he didn't understand anything that was happening. He asked her if she wanted to ride with him to the hospital.

"Oh, sweetie, I wish I could. I've got a girl coming by this morning for an interview. Plus, the downstairs heater is on the fritz, so I've called the repairman. He should be here soon. I hope he can fix it before Christmas. You'll give her my love, won't you?"

"Yes, ma'am. I will."

Chad hung up, dashed out the door, and was backing the truck down the driveway before he'd even shut the door. It wasn't until he reached the intersection near the hospital that he glanced in his rearview mirror and realized, in his haste, he hadn't shaved or combed his hair.

"Really smooth, man," he said to his reflection, trying his best to tame his out-of-control mop, glinting ginger in the morning sun.

He sprinted from the parking lot to the elevator bank, banging on the button ten times in quick succession in an attempt to make it arrive faster. Finally, he stepped on the elevator and the doors shut, making him glad he was alone. The mirrored glass doors revealed a misbuttoned, untucked shirt, in addition to the stubble on his face. He raised one arm and took a quick sniff to assure himself he'd indeed applied deodorant. Yes. He'd take any small victory.

With a deep breath and a silent prayer, Chad righted his appearance as much as possible before stepping out of the elevator onto the labor and delivery floor.

⌀ ⌀ ⌀

That afternoon, Alex's daughter made her appearance, telling everyone the news with a hearty cry. Through her exhausted tears, Alex laughed in disbelief as she held the tiny little girl. Charmain was so overcome with joy, amazement, and respect for Alex that she had to sit down. Then she remembered her promise to her brother.

"Oh, I'd better go let Chad know everything is good," she cried, jumping up from her seat and rushing toward the door. She halted, hand on the handle. "It is good, isn't it?" she asked looking around the room at the many medical professionals present.

"Yes, it is," answered Dr. Sheffield, looking relieved to have this stressful delivery behind her with a positive outcome. "Mother and baby are both doing well. They'll be in a room within an hour, but no visitors until tomorrow," the doctor declared.

"But Dr. Sheffield, Chad and Charmain brought me here. They're practically the only family I have…well, except for Miss Matilda, of course," Alex explained.

"Well, I suppose I can make a tiny exception this once. But just ten minutes. Then you're going to need your rest."

"Yes, ma'am," Alex answered. Charmain, who'd remained at the door to hear this exchange between patient and doctor, scurried to tell Chad the great news.

⌀ ⌀ ⌀

Chad knocked softly at the door. He and Char entered when he heard Alex call for them to come in. She was propped up on several pillows, her hair plastered to her face in ringlets, the precious bundle swaddled in a soft pink blanket in her arms. She beamed at them as they approached. She had never looked more beautiful.

"Hey, y'all. Thanks for hanging around," she joked. They all laughed in whispers so as not to disturb the sleeping child.

"Alex, you did such a great job!" Charmain gushed as she stroked the tiny fingers.

149

"I didn't have much of a choice, did I? But thanks. To tell you the truth, I'm kind of glad this is behind me. I know I've got some challenges ahead, but at least I've got this tough part over with." She sighed as she leaned her head back on the pillows. The exhausting day was beginning to catch up with her.

Charmain excused herself to go to the ladies' room before she and Chad said their goodbyes. Chad took her spot beside the bed and ran the back of his finger along the baby's cheek.

"She's beautiful, Alex. Congratulations."

"Thanks, Chad. And, thank you for all you and Charmain have done for me. It meant more than you can imagine to have you here with me last night. I don't know what I would have done without you."

She held his gaze, but there was so much in her eyes that he couldn't read. Did she reciprocate the feelings he had for her? Was he just a friend? He wanted so badly to know where he stood with this incredible woman who amazed him at every turn, but today was not the right time.

He'd wait.

But soon, he would find out, one way or another, if Alex cared for him.

Chapter 16
Good for Something

The next day, Miss Matilda heaved herself up into Alex's vehicle to visit the cherished baby she'd been waiting on since the day she'd seen her tiny heartbeat. She'd asked some of the girls to install the car seat/carrier combo contraption Alex had purchased several weeks ago as soon as Chad had called her, happy for the distraction.

Of course, Matilda loved all of her residents, and the good Lord knew she'd seen her share of trials and tragedies come through Together for Good. Somehow, though, Alex's sad story of betrayal and pain grabbed her heart in a special way. As she drove the route she'd travelled many times over the years, she reflected on the circumstances she'd witnessed in her long stint of caring for girls with nowhere else to turn.

She'd met ladies who'd made poor choices and admitted it. Others were so strung out on drugs, all Matilda could do was call Dr. Sheffield, seeking medical intervention. Some were running. Running from abusive partners, pimps, parents. Sometimes, the ones they ran from found them, requiring law enforcement to intervene.

But always, Matilda prayed. She prayed for the young mothers, the fathers, and, most of all, the babies. Those precious little ones had no choice in any of the situations, so she petitioned the Lord the most fervently on their behalf.

Matilda never betrayed a confidence. Her sister taught her this hard and fast rule before she died. If a girl took Matilda into her confidence, she knew her secret was protected, unless it was a grave matter of safety. She'd shouldered so many burdens over the years. Often, as the girls had their babies and started their new lives, she released any of the pain and sorrow she carried while they were under her care.

Although she'd never admit it to anyone, some of the secrets she'd harbored for decades continued to gnaw away at her even now, holding her tight in the grip of a guilt she couldn't escape. The Lord knew, and she asked for His forgiveness all the time. But no matter how hard she tried; she couldn't forgive herself.

Matilda shook her head to deflect her thoughts from her own mental anguish and instead thought of the young girl she'd see soon. Chad's short answers on the phone yesterday hadn't allowed Matilda to glean much information. He'd seemed frazzled, preoccupied, and hurried. She understood. He and Alex obviously cared for one another, but they continued to dance around their feelings. Matilda didn't understand kids these days. Why play these games? If you care for someone, tell them!

Matilda parked in a new mothers parking space and walked the short distance to the elevator. Once she reached her floor, she was surprised to see Alex's door standing wide open. She knocked anyway. What greeted her was a sight to behold.

Alex had risen early, showered, dressed and gotten her daughter dressed in the tiny clothes she had packed in her bag. She looked up at Miss Matilda's tentative rap at the door, pleased to see the lady who'd become her friend and mentor in a few short months. After hugging her in greeting, Alex led Miss Matilda to the little bassinet where her daughter lay staring up at the world. Matilda smiled as tears stung her eyes.

"Oh, Alex. She's gorgeous. It reminds me of when Terry was born. I think it's because of all her dark hair," Matilda spoke but never took her eyes off the little girl. "Have you given her a name yet?"

Alex explained to Matilda how her Sunday school class had been studying the book of Acts and Paul's missionary journeys. She was moved by the difference he had made not only in the world for the gospel, but also in those who heard him preach.

"I was really impressed by the woman in Thyatira whose whole household believed because of her. I want my daughter to have a special namesake to live up to, so I've named her Lydia. Lydia Faith. Because she's a living example of how my faith in the Lord has grown."

"Well, her name is just as beautiful as she is," Matilda dabbed her eyes with a tissue, hugging Alex one more time. "I spoke to the nurses on my way in. They said you've been cleared by Dr. Sheffield to check out."

"OK. I need to call Charmain and ask her to bring the car seat. I don't want you to have to go all the way home just to get it," Alex said.

"I'm a step ahead of you!" Matilda responded confidently. She shared the story of the Whites driving Alex's car to the home and the struggle that ensued with the three of them trying to install the car seat. Alex threw her arms around the old lady, her gratitude evident in her embrace.

∅ ∅ ∅

Alex marveled at the kindness of people who hadn't even known her this time last year. If it hadn't been for Miss Matilda, her nephew, and the Whites, her life's course would no doubt have taken a different, probably darker, direction.

On the drive home, Alex sat in the back seat beside her daughter and told Miss Matilda about her plans for moving into the White's guesthouse. Matilda agreed it sounded like a perfect solution for Alex and Lydia, although she'd miss having her around the home. Reminding Alex that Christmas was only a few days away and no new residents were scheduled to arrive until after the new year began, Miss Matilda invited Alex to stay with her until after Christmas, giving Chad and Charmain a chance to ready the little house for their new tenants.

"That would be great, Miss Matilda. Thank you so much."

Alex stroked her bundled up baby's soft cheek, tears spilling down her face as the full impact of her new role in life hit home. *Mommy. Her title from now on.* Could she do a better job of it than her own mother had done? Determination surged up in her, and she decided she not only could but would be the best mommy ever to this perfect little girl.

Another wave of gratefulness welled up within her remembering that Miss Matilda had insisted she sit through three long days of parenting class before Thanksgiving. Having never spent much time around small children, Alex had very little clue about caring for an infant.

Learning, on the other hand, was where she excelled, and she'd soaked up the information like a sponge. Even though she knew she'd

153

never win Mother of the Year, she felt more confident in her abilities to take care of her little girl once the class was over.

The only catch was now she had to figure out how to do it in real life.

✄ ✄ ✄

The days leading up to Christmas proved more hectic than usual for Matilda. A new baby, an impending move, two mothers-to-be sitting on go and awaiting their babies' arrival any minute, last-minute shopping, more baking. It seemed the list never ended. But Matilda wouldn't have it any other way.

The Saturday before Christmas, the sun couldn't penetrate the thick clouds, and it was colder than in recent days. When she heard her front door open, Matilda looked up from her baking and smiled at the sight of Terry entering the kitchen, bundled up in a coat and scarf and carrying a long narrow white box.

"Hey, Aunt Tilley. It smells fantastic in here. You got any duds you need to get rid of?"

This running joke between them had started when Terry was a young boy and Matilda would make some of the cookies look bad on purpose, making them unfit for gift giving. She'd tell Terry they were duds she needed him to take care of. This ruse had continued through the years, reminding them both of their shared past and deep affection for one another.

"I think I already threw them away," she said with a straight face. The crestfallen expression on Terry's face was exactly the response she'd been hoping for, and her belly shook with laughter. The sound of it set off Terry's deep, rumbling laugh. He accepted two of the proffered cookies and poured himself a glass of milk.

"By the way, happy birthday, dear," Miss Matilda said over her shoulder. "I hope you don't mind, but we'll do like always and celebrate after Christmas when we can focus on you. Does that suit you?"

She always felt guilty postponing his birthday celebration a week or so, but it made it so much easier to give him a proper birthday party instead of what felt like a combined celebration. Besides, celebrating on his actual birthday was still painful for her, though he didn't know that, even after all these years.

154

When will you summon your courage to tell him? Her small inner voice pressed for an answer. She pushed it away for the thousandth time.

"You know you don't have to go to any trouble for me, Aunt Tilley," Terry was saying when Alex entered.

"Hi, Terry," she said, glancing around the kitchen. Matilda knew the girl needed to verify Gail wasn't with Terry. Who could blame her?

Matilda watched two of her favorite people in all the world.

𝄢 𝄢 𝄢

"Hey, Alex. I brought you something." He handed her the box.

"Thank you, Terry. You didn't have to get me anything," she responded, accepting what appeared to be a box of long-stemmed roses.

"I know, but since we're business partners, I wanted you to know I'm thinking of you and wish you and the baby well."

Terry took a bite of cookie and a gulp of milk as he watched Alex inspect the box. She lifted the lid, and her mouth dropped open in disbelief. This bouquet was made of flowers fashioned from paper money!

"Someone once told me new moms are stretched for time, so I thought real flowers might not be the best choice. When I saw this at the florist, though, I knew it was just what I was looking for," Terry said, still chewing his huge bite.

"Terry, I can't thank you enough. It's so generous. I almost hate to take it apart; they're so beautifully made."

"Maybe you can keep one of them just to remember what they looked like," Miss Matilda suggested. Alex nodded in agreement with Miss Matilda's practical solution to the situation.

"Great idea. Thanks again, Terry. I'm going to take these up and put them with the stuff I'm packing. If Lydia's awake, would you like to see her?" Alex asked.

"Of course. I can't wait to meet her."

Once Alex was out of earshot, Matilda turned to Terry.

"Does Gail know you got a gift for Alex?"

"Yes, I told her I was going to the florist to get something for her and coming over to see the two of you. She wasn't happy, but it's her own doing she's not welcomed here. I feel kind of responsible for

Alex. If I hadn't made a business offer, she would have been free to go out and find another job."

"Is there a problem with the business?" she asked, voicing her concern to her nephew.

She had told Terry how Alex making her "found treasures" creations had sparked a renewed passion in Alex that had been absent when she arrived in Burton. Matilda hoped the business venture wasn't in jeopardy.

"No. Well, unless Alex can't keep up with the huge demand for her work. She has a great eye; she knows what folks want. Her stuff is easy to sell because it's such a perfect fit in the homes I design." He thought back to the day he'd struck the deal with Alex. He seemed pretty smart for recognizing her talent and artistry, but in reality, he knew how to listen to what people wanted.

Alex did, too.

They heard Alex's footsteps descending the creaky old stairs, and she appeared in the kitchen doorway smiling from ear to ear and holding a wiggling bundle.

"Come and meet Mr. Terry," she cooed to the baby, which she placed in Terry's arms. Terry tried to hide his astonishment. He didn't hold many babies. It only forced him to relive the sense of loss he felt each time he recalled the day Gail made her "baby announcement," as he called it. Looking into the precious little eyes staring up at him, he remembered it as if it were yesterday.

They'd been married five years, still young and managing budding careers. Gail worked day and night to make a name for herself in the world of commercial real estate, a less-than-booming market in the small town of Burton, South Carolina.

She branched out to her precious and familiar hometown of Atlanta, attending the parties, corporate functions, weekend events...whatever it took to get ahead. Terry stayed in Burton, building his architecture business from small remodel jobs to spec houses and then, finally, luxury homes.

Within a few short years, he solidified his position as one of the most respected and requested residential and commercial architects in the area, not only because of his talent and excellent designs, but also because of the respect and courtesy he extended to his clients.

When they were both established in their fields, Terry had approached Gail about starting a family. She stalled at first, offering up one flimsy excuse after another. One day when she returned from a week-long business trip, he told her he was tired of the delays. He felt he deserved an answer. That's when she voiced the truth he'd already guessed.

She had no intention of derailing her career trajectory for a baby, not then and not ever, crushing Terry's hopes. He suggested adoption, but she pointed out that a child, regardless of how it came into your life, required constant care. She also reminded him that the home visits needed to qualify for adoption would rule them out when it became evident how much the mother of the household was absent.

Her exact words to him had been, "Why do you think we've never even gotten a pet? I don't have time to deal with such nonsense."

His dream of being a dad died that day, but he'd had other dreams die before. He knew how to reimagine dreams to make them if not as good as new, then at least good for something. He redirected his energies and resources on his Aunt Tilley's place, his own childhood home. By then, he had no financial worries. Just the opposite.

His modular housing systems had received a patent and were being installed in third world countries at a pace that astounded even him. If God's plan for him didn't include having his own child, then he vowed to ensure the at-risk babies and young women under his Aunt Tilley's roof were well cared for.

Only Aunt Tilley was aware he was the majority benefactor of Together for Good. Well, Aunt Tilley and Gail. The first month his wife had seen the bank statement documenting how much he intended to give to the home each month, she blew a gasket. He flatly refused to be dissuaded, though. By the time Gail could register her disapproval, Terry had set the wheels in motion with his lawyers, his investment advisor, and several service providers in town.

A plumber, an electrician, and a carpenter agreed to be on permanent retainer, thanks to Terry Lovell's tidy monthly fee. This ensured Aunt Tilley that all she ever had to do was pick up the phone; if she needed anything, she'd be taken care of.

This benevolence came at a price higher than the money it cost him. With his marriage little more than a sham, Terry's arrangement for the home was a bitter pill for Gail to swallow. She'd always hated the home, looking down from her ivory tower of self-imposed moral superiority at the girls who found themselves in situations they couldn't handle alone.

For a while, she feigned civility to Aunt Tilley in person, but berated and belittled her behind closed doors for condoning and encouraging what Gail considered the girls' unacceptable behavior. Finally, Terry refused to listen to Gail's rants, and she resorted to snide comments under her breath, thinly veiled insults, and voice inflections meant to telegraph her true feelings. Poor Alex was the victim of the final straw.

"Terry?"

Both Alex and his Aunt Tilley were looking at him as if he had three eyes. He must have zoned out while his past played like a movie in his mind. Looking at the beautiful baby in his arms, he smiled.

"Alex, she's perfect. I know some people say babies look alike, but I swear there's something familiar about her." He looked into her sweet face, and she looked back. He had no idea why Alex had ended up at the home, but he hoped she could see the blessing this little person was.

"I hope she looks familiar. She looks like me, right?" Alex teased as she eased Lydia out of his arms and excused herself to go upstairs to feed her.

The thought continued to nag at the back of his brain that it wasn't Alex Lydia reminded him of.

🕉 🕉 🕉

J.T. chopped veggies and browned ground beef to make chili. Bad weather had grounded his crews, allowing him to work in the kitchen while Karen went outside to place a festive garland and bow on the mailbox post.

"J.T.," she called, slamming the front door behind her. The warmth of the house welcomed her from the icy outside. "Who do we know in New York City? This Christmas card is post-marked from there, but there's no return address."

J.T. walked into the room wiping his hands on a kitchen towel.

"Well, open it, honey, and find out," he said smiling. His grin quickly faded when he saw the signature on the card. *Alex.*

"Do you think she went to New York to be with Brittany?" Karen asked.

He'd finally calmed Karen down and convinced her to accept her daughter's decision to leave, but he could see her getting spun up really fast. J.T. groaned inwardly. He recognized Alex's attempt to let them know she was doing fine, but what it accomplished in this house amounted to utter turmoil.

"No, dear, I don't. I saw Brittany at the grocery store yesterday. I'm not sure why it came from New York. Maybe it got lost." The excuse sounded lame even to his own ears. He returned to the kitchen to finish the chili and wonder how Alex had pulled this off.

ØØ Ø Ø

What J.T. didn't know was Alex and Brittany had worked out a plan to mail the card from New York. Alex placed the signed, stamped, addressed card in a larger envelope addressed to Brittany at school. Brittany removed the card from the outer envelope and placed it in the mail the day before she returned home for winter break, ensuring she'd be home by the time the card arrived at the Wickhams'.

It accomplished its intended purpose of assuring them she was safe while also throwing them off her trail.

ØØ Ø Ø

Alex reached into the nightstand drawer and pulled out the little diary. It had remained untouched since the day she'd found it. Deciding to read another entry while she fed her daughter, Alex settled into the rocking chair, then opened the book to where she'd left off.

June 2, 1963

After me being sick to my stomach for five days, Mother is beginning to worry I might be really ill. Although I'm not running a fever, I'm tired all the time and can't hold down solid food, with the exception of a few crackers. I insisted on attending school today, even though Mother argued against it.

"What if you're contagious, Carol Ann?" she asked.

I tried explaining that I can't miss school now. We're preparing for finals. So she wants someone to bring my schoolwork to our house.

"Well, if I am contagious," I pointed out, "that won't help them much. Besides, I have the highest marks in math class, and nobody else in the class understands what we're doing in there except for me. So,

159

they wouldn't be able to explain it to me. I'll be fine, Mother." Parents just don't understand things sometimes!

Mother agreed to let me go to school on one condition. I have to promise to come home if I start feeling bad. I promised, kissed her goodbye and headed out the door. I hate keeping secrets from her, but I'm certain she'd have a nervous breakdown if she had any inkling of the concerns lurking in my mind.

Not only do I feel horrible, but I'm beginning to worry something could be wrong other than what I'm almost certain is wrong. I want to see Jimmy and speak to him alone before school lets out.

June 3, 1963
This is the worst day of my life!

Walking home from school alone, I contemplated my next move. Jimmy had been busy at school with finals, graduation preparations, summer plans, and talking to his friends about college. There never was a good time to talk to him alone to discuss my concerns.

Besides, what would I say? Following our picnic and what had come after, we had both agreed to never again mention what we'd done. We've continued to talk of our plans to marry as soon as I finish high school. Jimmy assures me the college he's attending has housing for married couples where we can live. It sounds wonderful.

When I was almost home, I noticed Daddy's car parked in front of the house—strange for a Monday afternoon. Daddy usually takes his lunch with him to work, and then Mother cooks a big meal for supper. I couldn't figure out why he had come home for lunch. Maybe he was sick. I quickened my pace, the queasiness that's my constant companion mounting at the thought something might be amiss.

I opened the kitchen door and set my books on the table, still wondering what was going on. I was startled to hear Mother tapping across the kitchen in her good heels, dressed to go out with her hat in place and donning her white cotton gloves in short, jerky movements.

It's rare for Mother to go out after I get home from school. We usually sit for a few minutes and discuss the day while I start my homework, and when I'm done, I help her make supper. But today, Mother's lips were pursed as she greeted me.

160

"Get an apple or a cookie if you're hungry, then get in the car."
She sounded harsh. I decided her concern for me was taking a toll.

When I asked where we were going, she told me she'd made an appointment for me to see Dr. Jones.

"We need to find out what's wrong with you," she replied as she breezed out the door, keys in one hand, purse in the other.

My knees buckled and my vision blurred. I was pretty sure life as I knew it was about to change forever.

Two hours later, I sat on the exam table with tears streaming down my face. The doctor's examination confirmed my worst fears. What was I going to do? It seemed impossible this could be happening to me. The room whirled around, and I heard a droning in my ears. It was Dr. Jones speaking to me. Blinking, I tried to focus on what he said.

"By my calculations, I estimate you're about two months along. Is that about right, hon?" he asked me, as he made notes in my chart.

"My chart," I thought. "The place where he wrote about my broken arm when I fell out of the tree house and the chicken pox when I was eight; but I never thought he'd have to write this! I'm only sixteen. Well, seventeen in a few weeks."

Unable to hear my thoughts, Dr. Jones continued looking at me, waiting for an answer. All I could do was nod as the antiseptic scent of the small room assaulted my nostrils, making my stomach flip. I bolted off the examination table into the bathroom, emptied my stomach, splashed my face, rinsed my mouth, and returned to sit on the edge of the table again, tears still flowing.

"Doc Jones, do we have to tell Mother?" I whispered.

Even to myself I sounded like a scared child. Dr. Jones, a seasoned small-town doctor in his mid-sixties with a thick shock of white hair, patted my knee, smiled, and replied, "Sweetie, this isn't the kind of thing you can hide. A baby is a miracle, a blessing. You may not see it right now. But you, your parents, and a young man need to figure out how you plan on handling this blessing. I'm going to bring your momma in here. Do you want to tell her, or do you want me to do it?"

"I'll do it," I said with more bravery than I felt. "But would you please stay in here with me?"

"Of course. I want to give y'all some information before you leave."

I never knew what heartbreak looked like until I stared into Mother's eyes and told her I'm going to have a baby. I wonder if she

161

would've taken the news any worse if I'd told her I, her only child, was dying. As soon as the news left my lips, Mother slumped in her chair, exhaling fast as if punched in the gut.

She closed her eyes, and I watched a single tear roll slowly down her cheek. After about half a minute, she took a deep breath, sat up straight, looked at Dr. Jones, and spoke in a clear, authoritative tone.

"Okay, so what do we do next?"

Dr. Jones began to tell Mother about a baby being a blessing, and us having decisions to make. Then he talked about nice homes where I'd be very comfortable until the baby arrives and handed Mother a handful of pamphlets. He finished up with the final blow, bringing the whole conversation crashing to a gut-wrenching conclusion.

"And if she chooses adoption, there is information about that here as well." Dr. Jones spoke of these life-altering decisions as though talking about the weather. "You may want to discuss with the young man the course of action you plan to take."

Homes. Adoption. This is so new to me.

I've never known of anyone my age who had a baby, but I've heard rumors of girls being shipped off to homes for unwed mothers to live until their child is born. The family always tells people back home the girl has gone to "visit an aunt" or some other implausible story. The baby is placed for adoption, and the girl returns home and goes on with her life. The thought of it makes my stomach roll, and the tears fall again as I write this. Mother reached for the literature and placed it in her purse, rising to leave and signaling me to do the same.

"I can assure you, doctor, the young man responsible for this has done more than enough and will be included in no more decisions from here on out," she announced. "We appreciate your seeing us on such short notice and trust this visit will be kept in the strictest confidence."

"Of course, Beverly. And, if you'd like me to make a call to this home," he said as he indicated one of the brochures, "I know the director. I think you'd be very pleased," the kind doctor continued as he rose to walk us to the door.

When I heard Mother say that she meant to exclude Jimmy from all future decisions, my sobs came from deep within me. Dr. Jones recommended Mother bring the car around to the back of the office to pick me up. After I got in the car, Mother walked with the doctor back to the office door. I rolled down the window just a little bit to hear what they said. I know it's rude to eavesdrop, but this is my life they were talking about.

"Could you please call the director you know and see if we can get Carol Ann in tomorrow?"

This was the first time Dr Jones' cool exterior faltered.

"Don't you think you're rushing things a bit? Wouldn't you like to look over the rest of the literature? Think about it? Discuss it with your husband?"

"No." Mother's answer was firm, her mind made up. There was no deterring her. "We leave in the morning. Call me if there are any problems with placing her there. Money will not be an issue. We're going home to begin packing."

The doctor handed her a slip of paper with the directions to the facility. She tucked it into her purse and closed it with a click, pivoted halfway toward the car, and then paused.

"Doc Jones," she said in a whisper so soft I almost didn't hear. I could see her eyes shine with unshed tears, "am I going to make it through this?"

The doctor sighed, then smiled the saddest smile I've ever seen.

"Y'all will be fine, Beverly. Don't forget to love your daughter. Remember she's hurting and scared."

Those words snapped Mother back to the painful reality of the situation, the reality of having to be in charge of getting an ugly business dealt with as soon as possible before anyone in this small Southern town found out. Because if they did, you could be assured my mother would never show her face in public again.

Icy silence permeated the drive home. Mother maintained a death grip on the steering wheel, never letting her gaze veer from the road. Tears coursed down my face. Shame assaulted me in waves. I know what high hopes my parents had for me, and now I've ruined everything. This will crush Daddy.

If only Jimmy could talk to them and explain our marriage plans. I ventured a glance over at my mother a block from the house, and her face was red and splotchy, the way it gets when she's truly upset. Parking the car, Mother turned to me with a mixture of exhaustion, sadness, and bitterness in her eyes. She spoke through clenched teeth.

"How could you do this to your father and me? Carol Ann, I just don't understand what would make you think this was acceptable. Haven't we taught you better than this? Do you realize we'll be the

163

laughingstock of this town now?" She worked herself up to an almost hysterical frenzy by the time she finished her rant.

"Mother, maybe we should go inside. Folks are staring at us," I whispered, looking around at people on the sidewalk and in a few neighboring yards who were craning their necks to see what had caused Mother's outburst.

We exited the car, Mother slamming the driver's door with much more force than necessary, and went inside. She told me Daddy had ridden to work with a friend and would be home within the hour. She set about chopping vegetables for soup. As she busied her hands with meal preparations, I stood wondering what would happen next. I didn't have to wonder long.

"Go get the big suitcase out of the spare bedroom," she commanded, "and start packing. I asked Dr. Jones to arrange for us to leave tomorrow."

"Tomorrow?" She'd been serious! My hands flew to my mouth, trying to hold back my anguish. It was too much to take. "Mother, can I at least say goodbye to Jimmy?"

The mention of his name sent her into a rage. She turned on me with wild-eyed fury.

"Don't you mention his name to me ever again, do you understand? We welcomed that boy into our home, trusted him with our precious daughter, and how did he repay us? Not to mention how he disrespected you!" She paused to take a breath, and I saw what might be my only chance to get a word in.

"But, Mother, we're going to get married after I graduate. It's just a year away."

My argument fell on deaf ears. Mother would hear nothing about marriage, babies or Jimmy. I knew when I'd been beaten. I retreated upstairs, humiliated and exhausted, to begin the task of packing for my extended absence.

I found the suitcase and began throwing clothes into it, feeling as if I were in someone else's skin or maybe like I had watched this whole day in a movie. As I picked up a skirt, it struck me that most of my clothing will be useless once the baby begins to grow within me. At least my socks, nightgowns, and sneakers will all fit.

Soon I heard the sound of my father entering the front door and his footsteps making their way down the hall toward the kitchen. Muffled voices floated up the stairwell, and I knew Daddy was hearing the news. The scraping of the kitchen chair from underneath the table told me he needed to sit down.

The one thing I was counting on was that he might be able to somehow convince Mother that leaving tomorrow is not a good idea. I think if I had a few more days at home, I could talk to Jimmy and we could figure this out together.

"Carol Ann, come downstairs. We need to talk to you," I heard Mother call up from the bottom of the stairs.

When I was halfway down, the shrill ring of the telephone sounded from the living room, followed by Mother's heels clacking across the kitchen floor as she hurried to answer it. She reached it on the third ring.

"Hello," her calm, cordial tone belied the turmoil brewing in our home. However, as she listened to the caller, her face contorted into a picture of loathing.

"No, you may not speak to her. Never call here again. Do you understand?" She slammed the receiver into the cradle so hard I was surprised it didn't break.

I stared at my mother in stunned silence. She isn't even going to allow me one final phone conversation. I was all cried out, but the hurt extended so deep I felt sure I'd dissolve into a puddle. My heart is being ripped from my chest, and my very own mother is the one doing it.

Mother dabbed her eyes and nose with her handkerchief, took a deep breath, then turned, surprised to see me standing in the doorway. Walking toward the kitchen, she motioned for me to follow her. We found Daddy still sitting at the kitchen table staring into space, dazed.

Somehow, the family made it through the familiar routine of the evening meal. Nobody ate much supper or even spoke, each of us lost in a silent reverie of "what if?" and "what next?"

As everyone attempted to avoid eye contact with one another while cleaning the dishes, the telephone rang once again. Mother stiffened as she wiped crumbs from the counter, her eyes snapping to me.

"I'll get it," she said as she tossed the dish cloth into the sink, whisked off her apron, and scurried into the living room, prepared for yet another confrontation with Jimmy. I retreated to the top of the stairs, not wanting a front row seat for the showdown that was sure to ensue. This time Mother's greeting was not as cordial, which she regretted. It was Dr. Jones.

"Oh, hello, Doctor. No, we're not eating," she replied. "We were just finishing with the dishes. Is there something I can do for you?"

This is where I got very nosy. I picked up the extension in the upstairs hall and listened in on the rest of Mother's conversation. I've never eavesdropped in my whole life, much less twice in one day! I just couldn't help myself. It was my future they were discussing as if I weren't even here. Dr. Jones had called to tell Mother the details about the home they're taking me to.

"Yes, I just wanted to let you know I spoke with my friend at the home in South Carolina. His name is Charles, and they have an available spot for Carol Ann. I think she'll be comfortable there. Charles is a pastor, and he and his wife started this ministry a few years ago."

I could hear Mother hesitate. We've never been what you would call very religious people.

"Beverly?" Doc Jones called her name. She'd wandered off into her own thoughts again.

"Yes, Doctor. I'm here. Thank you so much for making the arrangements for us. I don't know how we can ever repay you. You've been so kind through this whole ordeal," she said, and I could tell she meant it. Dr. Jones had been the one calming, steady influence in the hurricane rocking our world.

"Don't mention it. Keep me posted on how she's doing," he said as he wished her a good night.

Mother hung up the phone as I replaced the other receiver without a sound. How would a bunch of Christians accept a girl who was pregnant out of wedlock? Then the cold truth hit me. They were there to accept me and other girls just like me.

It was my own mother who was turning me away. Why was she doing this to me? Was her reputation so much more important to her than her own daughter?

Deep down, I know the answer.

I was still sitting at the top of the stairs when I heard Daddy shuffle into the living room looking for the newspaper. I could see him go to her and wrap her in his arms. They sobbed until they were spent. She stared at him with swollen eyes, voicing her concerns.

"Are we doing the right thing, Tom? Sending her away?"

"I don't know," he admitted, shaking his head of salt-and-pepper hair. I always thought my dad had aged much better than the other

166

fathers his age. Tonight, in his anguish, I could see the ruthless fingers
of time begin to claim his countenance.
How could I have hurt them so deeply?

Alex didn't even know Carol Ann and she felt sorry for her. She'd been there herself. She understood the feeling of cold fear running through her body, realizing that the life she was accustomed to had ended and something terrible was about to happen.

Alex looked down in her arms.

This beautiful person, now sleeping with her hand resting against Alex's bare skin, was not something terrible. Quite the opposite. Alex watched Lydia sleeping, wondering how she could have ever contemplated ending this life.

They belonged to each other.

Chapter 17
Moving Day

Christmas passed in a blur of gifts, food, people, and, for Alex, packing up to move for the second time in less than a year. This time, Alex felt at peace about her move even though her life seemed upended by moving into a new house, growing a new business, and beginning life as a single mom.

She believed Chad and Charmain would be there for her if she got in a jam, and Miss Matilda was only a few minutes up the road if she needed experienced assistance. Plus, Lauren had decided to remain in Burton and finish her tech school education. Alex realized how rich her life had become with the addition of so many dear friends. All too soon, however, she had everything packed, and it was time to say goodbye to a place and people she'd grown to love.

The morning of her move, while Lydia slept, Alex hurried downstairs after her shower to grab a cup of coffee and a banana. She saw Miss Matilda pouring her morning brew and stopped to say a prayer of thanks for the deer that ran out in front of her half a year ago, bringing her together with this wonderful lady.

Although Alex now had a better understanding of God's sovereignty, she hated to think she could have somehow ended up all the way on the west coast, doing heaven knows what, with heaven knows who. She cleared her throat as she came into the kitchen, so as not to startle the older lady, who appeared deep in thought as she stared out the bay window.

"Good morning. You seem lost in the clouds. Everything all right?" Alex asked as she grabbed a mug and poured a steaming cup, the fragrance awakening her senses before the caffeine had a chance.

"I'm fine, dear. Just a little sad to see you go. I know it happens with all of you girls, but it's so difficult sometimes." Her gray eyes misted over, and Alex, already hormonal from having just given birth, didn't think she could deal with a whole morning of teary goodbyes. Miss Matilda was as bad as Brittany!

Alex wracked her brain to think of a way to distract Miss Matilda from her impending departure. In a flash of inspired brilliance, she remembered the diary. She'd wanted to get Miss Matilda's thoughts and recollections on it, and the Christmastime rush had distracted her at every turn. Now was as good a time as any.

"Miss Matilda," Alex started, peeling her banana and trying to act nonchalant, "I know you couldn't remember all of the girls who come through here, but do you, by any chance, remember a girl by the name of Carol Ann?"

Matilda's coffee cup crashed to the floor, and Alex thought for a split second the dear woman might follow suit. Her face turned an ashen white as she spun around to face Alex. Terrified something was wrong, Alex set her breakfast on the counter and grasped Miss Matilda by the shoulders to steady her. They walked to the table, where Alex pulled out a chair and eased Miss Matilda into it, the mess by the counter forgotten for the moment.

"I'm so sorry if I said something to upset you, Miss Matilda." Alex, scared and shaken, knelt at her friend's feet.

"No, no, no. I just don't understand how you could know about Carol Ann. I mean, you're from the same town, of course, but she left so long before you were born..." At the bewildered look in Alex's eyes, Matilda stopped.

"What do you mean we're from the same town?" Alex was confused.

"Carol Ann was from Woodvale. Your hometown, right?" she asked Alex.

"Yes, ma'am. But how do you know?" Alex said, knowing she guarded the secret regarding her past with all her might.

"I saw your driver's license at the auto shop the first day you were here. I thought then how strange it was the Lord would send another girl all the way from Woodvale to us. But how do you know about Carol Ann if you didn't know she was from your town?" Confusion clouded Matilda's face as Alex sat in the chair next to her.

"When you gave us those Christmas decorations, my box had a little journal tucked away at the bottom. It had her name on it." Alex was unwilling to divulge any more information at this point. She didn't want Miss Matilda to know she'd started reading someone else's personal thoughts, particularly if there was any chance she could return it to the owner. "So, she lived here?" Alex asked, hardly wanting to speak the words.

Matilda nodded.

"How much have you read?" she asked Alex.

"A few entries," Alex answered. Matilda nodded, somber, seeming to contemplate her next move.

"I believe Carol Ann's last name was Miller. By the way, do you know if there are any Wickhams left in Woodvale?" Matilda asked.

A punch to the ribcage wouldn't have knocked the wind out of Alex any more effectively than Miss Matilda's question did. She struggled to catch her breath at the mention of the name; her heart raced at what she was certain was an unsafe rate. She couldn't conceal her reaction, and she knew one so accustomed to picking up on subtle cues would sense her discomfort.

Matilda asked again if Alex knew the Wickham family, which Alex answered with a mute nod. Without realizing it, Alex assumed the same protective posture she had taken when she first rode to the home, shoulders hunched, arms wrapped across her body. Alex admitted her stepfather's last name was Wickham, but she also informed Miss Matilda that Lydia's last name would be Powell, the same as Alex. Revealing this information burst a dam in Alex's heart.

As they cried and held one another, Alex began to ramble about her childhood, growing up, growing to trust her stepfather, and then the ultimate and horrific betrayal at his hands. This last part wasn't a revelation to Matilda, who'd heard Alex's story the day she arrived in Burton. But what Alex said next was almost Matilda's undoing.

"I thought of J.T. as my own dad," she said. Her defenses down in her distress, Alex let his name slip for the first time since her arrival.

Miss Matilda stopped patting Alex's back. She pushed back from the girl, looking her in the eye.

"Alex, dear, this is very important. What is your stepfather's full name?"

Horrified she'd divulged even this much crucial information, Alex jumped up from the table and pretended to busy herself with cleaning up the spilled coffee and broken cup, avoiding the question.

"Alex, I understand you have your reasons for the secrets you keep. But I have my own reasons for needing to know. If you change your mind, you'll tell me?" she asked.

Alex nodded and rushed out of the kitchen.

∅ ∅ ∅

Pieces to a puzzle only the older lady knew about began to fall into place for her. The sense of doom that had lurked in the shadows for years began to seep into Matilda's bones. With it came an inexplicable knowledge that soon things wouldn't be the same ever again.

∅ ∅ ∅

This changed everything. In her room Alex tried to sort through what had just happened. How could she have been so careless as to say J.T.'s name? And then it spooked her so much she left without even finding out the connection. For all Alex knew, Carol Ann could still be living in Burton and was a good friend of Miss Matilda's.

But Alex couldn't make sense of the connection to Woodvale and the Wickhams. She'd met J.T.'s parents when her mother first married him, but they'd passed away not long after. How were they connected to Carol Ann?

Lydia's soft whimper interrupted Alex's musings. Looking at her sweet little girl brought a smile to her face. As she settled into the rocker to nurse her baby, she pulled the diary from the nightstand drawer.

Maybe, Carol Ann could give her some answers.

June 4, 1963

Before the sun rose, we were loading the car with my luggage—my overnight bag filled with toiletries; a duffel bag with sheets and a pillow; and a picnic basket full of sandwiches, apples, and a big thermos of sweet tea. By leaving under cover of darkness, Mother and Daddy were hoping to avoid the prying eyes of any friends, acquaintances or just plain nosy neighbors. I'm so tired, though. I was up late writing, trying to make sure I never forget what I'm feeling.

The sun was just beginning to blush the horizon a beautiful pink when Daddy started the car, and we pulled out of the driveway. I pressed my forehead against the backseat window, trying to commit to memory every detail of my home and the small town where I grew up so I could recall them during the long months ahead. I couldn't stop the fresh tears from flowing as everything I've ever known slipped away.

We turned the corner to head out of town, and in the dim light I saw a familiar figure striding toward us. Carrying schoolbooks in one arm and a huge bouquet of flowers in the other was Jimmy. It was his last day of school before graduation.

We approached him and his eyes lit with recognition when he saw our family's car. He stopped on the sidewalk and waited for us to pull up alongside him. When Daddy continued to drive by, with my tear-streaked face and one hand pressed to the window, he looked at us in horror and disbelief.

He started to run after the car, though there was no logical way he could ever catch up as Daddy pressed the accelerator. Jimmy raised his hand in a final goodbye wave as we turned the corner a block later.

Alex's heart broke for Carol Ann. How terrible to be torn from your life, your home, your love. She realized this was akin to what had happened to her; the difference being, for Carol Ann, it had been a forced separation. Alex's exodus was more out of self-preservation. She switched the baby to the other side after burping her and continued reading, noting the long time gap between entries.

October 9, 1963

I haven't written in a long time. I'm going to try to do better. I know once the baby gets here, I won't have much time to write anymore. Looking back through the entries, I realize if Mother ever found this diary, she'd die a hundred deaths. I think I'll just burn it before I leave to go back home.

While I sat out on the porch today, I rubbed my hand over my swollen tummy. To my surprise, I was rewarded with an answering nudge from the tiny life growing in me. This made me smile as I watched the fire-colored leaves drift to the crunchy brown lawn of the girls' home. The porch rocking chair is one of my favorite spots.

From there, I can see most of the small farm that keeps the operation functioning. Somehow, I've grown to love everything about this place: the animals, the gardening, even learning how to preserve the produce we grow. We're all expected to help with chores until our eighth month, so I still have a couple of months of activity ahead of me. But I don't mind at all. It's now a part of my everyday routine. As I sat there, I let myself remember the day I arrived at Together for Good.

The sound of my crying had been the only sound during much of the long trip, until I finally had no tears left. Then, physically and emotionally spent, I slept for two hours of the journey. Daddy woke me for a quick roadside stop to eat our packed lunch, then we were back on the road.

It was just about suppertime when we pulled into the quarter-mile long drive leading up to a quaint two-story country home with white clapboard siding and black shutters. The big front porch is standard Southern issue. As our car crunched the gravel out front, the screen door flew open and a couple who looked to be in their early thirties rushed down the brick steps to greet us.

Charles and Sara made me feel welcomed at once. I can't put my finger on it, but something drew me to them. And, though my heart was breaking at what was happening, I felt a strange sense of calm, a peace affirming I was where I needed to be.

I put that strange emotion aside and decided to explore it later. My belongings were unloaded to the room I share with another girl, something I've never done before as an only child. Daddy hugged me and cried, also something I'd never experienced before. Mother kissed the air by my cheek and asked me to write—no more tears from Mother. And, then they were gone.

Today, with the crisp hint of fall in the air, I can see the wisdom in their brusque departure. No need to draw out sad, tearful goodbyes. They don't accomplish anything. It was better, instead, to begin the task of settling into my new, if temporary, life.

Under Sara's loving and watchful eye, all ten of us girls at the home have learned how to grow vegetables in the garden, cook, do laundry, gather eggs, and even sew. I've made new friends. In the evenings, the girls gather around the big kitchen table for Bible lessons. It was during one of these lessons last week that Charles explained why everyone needs a Savior.

"Well, of course, we need a Savior. All of us have sinned. Just look at us," said Ella, who is eight months along and ashamed of her past. We've all grown close and don't feel the need to hide much from each other.

"Ella, what I'm telling you is the Bible says everybody is a sinner, including Sara and me. We all need a Savior. Without one, we're separated from God forever," Charles answered, looking around the table.

That night, I accepted Jesus as my Savior. Charles gave me a Bible of my very own, and I've been reading it with a hunger unlike anything I've ever known. I'm learning and growing in my faith, even as my baby is growing within me. But my doubts about the future are also growing.

As I've watched my new friends have their babies, one thing has become clear. Although not required, it's expected that most girls will place their child for adoption with a Christian family. I wouldn't want my baby to go to any parents other than Christians, but now that I can feel this child moving inside me, the thought of not holding my baby, watching him or her grow up, being a mommy…well, it's almost more than I can bear.

I've poured out these fears to Jimmy in many letters. I've given the letters to Sara to take to the post office in town, but, as the months have slipped by, I've received no response. Has he forgotten me? Could so many letters have gotten lost in the mail? Maybe his family moved.

This problem may be up to me to figure out alone.

Instead of answers, Alex had only more questions after this entry. She smiled when she read about Charles and Sara, Terry's beloved parents. Terry must not have been around yet. She rejoiced for Carol Ann that she, too, had found Jesus as her Lord and Savior. Together for Good had truly been doing good for a very long time; that much was obvious.

The last part about Carol Ann's letters, though, was puzzling. If Jimmy had loved her as much as he claimed, why hadn't he answered her letters? Alex's opinion of Jimmy began to diminish, and in her mind, she painted a picture of a carousing college kid who had rid himself of the problem he'd created. By the time she changed Lydia's diaper and put her back in her bassinet, Alex was seething at this unknown boy who'd used an innocent, naïve girl.

She needed more answers and intended to get them by scanning through the few remaining entries before finding Miss Matilda again.

November 2, 1963

I woke in a sour mood today. I haven't slept well the last few nights due to my huge tummy and having to visit the bathroom several times each night. Being awake so much at night has given me plenty of opportunity to contemplate what the future might hold for my baby and me.

With no word from Jimmy, I'm forced to believe he's changed his mind about us. At first, my heart felt like it was breaking into pieces. But I've mulled over the situation in my head through the night hours, and ideas that would make no sense in the light of day have somehow formed in my mind with perfect clarity.

So, what if Jimmy has abandoned us?

I can raise this baby by myself. Maybe it's unheard of for a girl my age to keep her baby, but there has to be a way.

Frustrated, hot and tired, I arose when the rooster began to crow. I checked myself in the bathroom mirror one last time before going downstairs for breakfast and saw the ugly dark circles under my eyes. And to go with that ugliness, I carried a rather ugly, cranky disposition.

Later, Sara asked the other girls to cover the outside chores while she and I folded the laundry. She asked if I'd heard Ella had her baby, a healthy little girl. I grunted as I folded, avoiding eye contact with Sara.

"The couple who adopted her baby have wanted a family for a very long time. That little girl is such a gift from God, and they are so thankful to Ella," Sara continued, pretending not to hear my rude response.

We kept working in tense silence for a few minutes. When I couldn't bear it anymore, I stopped and looked right at Sara and asked, what if my baby and I want to be "together for good." I told her I thought the name of this home was all about being together for good, but that I had never seen any of the girls so far decide to stay with their babies.

I didn't understand.

I thought I'd lose control of my emotions as I talked to Sara. I have such a shaky hold on my feelings these days, and coupled with the

176

lack of sleep, I'm a complete mess. Sara answered my question something like this:

"Sweetie, every girl who stays here can keep her child if she chooses to do so. But we find loving, Christian parents for their babies, if that's what they want. Most of the mothers are young girls themselves, like you, who just want to go back to their lives as they were before the baby came along. It's a very difficult decision to make. But I'll tell you this, the parents who adopt these children recognize how incredibly blessed they are to welcome them into their lives."

Sara's eyes shone with unshed tears and her voice shook as she spoke. Still, I couldn't help but ask the question continuing to plague me.

"What about the name, though? Why Together for Good if the mothers and their babies are separated at birth?"

She explained I had the wrong understanding of what the name meant. I'd been thinking of it as "always together," but Sara explained the meaning based on a biblical reference.

"The name comes from Romans 8:28. Paul told the church in Rome: 'And we know that all things work together for good to them that love God, to them who are called according to His purpose.' Do you understand the difference in the two meanings?"

"Yes." I took several seconds to consider what she'd said. "I wanted to believe that maybe my baby and I could stay together, but God might have different plans for this baby."

It was a harsh truth, but Charles' last few evening talks have focused on the sovereignty of God. I have to trust He is in total control of my situation. Of every situation. It's so hard, but what choice do I have? I have nothing to offer a child, no way to support myself, much less an infant. The force of understanding the choice I must make almost left me breathless.

I asked Sara if she believed God had intended for me to come to the home. Sara stopped reaching for the next item to fold and looked me straight in the eye, holding my gaze before answering.

"Honey, I believe God doesn't make mistakes, and He's never surprised. He knew about your beautiful baby," she said as she rested her hand on my protruding abdomen, "before time began, although He's not so thrilled with the circumstances of how he or she came to be."

I dipped my head.

A few of our evening Bible studies have focused on God's plan for the marriage relationship. But Charles has also taught us of His forgiveness when true believers are willing to repent of the things they've done that go against biblical teaching.

"So, knowing all that," Sara continued, "I think, yes, He must have intended for you to come here. Why? Well, I can't even begin to understand God's purpose. But remember...Romans 8:28," she encouraged with a smile.

I hugged her, feeling much more at peace, the same strange peace I'd felt the first day I arrived. As we finished the folding and carried the stacks of laundry to the various rooms, I shared with Sara what a restless night it had been and the toll it had taken on me today. Sara reminded me of what the doctor had told me about increased discomfort as my final months stretch ahead of me.

"I wish my baby could have a mom as great as you," I said as I placed a stack of laundry on one of the beds. When I turned around, I noticed Sara blotting her eyes. I don't think my compliment should have made her cry, so I wonder if something is wrong.

Alex's heart ached again for everyone involved in this sad situation. The 1960s were a different time than today, and it wasn't as socially acceptable, or even feasible, for a very young girl to attempt to raise a child by herself. How painful it must have been for Carol Ann to know she'd soon to be separated from her child or forced to raise it alone in a culture unaccepting of single parents. Alex glanced at the baby sleeping in the bassinet and again couldn't imagine not having her here. Not just here with her, but alive and breathing, living and growing every day.

She considered Sara, Terry's wise and kind mother. From Alex's brief glimpse into the life of this hard-working, dedicated woman, she and Charles were so deeply loved and gave love to every resident, making them the perfect couple to run this home. Losing them must have left a gaping hole in the hearts of those who cared about them.

Alex considered the many similarities in hers and Carol Ann's stories: they both left all they knew; they both leaned on one of the sisters, Sara or Matilda, for wise advice; and they both came to know Jesus while living here. Her heart resonated with Carol Ann, even though she'd never met her. Alex had one final entry left to read. Sad to be finishing but eager to learn the ending to Carol Ann's story, she continued.

December 22, 1963

Days have melted into weeks. Some of the girls have had their babies and left. New girls have arrived. Before we knew it, Thanksgiving was over and we're getting ready for Christmas. Last week Charles found the perfect tree at the back of the farm, then we made popcorn garland while Sara hung stockings at the fireplace for each of us.

Several of the other girls received packages with Christmas gifts from home or cards with spending money to take into town. My card was signed, "Love, Mom and Dad." Nothing more. I know I hurt them, but for them not to have written even a short note was more than hurtful.

It was downright cruel. I'm in my last weeks of my pregnancy now, my nerves a roller coaster. I admit I have little tolerance for even the smallest offense, but the jab from my parents cut me to the quick.

Without thinking, I tossed the card into the fireplace, watching the flames lick the red and green ink. I regretted my decision almost at once. Despite the hurt they caused me; I still hope perhaps they're planning a surprise visit to see me in a few days on Christmas.

I'm about two weeks from my due date, so I've decided today the girls and I will do the Christmas baking, maybe distracting me from the hurt in my heart. I've never done much baking, but I think with Sara's help I'll be able to get through a few dozen cookies, a couple of cakes, and a few pies.

Alex smiled remembering their baking day not so long ago. She wondered why Carol Ann hadn't written anything else in her diary. Alex flipped through the remaining pages, but saw nothing. Had Carol Ann's parents come to visit? Did she give her baby up for adoption? With one last glance to be sure Lydia slept soundly, Alex went in search of the one person who may have the answers to these and other questions.

She had no idea how much life would change as a result of her answers.

Chapter 18
More Secrets

Miss Matilda sat on the ottoman in the living room sorting through old photos. Her thoughts were a hundred miles away…or maybe it was a hundred years. Arthritis-gnarled fingers picked up one of the photos among the sea of memorabilia spread out on the floor and held it to her chest. When she looked up, Alex stood in the doorway, apparently not wanting to disturb her friend or intrude on her reminiscing.

Memories flooded back to Matilda's mind, raw and fresh. She should have known something like this would happen. She'd tried to avoid the pain, postpone forever the task others before. Now she didn't believe she had the courage to face it. Delaying any longer wasn't an option, and she knew it.

Oh, Lord, I'm scared. Be my strength and my protection.

She drew a deep, calming breath and released it slowly. "Come in, dear. I want to show you something." She motioned to Alex to join her on a nearby chair.

"Miss Matilda," Alex said, sitting beside her friend. "I'm sorry I ran away earlier. You caught me off-guard. I guess at some point I'm going to need to talk about my past if I want to get over it."

Alex had been to a few counseling sessions with Reverend Drummond at Miss Matilda's urging, and he'd suggested verbalizing her past hurts to a trusted friend.

"You'll get there, Alex. And, I will, too. There are some things I need to tell you…"

Punctuating Matilda's sentence, the front door blew open, swirling a blast of icy air around the room. Terry walked in, stomping his shoes on the mat, calling to see where everyone was.

"In here, sweetie," his aunt called from her little perch.

Terry stopped at the living room doorway, saw the two of them surrounded by the pictures, and started to walk out again.

"Come join us, dear," Matilda beckoned him.

At Terry's dubious expression, Matilda smiled. She'd subjected him to all-day walks down memory lane in the past, and he'd been happy to escape for any reason.

"Aunt Tilley, I'm just here to help Alex move," he said, glancing at his watch as he clarified the intent of his visit.

"I know. Have a seat for just a minute. I want to talk to both of you."

Summoning her courage and saying a final prayer, Matilda pressed on to what she knew would be one of the most difficult discussions of her lifetime, with two of the people she cared about most. She didn't miss the questioning look and shoulder shrugs Alex and Terry exchanged.

"I found the photo I was looking for."

"That's great," Terry acknowledged, hoping his feigned engagement with this process would speed it along. He took a seat on the floor beside Alex.

"I'd like for y'all to take a look at it." She handed them a picture of an infant. The paper was yellowed with age. Alex studied the image more closely.

"It looks a little bit like Lydia," she said.

"But I know it's not Lydia because this is the same picture of me you gave me for my thirtieth birthday." Terry was confused because he saw the resemblance too. The shape of the eyes. The curve of the forehead.

"The truth is, you're both right," Matilda said.

Alex and Terry looked at each other again, more confused than before. Matilda, shaking now, dreaded the daunting task ahead of her. She knew she risked great pain for these two, perhaps even to the point of driving them from her forever. She didn't think she could face such a pain. But this wrong had to be rectified, and she had to do it. The wheels had been set in motion.

"I'm going to tell you a story. Alex, you know the first part because of the diary."

"What diary?" Terry asked, his curiosity piqued.

"A diary belonging to a girl named Carol Ann. She was a resident here in 1963," Alex said.

"The same year I was born," Terry noted.

Matilda ignored his comment and forged ahead with her self-appointed task. She related the story of Carol Ann's journey to Together for Good, her relationship with Sara and Charles, and her numerous letters to Jimmy. This brought Terry up to speed, so Matilda continued the story.

"I was here at the home on Christmas break helping my sister that year. Carol Ann was so excited to learn to bake." Her voice broke as the emotions and memories flooded back, transporting her to that day in the kitchen.

Tears streamed down Matilda's cheeks. Terry hurried to the kitchen for a glass of water while Alex offered Miss Matilda a box of tissues. Once everyone was settled again, Matilda continued to relate the events of the day of Christmas baking. She launched into her description of that fateful day; her eyes lost in the past as her voice told the story and her mind re-lived it.

Sara had told her sister they planned to make cookies. Several of the girls were coming in from gathering eggs. Carol Ann had admitted she didn't know anything about baking, but she felt the need to be doing something. Sara had looked at Matilda and mouthed the word "nesting" to her, and Matilda had nodded. They both knew it wouldn't be long.

Sara had confided to her sister weeks before that, although she loved all of the girls who came through the home, she'd miss this young mother in a different way. They'd grown close, with Carol Ann confiding in Sara, telling her she'd never been able to confide in her own mother. Matilda had seen the two form a special bond and knew it would be difficult to say goodbye.

When Carol Ann asked where the vanilla was, Sara directed her to the pantry. The girl reached to the top shelf, and when the other girls heard liquid splashing on the floor, they thought she'd spilled something. But Carol Ann began screaming in panic, feeling the damp warmth on her legs and knowing her water had broken.

With an experienced calm, Sara rallied the other girls into action, dispatching one to fetch Carol Ann's bag, two others to prepare dinner, and one to call Charles at the church where he was finishing his Christmas Eve message. All this happened while Matilda escorted Carol Ann to the car and got her comfortable in the back seat for the forty-five-minute drive to the hospital.

Charles would meet them there, and Matilda would come back to stay the night with the girls at the home. With first babies being notorious for taking their time coming into the world, they all expected it would be quite some time before they had anything to worry about.

They couldn't have been more wrong about Carol Ann having more time. They'd almost reached the city limits when it became clear time was definitely not on their side.

Sara pressed the accelerator to the floor as Carol Ann writhed in pain, contractions coming so fast she couldn't catch her breath. Sara had never seen such a quick labor. She sped down the rutted country dirt roads as fast as she dared, but every time she hit a pothole, it elicited a groan of agony from the poor girl. Sara and Matilda exchanged a worried look.

During one of the louder screams, Matilda asked her sister if Carol Ann was going to be all right. Sara tried to reassure her. But her white knuckled grip on the steering wheel belied her calm exterior.

When they pulled into the hospital, Sara glanced in the back seat and saw Carol Ann drenched in sweat and doubled over.

"Sara," Carol Ann had gasped, "I don't think I can make it in there."

"We'll get you a wheelchair, sweetie," Sara still tried to remain as calm as she could so the girl wouldn't see how nervous she was. Matilda knew this had happened way too fast. Something had to be wrong.

"No, you don't understand. I think I'm going to have the baby now," Carol Ann wailed.

Matilda took off at a sprint to the front desk, screaming for help. She was followed back to the parking lot by two orderlies with a gurney who lifted the girl and whisked her away, barking instructions to Sara to get the girl checked in. The two women ran into the hospital and could still hear Carol Ann's screams as she disappeared through two swinging double doors.

A few minutes after Sara had registered Carol Ann, Charles came walking into the waiting room. When he saw Sara's and Tilley's tear-streaked faces, he knew something was terribly amiss. They filled him in on the whirlwind of events, words tumbling out so fast he had trouble making sense of what had transpired. In disbelief, he asked if they'd heard any news of her condition since arriving, and Sara shook her head. It was then she remembered they had not yet contacted the adoption agency they partnered with.

Matilda paused at this point in the story to explain about the adoption procedures of that time. Applicants from across the Southeast underwent a rigorous screening process, followed by an even longer waiting period before being contacted.

Sometimes, when one of the girls delivered before her due date, the call could come with little or no warning. Charles and Sara made it their policy never to meet the prospective parents or even know their names. The adoption agency handled all those details.

Charles volunteered to go to the pay phone outside and make the necessary notifications. However, before he could leave Dr. Simons, the gentle and patient doctor who made house calls to the girls' home to check on them each month, walked through the swinging double doors.

A fine Christian man, he'd become a good friend to Sara and Charles, which was why the grim set of his jaw and the strained look in his eyes worried Sara. She jumped up from the uncomfortable chair and rushed toward him.

"Doctor, is everything all right? Carol Ann? The baby?" The questions poured out faster than the doctor could answer. He wouldn't meet her gaze, confirming her suspicion that there was a problem. Charles and Matilda stood close behind Sara, each with a hand on her shoulder.

"I'm so sorry," Dr. Simons began, shaking his head, looking up, and locking eyes with Sara. "By the time she arrived, she'd progressed so far, there was little we could do. She was bleeding internally, and we didn't realize it. We tried everything we could to save her."

Sara later told Matilda she wasn't sure what happened next. Dr. Simons seemed to be speaking at the end of a very long tunnel, and he kept getting further and further away. The last thing she heard him say before she hit the floor was something about the baby boy being fine, and they needed to contact the adoptive parents.

$$\mathcal{O} \; \mathcal{O} \; \mathcal{O}$$

Spent, Matilda's shoulders shook with sobs at the memory of their friend's death. Alex cleared a path through the photos and knelt beside her, holding her close and patting her back.

"Miss Matilda, it wasn't your fault. You did everything you could," she told her. By now, Terry was at his aunt's other side, rubbing her back and whispering his own reassurances.

"But you haven't heard the end of the story," Matilda wailed. She dabbed her eyes and blew her nose.

"Well, then," said Alex, returning to her seat. "Tell us the rest."

"Just know what I'm about to say will change both of you forever. I love you both. Please remember that," she begged them as she looked from one to the other.

"Aunt Tilley, you're scaring me. Whatever you've got to say, it can't be all that bad." Matilda held up her wrinkled hand to silence him, then continued.

"Charles began to make the necessary arrangements. He called Carol Ann's parents, who said they'd come for her body after Christmas." Here her voice cracked with a stifled sob. "Then he called the adoption agency to find out which couple was next in line to adopt a child. He learned a couple who'd been waiting for a very long time, not having been able to have any children of their own, would have their dreams come true that Christmas."

"Who was it?" Alex asked, enthralled by the story now.

"Charles and Sara Lovell." Matilda buried her face in her hands, unable to look Terry in the eyes.

Terry's face turned an ashen shade of gray as he processed this information.

"I was adopted?" he whispered, the implications still too much to grasp.

All Miss Matilda could do was nod as she looked up, finally able to bear the weight of his disbelieving stare.

"But why...? Why didn't Mom and Dad tell me?"

"They were going to. There just never seemed to be the right time. And then...well, you know. I couldn't bring myself to do it after the accident. I thought since Carol Ann had died, there wasn't any chance you'd ever find out."

Terry's expression went from confusion to something harder. Anger? Disappointment? Alex jumped in with her own questions.

"So where do I come in?" she asked.

"When Carol Ann's parents came for her body, they handed Sara a huge stack of letters—the letters Carol Ann had sent to Jimmy...all unopened. You see, when they'd first brought Carol Ann here, her mother had given Sara an address where all correspondence was to be sent. Sara sent all of Jimmy's letters to a post office box in Woodvale. When we saw Carol Ann's mother at the funeral home, she explained she'd never had any intention of sending those letters to Jimmy, and we could do whatever we wanted with them. I've still got them." More tears as Matilda pulled a wooden box toward her and opened the hinged top. She pulled out one of the yellowing envelopes from inside and handed it to Alex. It was addressed to James Terrence Wickham.

Even as her head spun, the full import of this news dawned on her. Jimmy. J.T.

He was the same person! This meant Lydia was…

"Terry," she turned to face him. "You have a sister," Alex said, choking on the calm façade that masked the turmoil rumbling inside her.

"A what? Where?" He was still shaking his head as he tried to comprehend the years of being left in the dark about his parents.

"Upstairs, sleeping in a bassinet." Terry looked as if he might pass out.

⌀ ⌀ ⌀

It was Alex's turn to rid herself of the burden of closely guarded secrets, washing them away with a river of tears and a long account of her childhood, ending with the shame-laden confession of how her innocence had been ripped from her. Matilda, in need of some sustenance, disappeared to the kitchen to put on the kettle for tea.

"Alex, you do realize what happened to you is in no way your fault? What kind of sick man would do such a thing to a girl he considered his daughter?"

It dawned on Terry after he spoke the words that it was his own biological father who'd committed the dreadful act, and he felt ashamed of a man he didn't even know. An hour ago, he didn't even know the man was his father.

Terry knelt beside Alex, handed her a tissue, and brushed her short curls back from her face. She'd taught him so much since coming to Burton. Her independence and determination were forces to be reckoned with, and when throwing her incredible talent in the mix, she was a phenomenon. As her business partner, he couldn't be prouder. And now, they shared an even deeper bond. Family.

Matilda bustled in from the kitchen carrying a tray laden with mugs of tea for the three of them. Without warning, the front door flew open again, cold air rushing into the front rooms. They all looked up as Gail's heels beat their quick rhythm across the foyer to the living room doorway, followed by Chad. Terry still knelt beside Alex, one hand on her back.

"See, Chad, I told you," Gail shrieked, pointing an accusing finger at Alex and Terry.

The pair on the living room floor looked up in confusion at the newcomers in the foyer, unable to understand what was going on, due in no small part to the bombshell news they were still trying to assimilate. Matilda set the tray on the coffee table and addressed Gail.

"I seem to remember you are not welcome in this house," Matilda said, staring at Gail. A bitter cold rivaling the winter wind frosted Matilda's words. Alex had never seen her friend so angry. Gail's tirade, however, gained momentum with every word she uttered.

"I've come to save Chad from a mistake even worse than the one I made."

⌀ ⌀ ⌀

"Exactly what mistake would that be?" Terry rose from the floor and approached his wife. Beneath the modulated calm of his voice, a roiling anger raged. Terry clenched his fists then flexed his fingers, trying anything to help him regain some semblance of control over this bizarre situation.

"When I found out that girl was going to live in the White's guesthouse, I went over and tried to talk Chad out of it. I've been trying to make him see reason all morning. Then I brought out my evidence," she said, pulling a framed photograph from her cavernous purse.

"Did you go to my office and take this photo off the wall?" Terry asked, swiping the frame from her hand as he marveled at the depths to which she would stoop.

"Don't get all high and mighty with me, Mr. Lover Boy." Gail's face turned red as she flailed her arms.

"Gail, what on earth are you talking about?" If this day's events got any weirder, Terry thought his head might explode. His wife had finally lost her mind, and he had no clue what she was ranting about.

"I'm not stupid, Terry. And I'm not blind. I know how much you've always wanted a family. But, really, Terry. Turning to an eighteen-year-old girl to fulfill your dreams? Did you pay her to have the child? Are you going to raise the baby as your own? How pathetic can an old man get?" Gail stood with arms crossed, as if prepared for battle.

Alex, Matilda, and Chad watched this spectacle unfold with something akin to fascinated horror. They didn't dare interrupt, and yet, they also didn't dare try to make a stealthy getaway. When Gail flung these final accusations, however, wounding both Terry and Alex with one blow, Matilda could stay silent no longer.

"Gail Lovell," she said, teeth clenched against her anger, "you take your heathen self out of my house forever. Don't you dare darken my door again. Do you understand me?"

"Gladly, Matilda. First, though, do you remember the picture you gave Terry? Do you see any resemblance with a certain baby? Chad agrees. Don't you, Chad?" Gail spun around, fixing Chad with her crazy-eyed gaze.

Chad looked at the floor, not daring to meet Alex's hurt stare. Terry, knowing the truth now, ached for this girl who'd already suffered so much pain. Ashamed of and infuriated at his wife, Terry strode toward her with every intention of bodily removing her from the premises. Seeing him approach, she turned on her spike heel.

"I'm leaving y'all to work this out," Gail flung over her shoulder. She clacked back to the front door, leaving with a resounding slam.

Terry saw his aunt shoo away a group of girls gathered at the top of the stairs to witness the debacle. They shuffled away. Matilda announced she needed an aspirin, and Terry volunteered to go with her to the kitchen, leaving Alex and Chad alone in the living room.

Ø Ø Ø

Alex, the pain evident in her big brown eyes, stood facing Chad. She needed to know how he felt if she and her daughter were going to go through with today's move. She couldn't live there knowing, or even thinking, Chad believed Lydia was Terry's child.

"Do you believe that stuff, Chad? Do you believe those accusations Gail made?" she asked him. While she'd never been forthcoming with the details about the circumstances that brought her to Together for Good, she hoped he wouldn't give credence to the awful accusations Gail had tossed around.

"Alex, I don't want to believe her. But you gotta admit, there's a close resemblance to Lydia and Terry's baby pictures. Also, the timing of things after your arrival in Burton was a little strange. You got here, then all of a sudden Terry offers you this crazy business deal. If he

189

didn't know you, how did he know he could trust you? And, why did you trust him? Things just don't seem to add up."

Chad paced the length of the room, rubbing the back of his neck, seeming to try to make sense of the scenario in his head. Alex knew he couldn't, though, because he lacked a crucial piece of the puzzle. She couldn't believe her ears. Chad thought she and Terry...

Alex respected Terry's business sense, admired his commitment to the institution of marriage, and appreciated his deep affection for his beloved aunt. But she'd never shown or harbored any other feelings toward him, and Chad knew this. Gail's sick and twisted ploy to assuage her own guilt now somehow made sense in Chad's head.

Rolling today's revelations around in her head, Alex seethed to think Chad would justify some scheming woman's nonsense by hearing her out before he had the decency to give Alex a chance to defend herself. A niggling little voice in the back of her head reminded Alex he'd asked her on more than one occasion to open up, share her hurts with him.

She pushed the voice of reason aside, giving full wind to the anger building within her. Then, with the heightened hormones of a post-partum mother and a wounded teenage girl, she turned on Chad.

"How dare you," she said, her voice low and her lips barely moving for fear they might tremble as a precursor to the tears stinging her eyes. "You think nothing more of me? And what about Terry? He's married! Chad, I'm going over and over in my mind how you could even find this scenario plausible, knowing me as you do, and I don't know what to say."

The tears flowed freely down her face now.

Chad stopped his pacing in front of her, so close she could smell his spicy aftershave. The day he unburdened his heart about his mom, she'd seen a broken man before her. Today she saw instead a man with a broken heart.

"Maybe that's the problem, Alex. Maybe I don't know you at all," he said before turning and walking out the front door, leaving Alex to wonder what happened next.

✿ ✿ ✿

Matilda made two more mugs of tea and joined Terry at the table. They'd decided to go to her little cottage to allow Alex and Chad some privacy. Matilda looked at her nephew staring into his cup, lost in thought, and felt her heart might burst. She loved him so much, just as a mother would.

To think she'd caused him pain wounded her deeply.

"Sweetie, is there anything you'd like to ask me?" She tilted her head, trying to look him in the eye. He gave a mirthless laugh, more of a grunt, and raised his head to stare at her.

"Aunt Tilley, everything I've ever thought to be true has been turned upside down in the last hour. I'll never know my real mother and father, the people I thought were my mother and father lied to me their whole lives, and then there's you. You knew this whole time, and you didn't say a word."

Terry looked defeated, the underpinnings of his life seeming to slip away. Matilda knew she'd been the one he trusted more than anyone, and she'd kept a secret so monumental, it amounted to lying to him. Still, that didn't change certain facts about his life.

"Terry Lovell, you listen to me. Your 'real' mother and father died in a car crash when you were ten years old. They may not have been your biological parents, but they cared for you when you had the chicken pox, they encouraged your love of learning, and they taught you about the Lord. I've never seen two people who loved a child more than they loved you." Matilda needed Terry to understand Sara and Charles were devoted parents, not lying sneaks trying to keep secrets from their child.

"Why did Mom and Dad have to wait so long to adopt? If they ran the home, shouldn't they have gotten placed with a child sooner?" Terry was searching for answers, and Matilda wanted him to see God's hand in this.

"They could have, but they didn't feel it was fair to the other families who endured the process. They never knew the names of the next family in line to adopt. That ensured no communication with and, consequently, no disappointment for the adoptive family if the mother decided to keep her baby."

Terry nodded at Aunt Tilley's answer.

"Why did Mom and Dad name me Terry?" he asked. "I always thought it was a family name."

"In a way it was...for you. Carol Ann told your mother, no matter what the gender of her baby, she intended to call the child Terry. She planned to name you Terrence if you were a boy or Teresa if you were a girl. Your parents honored her wish when they adopted you by naming you Terrence Charles."

Matilda continued by telling him what Carol Ann looked like, where she was from, and what her parents had done when they came to claim her body. From what Matilda had been able to surmise from Beverly, Carol Ann's mother, they no longer lived in Woodvale after the "disgrace their child brought on them."

They made the decision to have her buried outside of Burton, saving themselves the expense and embarrassment of transporting her back to North Carolina. Terry asked to visit her grave, and Matilda agreed to do so when it warmed up a bit.

They talked for a long time about the adoption process, Carol Ann's parents, Alex, and Gail. Terry realized out of all of the revelatory information dropped on him today, Gail's outburst caused him the most pain.

"I'm going to file for divorce, Aunt Tilley."

After today, he couldn't live with a woman who not only didn't trust him, but who went out of her way to ruin his reputation and the reputation of innocent people. He knew what he needed to do, no matter how much it hurt.

Matilda sighed. She knew divorce was a difficult option for Terry, who'd done everything in his power to save his marriage. She also knew after seeing what Gail was capable of today, divorce might be his best option. She reached over and patted his hand. Nothing else needed to be said.

She hoped he knew that, no matter what, she still supported his decisions.

Chapter 19
Apologies

The cold air assaulted Chad's skin as he yanked Miss Mathilda's front door open and descended the porch steps two at a time. He took long, purposeful steps to his truck, slammed the door after getting in, and sat there staring at nothing in particular. He'd ruined any slim chance he ever had with the most wonderful girl he'd ever known.

It was all Gail's fault. Chad banged the heel of his hand on the steering wheel, sending waves of pain vibrating through his arm. She planted the crazy idea of Lydia being Terry's child in Chad's mind, sparking a jealousy unlike any he'd known before. He didn't want to believe Gail's ridiculous theory, but the more she sold it to him, the more sense it made.

He started the truck, gunned it down the long drive toward the highway, and spun out onto the main road, spraying gravel behind his tires. He was half way to his house before he took any notice of his surroundings. Realizing what a menace he could be in this state, Chad slowed his speed and paid more attention to the road.

Now that he'd cooled down, the memory of the hurt in Alex's eyes and the pain in her voice forced Chad to accept the blame that needed to be placed at his own feet for believing the conniving woman Terry had married. He hadn't given Alex the benefit of the doubt or even an opportunity to explain. He had just hurled accusations, and they must have stung coming from someone who told her he wanted to be there for her.

At a stop sign, another smack on the steering wheel brought tears to his eyes. He let his head fall back, exhaling in a huge puff. He knew whatever ghosts haunted from Alex from her past must be bad, but he had no idea what kind of hurt she wrestled with. Now he'd added to the problems in her life. He needed to make this right, and he needed to do it now. He wouldn't have any peace until he made amends.

Looking both ways, Chad made a U-turn in the intersection and sped back to Miss Matilda's house. He kept going over in his head what he wanted to say to her, but somehow, everything he came up with turned out all wrong. If he ever needed prayer it was now, but those words wouldn't come to him either.

He sighed. "Jesus, help me."

He'd barely stopped the truck before bolting out and running to the front door. He tapped on the door a couple of times and entered without waiting for a response. He saw her sitting on the sofa with her back to the living room door, her head turned and tilted to one side, looking down, her sweet smile curling her lips.

He stood very still and heard her softly singing. Chad knew he'd walked in while she was nursing her baby, and the tenderness of the act made him shuffle his feet, uncomfortable at having intruded.

He had no right to be here with her. He'd spoken with so much authority of trusting the Lord, yet when faced with a serious test, Chad had not only lost his trust in the Lord, but also in Alex.

She owed him nothing, and he knew it. And while the question of her baby's father burned a hole in his heart, he felt certain she would share it when she could. He needed to take his own advice and trust her, believing in time she'd tell him everything.

For now, though, he needed to make up for the horrible hurt he'd caused her. He'd seen it in her eyes; his willingness to believe Gail amounted to a betrayal Alex couldn't comprehend. *But could she forgive him? And, even if she could, would she?* Alex moved Lydia to her shoulder, rubbing the baby's back and continuing to sing. A hearty belch from the little girl elicited a giggle from her mom, and a chuckle from Chad.

"I don't want to see you right now," she said without flinching.

She'd known he watched her, yet she ignored his presence.

"I'm not going anywhere until you let me apologize."

He took a couple of steps toward the living room, cutting off her exit to the stairs. Alex returned Lydia to her carrier. She stood, approaching Chad with unshed tears shining in her eyes, along with many unanswered questions. A nod was all she could manage.

He watched as she came to him, guarded, closed off, distrustful. She assumed her protective posture, wrapping her arms about her middle, shoulders hunched, making her appear small, vulnerable, delicate.

He couldn't measure the depths of his foolishness at the choice he'd made earlier today. He vowed to do everything in his power to convince her how sorry he was for listening to Gail. With a deep breath, one final silent prayer, and a quick swipe of his neck, he dove in.

"Alex, I was so wrong, and I can't begin to tell you how sorry I am. I never should have believed Gail. I've seen firsthand how she treats you, how she treats everyone. I should've known she had some ulterior motive. She always does. But whether it was Gail or anyone else who brought some crazy story to me, I should have come straight to you for the truth, and I didn't. Can you forgive me?"

At this question, he took one final step that closed the gap between them and held her shoulders, looking into her eyes. He needed to know where he stood with her.

⌀ ⌀ ⌀

She looked up into his green eyes, wanting to forgive him, wanting to go back to how things had been before. Alex knew things could never be like they'd been before, though. She didn't want them to be.

Almost since her arrival in Burton, Chad had spoken honestly about his feelings for her. She'd never returned that gift. Alex understood now how hurtful her silence, her skittishness had been.

She also knew these actions had raised doubts in Chad's mind. Even though she and Chad had grown closer over the months, Alex had yet to level with him by giving him the details of the tragic, life-altering event in her past.

Yes, she could forgive him. Could he forgive her, though? Would he still feel the same about her when he learned she handled her problem by running away? True, she didn't run away from the ultimate issue. Alex glanced down at her sleeping daughter, so innocent and peaceful.

When Alex decided to have her baby and raise it as a single mom, she'd promised herself and her child that she'd be the best mommy she could be. She needed to make good on her new promise today by being transparent with this caring man before her. She owed him that much.

No more running.

Alex took a deep breath and prepared to give voice to her harrowing story for the third time in one day. She marveled again at how cathartic sharing could be.

$$\mathcal{S}\ \mathcal{S}\ \mathcal{S}$$

Chad sat on the sofa in Miss Matilda's living room, shocked and sickened by what Alex had endured. In the space of time it took Alex to tell the story, he'd gone from wanting to hold and protect her to wanting to strangle her stepdad. What kind of sick, demented man did such a horrible thing to a girl, and to a girl who trusted him like her own dad?

"What's your mom like, Alex?" He wanted to know how a caring mother could let such a thing happen.

"My mom," she rolled her eyes, "is a wonderful decorator, the consummate hostess, a fantastic fundraiser chairwoman. But when it comes to being a mother, quite honestly, she stinks."

Chad chuckled at her frank and candid assessment.

Sitting next to Chad on the couch, she noted it was the first time she'd ever admitted aloud Karen was subpar in the parenting realm, and it felt good to let it out. She giggled, which got Chad tickled, which made Alex laugh harder. Soon, the two were roaring with laughter.

The volume of their outburst startled Lydia, causing her to answer their mirth with a wave of high-pitched baby cries. Alex jumped up, scooped her baby from the carrier, and bounced her gently, whispering in a soothing voice. The effect was amazing and quick. Lydia soon rested, comfortable again in her mother's arms.

This quick emotional swing sobered Alex. Looking down at the beautiful bundle in her arms, she wondered what she knew about being a mom? Not one single thing. She'd gone to three days of classes and learned to change diapers, take a digital temperature, and install a car seat. There was more to it than that. Her brow furrowed as she considered the years stretching before her, clueless how she'd teach this child and if she could provide for her.

"Chad, what was I thinking?" Alex asked with an edge of panic in her voice. "I don't know anything about being a mom! I can't do this!"

Her breathing became shallow, and she feared she might pass out. No, she couldn't do that. Not while holding her baby! Chad leaned forward and put his elbows on his knees, lacing his fingers together. He looked so calm and handsome sitting there, while she sat there overcome by anxiety. She worried she'd inherited some deep character flaw or maternal deficiency.

"Alex, take a deep breath." She did as he instructed. Twice. "Good. Now, let's get some perspective here. God blesses folks with babies all over the world every day, right? Don't you think there are at least a few of them who have no idea what they're doing?" She nodded, encouraging him to continue. "Of course. And, I bet there's a whole bunch of them who don't have a great group of friends around to help out. See? You're ahead of the game on that count already."

He was ticking off the reasons to remain calm on his fingers. As he did so, Alex rocked back and forth, the motion comforting not only Lydia but her as well.

"Can't you see what an amazing job you're already doing with her?"

"Thanks, Chad. I needed someone to talk me through that panic attack," she said, still doubtful but appreciative of the pep talk.

She felt better as she placed her daughter back in the carrier. Turning around, she was startled to find Chad standing right behind her. He rubbed the back of his neck, a sure sign of nerves. She smiled up at him and took his other hand in hers.

"I know how hard it was for you to tell me about your mom. It was also really hard for me to tell you about J.T." Thinking she might not be able to keep speaking, she cleared her throat and continued after Chad took her hand in both of his. "That day in the garden, you said you didn't know my story, but you wanted to."

He nodded. "You told me you weren't who or what I thought you were."

It was burned into his memory.

"Well, now you know my story, and how I ran away when I got scared. Does it change anything?"

Terrified to ask, Alex had to know the answer. She'd opened her heart and shared her life story with this incredible man. Now, she needed to know if he thought of her as damaged goods or if he was willing to help her deal with the baggage she carried.

"Yes, it changes a lot, actually," he said.

197

Alex's heart sank. Why had she ever put herself out there? She wanted to crawl into a hole. Alex dropped her gaze to the floor, but Chad put a finger under her chin and lifted until she met his gaze.

"Alex, before today I thought you were a crazy talented girl who had come here looking to make a way for you and your baby. Now I know the true depth of your strength and courage. It couldn't have been easy to take off and leave everything you've ever known. But you make it look easy. You're amazing."

Chad took her face in both of his hands, and the way he looked at her made her heart almost stop. He leaned closer, close enough for Alex to feel his breath on her lips. Alex closed her eyes, anticipating his kiss.

Charmain blew open the front door, announcing her presence loud and clear.

"I have *got* to talk to that girl about her timing," Chad muttered, which rekindled their laughter as they turned to greet his sister.

Chapter 20
Settled

Alex concluded the tour of her little home by showing Terry the workshop. She opened the door from the kitchen, and they stepped into the spacious, well-lit shop, now outfitted with Alex's tools and some of her created pieces waiting on a table by the roll-up door. Alex could tell Terry was impressed as he strode around the space, stopping at the display table to inspect her latest items.

"These are fantastic, as usual, Alex." Terry shook his head in amazement. "I really don't know how you've managed to get moved in, settled, care for a baby, and start working again," he said. His protégé waved off the praise with characteristic modesty and a shrug.

"I had help from Chad and Charmain. Plus, a few of these things were in some stage of completion when Lydia was born."

She wrapped the items in bubble wrap and placed them in a box as she spoke. Terry would take them to his office, a few already spoken for and sold. He handed Alex a check for the sold items, and she accepted it with thanks.

"I've got something for you, too," Alex said, reaching into her pocket and pulling out a small book. Terry looked at it, puzzled. She extended it to him, and he read the word *Diary* on the cover.

"What's this?" he asked, taking it but not opening it.

"It's your birth mother's diary. It belongs to you." Alex knew this was the right thing to do, but hadn't had the opportunity until now. Terry looked unsure.

"But Aunt Tilley gave it to you…" he said, his reluctance clear as he spoke.

"She really didn't. She gave me a box, and it happened to have the diary in it." Looking at Terry, her brown eyes pleaded with him to take the plunge. "Read it, Terry. You'll be glad you did."

He nodded.

A loud rapping on the garage door made them both jump. Chad called from outside, "Hey, Alex, you told me to let you know an hour before the movie starts. See you in twenty minutes."

Alex blushed as Terry regarded her with eyebrows raised in question, a smile creeping onto his face. Terry couldn't resist just a little bit of teasing.

"A movie?" he queried, the inflection in his voice rising.

"So, we're going on a date, okay? It's no big deal!" Alex defended herself, fidgeting with her hair, packing the pieces, looking everywhere except at Terry. He burst into laughter.

"What's so funny?" she demanded.

"I've been wondering how long it was going to take you to see how much he cares about you. Just relax, Alex. Enjoy your date." He took the box from her and walked to the door.

On his way out, Terry asked Alex if she'd be willing to give a statement to a lawyer about Gail's behavior over the past months. Alex agreed she would and promised to pray for him.

"Give my little sister a kiss from me," Terry called as he drove off.

This was now a familiar refrain from him, and it never failed to make Alex smile. As she waved goodbye, she realized Lydia was living up to her namesake. Members of her family had changed and grown so much since she'd come along.

As soon as Terry was out of sight, Alex rushed inside to get ready. Her hands shook as she applied her mascara, requiring a dab of cold cream and a tissue to remove an under-eye smudge. *Why was she nervous?* This was the same Chad she'd known since the day she arrived in Burton.

And yet, she realized, things could be different after today.

She found her favorite skirt that fit her in-between body and paired it with a comfy sweater. A quick tooth brushing, a swipe of lipstick, a palm full of mousse to tousle her short hair, and a pair of gold stud earrings. She was done just as she heard a knock at her front door.

Chad stood on her front stoop rubbing his neck. Just out of the shower, his still-damp hair showed comb marks. Alex opened the door, catching a whiff of the delightful spicy scent she'd come to associate with Chad.

"Hi, Chad."

"Alex, you're not going to believe this," he blurted as he moved past her into the living room-kitchen combination. "Hey, it looks great in here," he said, looking around, not having seen the place since she started settling in.

"Chad, what's wrong?" He seemed upset.

"Oh, that girl. I don't know why I ever depend on her for anything," he carried on a conversation with himself, leaving Alex in the dark as to what was going on.

"Chad," she said in a soothing tone, touching his arm to try to get him to the present. "Why don't you tell me what's happened."

Chad explained Charmain had called to say she'd been held up in town on a job interview and wouldn't make it home until later in the evening. As a result, she wouldn't be able to babysit tonight. Chad was furious with his sister, but Alex took it in stride. She suggested they take Lydia with them, knowing she'd probably sleep most of the time anyway.

As Alex packed Lydia's bag for their date, Chad sat on the sofa, bouncing his knee. Alex smiled at his nervous behavior; glad she wasn't the only one on edge about this evening. Once Alex secured the baby in her carrier and collected everything she needed, she turned to Chad.

"All right, I'm ready," she said, smiling at him. She'd been anticipating this evening with nervousness, but excitement now welled up.

"You look beautiful," he said, walking toward her, taking the carrier, and placing it on the floor. She dipped her eyes and twisted an earring several times. He took her face in his hands again, and the memory of their almost-kiss at Miss Matilda's made her knees feel like jelly.

"Alex, I know it wasn't easy for you to trust me enough to agree to go out with me. I've done some stupid things. But I promise, I'll never hurt you again." He was whispering now, all traces of nervousness gone, gazing into her eyes with an intensity she couldn't escape.

"I know now God led me here for a reason. I'm still learning to trust Him, but I think I'm learning to trust you, too," she whispered back. "With all my heart."

He closed the distance between them, his gentle kiss a token of the solemn promise he had made.

Reader Questions

Thank you for taking this journey with Alex and her friends. Below, you'll find a few questions to help you delve deeper into the main themes of the book and to encourage discussion with others. Each question set is divided into information you gleaned from the book and truths you've experienced in your own life.

I hope you enjoy diving a little deeper.

B = Questions related to the book.

P = Questions related to your personal experience.

1. *Proverbs 3:5 says, "Trust in the Lord with all your heart and lean not on your own understanding."*

   B. At the beginning of the story, Alex trusts only in her own intellect and abilities to deal with her situation. How does her trust in others grow? How does her trust in the Lord mature?

   P. What are some situations in which you have trusted "in your own understanding," only to have God open your eyes to something infinitely better?

2. *Trust is a major theme that runs through the whole book.*

   B. Alex understandably has trust issues. What was the most important thing Chad did to prove to Alex he was trustworthy? What did he do to make her question her trust in him?

   P. What has someone in your life done (or <u>not</u> done) or said (or <u>not</u> said) that bolstered (or destroyed) your trust in him/her?

3. *Throughout the book, people reveal the secrets they've kept, some for a long time.*

   B. What could be some reasons, besides those she gave Terry, Miss Matilda kept her secret for so long?

   P. If someone revealed a long-kept secret that changed how you see yourself or others, how would you react?

4. *Our past shapes who we become in life.*

   B. How might Chad's past, including finding his mother and his strained relationship with his dad, have shaped the man he became and the choices he made?

   P. What event or situation from your past has God used to make you a better person?

5. *Sometimes we make decisions we later regret. Terry honored his decision to marry Gail, even when it meant the death of his dream of a family.*

   B. Why do you think Terry stayed with Gail for so long, even though he knew he was giving up his opportunity to have a family?

   P. Have you ever felt "honor bound" to a decision you made? Was it the best choice?

6. *Alex and Chad decide to let their feelings be known for each other.*

    B. Based on both Alex's and Chad's past experiences, strong faith, and current situation, what hurdles could they face in their budding relationship?

    P. What challenges have you faced in a relationship (family, friend, or romantic)? How did your faith shape your responses to those challenges?

Author LeighAnne Clifton and her husband Bill call South Carolina home. After meeting while both earning their degrees in chemical engineering at the University of South Carolina, the pair married and settled in Aiken. They have two grown children, a son-in-law, and a pair of spoiled cats. Before writing *All Your Heart*, LeighAnne wrote *The Little Vessel*, a modern-day parable for all who need reminding that God has a unique purpose for their lives.

LeighAnne, like Alex Powell, loves to upcycle old junk into beautiful, one-of-a-kind pieces. She shares her thoughts on Christian living, DIY projects, and the latest book news on her blog:
https://alive-leighjourney.com